FATE

Tales *of* HISTORY MYSTERY *and* MAGIC

ANNIE WHITEHEAD

JEAN GILL

MARIAN L THORPE

HELEN HOLLICK

ALISON MORTON

ELIZABETH ST.JOHN

R. MARSDEN

ANNA BELFRAGE

J.P. REEDMAN

DEBBIE YOUNG

With an introduction by Cathie Dunn

TAW RIVER PRESS

FATE

Tales of History, Mystery and Magic

If you had a crystal ball to predict what lay ahead,

would you be tempted to use it?

Or would you leave the future to the turn of Fate?

by (in order of appearance)

Introduction: Cathie Dunn. *Bramble Creep* by Annie Whitehead, *Six Pomegranate Seeds* by Jean Gill, *One Black Dog* by Marian L. Thorpe, *In the Shadow of Ghosts* by Helen Hollick, *A Fateful Encounter* by Alison Morton, *Following Fate* by Elizabeth St.John, *The Black Onyx Box* by R. Marsden, *Beware the Crows* by Anna Belfrage, *Dame Fortune's Wheel* by J. P Reedman, *Saints Alive* by Debbie Young

Endword: Helen Hollick

978-1-0687721-4-6 paperback

978-1-0687721-5-3 e-book

Published by Taw River Press

https://www.tawriverpress.co.uk

CONTENTS

FATE: Tales of History, Mystery and Magic

Introduction by Cathie Dunn author,
and host of *The Coffee Pot Book Club*

Endword by Helen Hollick

READERS - PLEASE NOTE:

These are adult stories intended for adults and/or older teenagers, and may contain coarse language, or scenes of an intimate or sensitive nature.

INTRODUCTION
by Cathie Dunn
author, and host of *The Coffee Pot Book Club* Author Services

Fate. Such a small word; plain, simple, almost unnoticeable – but with a big, complicated meaning since time immemorial.

What is Fate?

Through the ages, believers have relied on Fate – or the Fates – as a greater, unseen power that holds the secrets to their lives. People of all walks of life have always consulted priests and priestesses, gods and goddesses, wise women and men. They sought guidance, hints, and promises. And they wished to foresee – and thereby forestall –threats to their lives and livelihoods.

In the olden days, sacrifices, often bloody, were needed to appease (or bribe) the Fates. Coins were always welcome, of course, especially in temples. Did people receive the answers they expected, as a result of a more generous offering? *Honi soit qui mal y pense...* "Shamed be whoever thinks ill of it", the motto of the British chivalric Order of the Garter, the highest of all British knighthoods.

Wars have been decided at the whim of the Fates. Marriages and alliances were forged and broken. The existence of whole tribes and peoples depended on the guidance from the Fates – and those who spoke in their name. So-called 'wise' men and women, who read what Fate had in store for people, wielded great power. They decided over life and death. Was that kind of power prone to abuse? Absolutely. Because, ultimately, throughout history, human beings have pursued their own gains first and foremost, often at the detriment of those who revered them. Collateral damage for the 'greater good'. Blame those unfortunate deaths on Fate…

Fate implies that your life, my life, everyone's life is laid out according to a greater plan. In the ancient days, with a plethora of gods and goddesses, people trusted them to keep them safe, or to lead their people to greatness. Conquering other tribes or nations, to subdue or kill those 'enemies'? Well, tough. It's their Fate, of course.

In our era of Western monotheism, Fate is often referred to as God's will. Crusades were full of such talk. But who hears God's messages? Inquisitors? Priests? Ordinary believers? Yes, again, it's fellow human beings, and often still with an agenda, to this day.

Fate cannot be touched. It is abstract. We cannot taste or feel it. Does it truly exist? Do our lives really depend on the whim of some greater power that maps out our journey through life from beginning to end, with all its joys, trials, tribulations pre-determined?

Or do we just need something as an excuse to forge our own destiny, regardless of any damage done, thereby shifting any responsibility to this unseen force, Fate?

You decide. It's your Fate!

© Cathie Dunn

website: www.cathiedunn.com
Author Services: https://thecoffeepotbookclub.com/

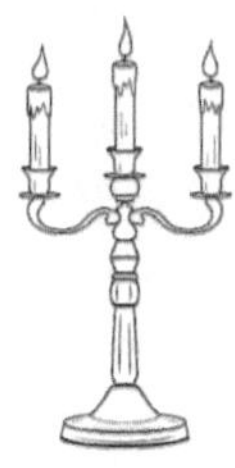

1
———

BRAMBLE CREEP

BY ANNIE WHITEHEAD

*When the Normans arrive at a peaceful Anglo-Saxon
village, do the women, children and old men submit...
or fight?*

October 1066

"Toi! La vieille! Tiens toi ici avec les autres. A l'instant!"

Grandmother, my oma, does not move. I know not
what the Northman is saying, but his yelling and the
flailing of his free hand make it clear enough; she must
stand up and join us all by the wall. His hairy fingers
dig deeper into the flesh above my elbow, five points of
jabbing heat which will show in bruises tomorrow. It
scarcely matters, when beyond this braying man, with
his honking way of speaking, the dawn light shines
through the open doorway and we can see the body of
our elderly reeve, lying face down in the dirt. These
invaders must have been marching overnight, or
camped outside our vill, waiting, watching. They felled
our reeve before he could raise the alarm. His boy, the
one who never fully had his wits, came running, using

one of his few words to say "No" over and over as he threw helpless punches.

From here, I can no longer see his feet, but I saw them earlier, kicking against nothing. It is a strange, unnatural thing, for feet to have naught but air beneath them and only happens when children swing for pleasure from the old oak branches or when men dangle from the gallows. My bowels feel loose and my throat, full of pent-up sobs, is throbbing. *Dear God, make Oma see sense.* She looks up, not at me but at the soldier, then she grips both sides of her chair, half-stands, lifts the chair, and without a word, turns to face the fire, showing him her back. The pressure upon my arm loosens and he pushes me aside, taking two strides into the room. *Oma please, turn around. Do as he says.*

The soldier raises his hand as if to strike, but then impotently punches the air. After all the fighting, all the burning, all the slaughter, the hangings and the stabbings, he and his kind will not be stopped by an old woman, surely?

The sudden release of his grip off-balanced me, and my clutching at the table edge has set the cups rattling. In the moment's silence, the rat-tat of metal on wood sounds dangerously loud. The clatter reduces, melts into the silence, a quiet that scares.

Leofing, dear Leofing, ever steadfast, speaks. "Lady, I beg you…" He does not need to finish his sentence. We are none of us safe. It's not as if there was even a war; the Northmen came, a battle was fought, King Harold was killed, and it was all over. Men have died. So many men that they cannot be counted and now my stubborn oma must insist on following them on their journey. Leofing looks at his hands, black as always. We both know he is only alive because he is the smith. They will work him and he will be useful to them. Oma is of no practical use to anyone. Still she does not turn.

Her voice chimes clear though. "Leave me be."

The Northmen shake their heads. They do not understand English. But I glance at Leofing and his raised eyebrow tells me that he is wondering, as am I, why she chooses now to speak in the Mercian tongue and not our southern dialect.

"I used to live on a road that many armies marched along. I moved here for a quieter life so you can all go and boil your arses."

With that last, delivered in the more familiar, to our ears anyway, West Saxon dialect, Leofing sucks air in audibly. In a heartbeat I've switched from wishing one of them spoke English to thanking God that they do not. There is more nasal honking and then the men shrug, their arms lifting and then slapping back down against their mailcoats. One waves a pointing finger at Leofing then mimes the squeezing of the bellows. *Back to work.* Another looks at me and it's clear from his jerky movements that he thinks I should pick up my besom. Buoyed by my oma's ill-advised but admirable resistance, I shake my head and walk from the hall. Let him find me in the weaving shed, for there is more important work to be done than sweeping. I will not stand on pride but sweeping is not my work. He seems not to know that I am the Lady of this steading. Perhaps they treat their women differently? I am the keyholder and it is for me to decide who will do what. I work, yes, because we all do, but sweeping is not high on anyone's mind at such a time as this.

Outside, it is as if someone has picked up our homestead and placed it in a foreign land. I hear not a word of English spoken as I cross the yard. All smells as it should: the ever present and comforting smoke of the forge, the musky, buttery warmth rising from the goat pen; the sweet scent of the apples, stored among the rafters of the hay barns, wafts down on the still warm October breeze. But the sounds are not right. We are used to the stillness when our menfolk are away. Now there are men we do not know, speaking words we cannot understand and the lightness of life has gone, leaving only a heaviness in our steps, in our souls.

I cannot see anyone who looks like a lord among these soldiers.

What, then, do they want with us? Are they making the place ready for the new lord? Then will those who work be safe? Reeve Ælfwine, who worked hard indeed but had no visible purpose, was not so lucky. He made a stand, defending the hall while my father was not here. Left behind when the call to muster came, too old to fight, he died anyway. Kneeling, I turn him over, gentle even though I know he is beyond pain, and unhook the keys from his belt. We shared them; he as overseer, me as Lady. His grey hair is sticking to his scalp, pressed down by thick blood. I press a kiss to my fingers and touch it to his brow before sliding my hand down to close his eyes. Will no one bury the poor man? And who will cut down his gentle, loyal, halfwit man-child from the top of the gateway? Must I ask the women to dig the graves? On my feet now, I hold helpless fists to my hips.

One of the intruders stares in my direction. He has a scar at the side of his mouth that makes him seem as though he is smiling. I point to poor Ælfwine and his son and mime the action of digging. 'Mark-mouth' grasps my meaning and shouts for men to cut down the hanged man and lift the reeve's body. To me he says, "*Église?*"

What does he mean? I shake my head.

He makes the sign of the cross and, understanding, I point to the churchyard. *Please God, let Priest Wulfnoth be there, alive, whole.*

Dare I follow them through the open gate? Someone should see whether the hazelnuts are ready to be gathered. I take a step nearer the gateway. Mark-mouth gives the smallest of nods. So, we are not prisoners. Yet our home is most assuredly occupied. I am out on the lane, walking more quickly now until the sound of the invaders fades away. All along the hedgerow the fruits of the season show themselves undisturbed by the changes. Haws, sloes, elderberries, blackberries, old man's beard, hop vines, rosehips. It could be as any other year. Except for the soldier behind me who takes a step along the lane a heartbeat after I take mine. I have come unprepared; with nothing else to use, my headcloth will have to become a makeshift basket.

As I pick, watched over by the men at the gate – I sense though that they are not only watching me, but that they are waiting for something, or someone – the long-legged harvest spiders dance away from the berries, scuttling from my fingers. Beyond the hedge, the Glynde Reach blinks blue in the sunlight, the water fresh and clear. Now, the minnows will be leaving to go upriver. As they go, so the fieldfare will come, settling on the hedgerow but I do not have the time to sit and wait, like I did as a child. Crossing the lane to the field, the soldier still following at a distance, I tread carefully, even though the adders should be asleep now until spring. The year is beginning to close, and there are fallen leaves on the grass. Horse chestnuts are here already and the big oak is full of galls. Will the scribes from the abbey still gather them to make ink? Will tomorrow be the same as today, with the sun rising and folk going about their chores? Only a few weeks ago, at Michaelmas, Old Mother Hildræd sent the children running to see what was inside the 'little oak apples', telling them that if they found a spider within, the crops would be sparse and ruined. Find a fly, she said, then the season would be blithe. A worm would show that the year would be calm, with all as it should be. They only found a worm and yet...

Returning with my bounty, I'm struck by how different even the smell from the stables is. Who would have thought that horses from another land would have their own odour? On the ground the dust is tainted red. Ælfwine's blood. I take the harvested fruit and nuts to the cook-house and leave them on the board without a word.

I reach for the weaving shed door with a shaking hand. My knees feel like limp rags that will not hold me up. Behind a slow blink, I see not only the shattered face of Ælfwine; now I have knowledge of what the rest of the men must look like, far away on that battlefield, strewn like unwanted bruised fruit across the ground, left for foraging creatures to pick what they will. Father, Edwin, Uncle Edric and his sons Ulf and Goda; none came home. We heard the hoofbeats and hoped. News came fast to our settlement, of King Harold's defeat, of the sons and fathers lost. The battle was not far away; just a day's ride, we were told. And Aldgyth went off to find her man. Is she, even now, trudging the battle site, trying to identify his mangled body? Will she find the other men? Do these invaders bury the dead?

They all rode out together, many weeks ago. We heard that they were heading north, and we did not understand how the fyrd came back south so swiftly. Edwin would not have minded; he was never happier than when in the saddle. As children, we would ride out often, sometimes paying for it with a scolding from Mother for neglecting our chores. Edwin cared less than I, teasing that I took life too seriously. I was ashamed, though, and stood before her with head bowed, cheeks on fire, for I wished always to be an obedient daughter. "Live a little!" Edwin would say, grinning so that his cheeks dimpled, and I would remind him that it was my duty to learn how to run the steading, his to learn to ride and fight. I did not realise how soon this would come to pass; did not expect our mother to die when Edwin and I were still so young. Then, he was not ashamed to weep. And I had to be the strong one, the one who held him, all snot and trembling. The one who comforted my father as the tears poured into his beard. Held him as if I were the parent, put my head against his soft hair, as he sobbed his loss into my shoulder.

And I must be strong now. I will not weep, for that would show that I believe them both to be dead now too. I cannot let myself lose all hope. And I must somehow persuade Oma to stop being so stubborn.

I join Eanflæd and we each work a side of the loom. The weights clack comfortingly as I pull the heddle, the wood warm and familiar in my hand, something known that I can clasp. It is less than a week since news arrived of King Harold's defeat and here we are, slaves all. At least while we are working the cloth, we can forget. But the movement is wrong; the loom weights clatter out of rhythm. Eanflæd, while separating the warp threads, has dropped the weaving sword on the floor. Glancing round the frame, I spot her tears and an odd pulsing at her throat as if she is trying to hold in a sob. She clutches the side of the loom for support. Bending to retrieve the dropped tool, I place it on the bench and hug my friend. We will work no more of our fine cloth today. Should we, I wonder, go instead to help with the wool carding?

Screams carry across the yard on a breeze that chills my bones.

It is a bigger concern even than Eanflæd's distress. She nods her acceptance that I must leave her. Rushing past the wort beds, where our leeks are growing fat and green, I am torn by the brambles which have crept too close to the beds. Rubbing at the scratches, I stumble into the hall.

Oma is not hurt, but she is causing an unholy row. The hairy-fingered soldier is taking away her treasured things one by one, picking up each item and waving it in front of her before throwing them in the fire. The wooden cup, that Opa turned on his pole-lathe for her and carved with love and care, spins as the Norman tosses it into the flames.

But then she stares up at him from her chair, nose and mouth moving as if someone has trodden a hound turd into the hall and she says, "Do you think I care? My husband gave me that and he's been dead these fifteen long years. I've no more need of it."

Memories rise, of tales told while we were sitting by this same fire, of Oma's life in Mercia as a young woman, how she met my greatfather, Opa, and how they upped and left with only a horse, a cart and a chest. Opa made wooden toys for me and Edwin. He would lull me to sleep telling me about their life in Gainsborough, but Oma would tell him "Shush" before he got to the part about why they left.

Hairy-fingers takes up the antler comb, kept always by the hearth. Opa carved the handle for her; this I know, because she would tell me whenever she combed my hair. I would sit on her knee while she gently pulled the tangles and braided my locks. Twisting love into my hair, she would say, the same love that she twisted into my mother's hair on the night she wed my father, thegn of Beddingham, and became lady of this vill. Now she makes the sound that Edwin and I always called her farting noise, a harrumph that makes her lips vibrate. "I'll not keen over that, for what need have I, with nary a wisp left on my head, for such a thing?" Sensing, no doubt, that he does not understand, she shrugs her shoulders with such dramatic flourish that she would put the gleemen who come at Yuletide to shame. To me, she says, without turning, "Go, my sweeting, back to the shed. Stay with Eanflæd and the others until it is time to eat." It is never wise to argue with her, so even though my hands are slick from cooling sweat and my legs are no stronger than a new-born foal's, I slip out of the room as Hairy-fingers reaches for another treasured item, a pot that I know was part of her morning gift when she wed Opa. It is hard to think of her as young and yet her eyes used to shine when she spoke of his gifts.

Throw it then, you silly man. Think I'll let you see that I care? Wait until you pick up that bowl, then you'll see me weep. Why? So that you don't know what is dear to me, and what is useless. So that you stay here, keep up your game, keep tormenting me, that's why. Would you have seen me if I'd meekly done as you bade me? Of course you wouldn't. Old women are not seen, are they? But our skin only shrinks round a body and mind that feel like they did when we were lithe and young. You will never know. You are a warrior and you will not grow old bones.

That's it, pick it up. Smash it hard and smash it well. It is worthless. But hear me as I wail. All you will know is that your taunting brings reward. So you'll keep it up. And you'll bide here in this hall with me. And it'll push my beloved grandchild to work with you against me. How else can I keep her safe?

Mark-mouth follows me outside. A gaggle at the gate are honking the word '*Robaire*'. Is this a name? Are they planning something for which this is the signal? They would have killed us all by now, surely, if that was their intention. They seem to want us to carry on working, to keep the landholding as if naught has happened. So it must be a day like any other. Ah, are they waiting for a new lord to come? If so, then my father truly is dead. And so it is not a day like any other and the world will never be the same again. I inhale, and the breath turns into a sob that makes me shudder and feels like an attack. I am close enough to the fence to grab the rail. With my back to them, I try to steady my shoulders so that they will not see that I am crying and the effort burns my chest and throat.

Here on the edge of the yard the fishpond, part of the old monastery, still holds some brown water. When I was little, Father would tell me tales of the monks who lived at the abbey in the time when Offa of Mercia ruled our kingdom of Sussex, before the West Saxons took us for their own. The monastery was burned down, folks say, by the Danish raiders who came not long after Offa's time. Oma always scoffed at the tale and would refuse to listen. She would never come down to the pond, even to chide us children when we were idly searching for fish when we should have been working. We knew we were safe, Edwin and I, and sometimes we would sit, take off our shoes and swirl our feet through the water, and I recall the way it tickled as it swooshed between my toes.

Daring to take a moment in a small act of defiance, I watch, and simply breathe. A wood pigeon flies into a pollarded ash grove while a dunnock beneath the hedge searches for insects, oblivious to the weasel who is lurking there, giving away his whereabouts only to me, a flash of brown at ground level, moving at speed.

At the field edge a vole is in the clover. The ditch is full of reeds and the teasel is still in flower. Edwin used to put dried teasels into my bed and, even in the midst of this terror, the memory of the prickles against my skin as I pushed my legs under the blanket, expecting no resistance, raises a smile.

The animals and plants have no notion of anything being amiss, yet the smoke on the air smells not of hearths but burned-out villages and brings my thoughts back to the knowledge that, like sticks thrown in the river, we are tossed this way and that with no control over the direction in which we now must travel. Never having been on the field of battle, I knew not what it was to see hatred and contempt in a man's eyes. I have seen it now.

Dear Edwin. One day my brother was stuffing prickles into my bed, and hardly a day later came the call came to join the fyrd and meet King Harold's men as they marched north. How can a soul be with you one day, gone the next? And what does it mean for us women, left behind, and now facing a new battle with no weapons to hand?

I could not swallow even a soft berry for my stomach would push it out again, but I do need to speak to Steapa the cook about the meal. Loaves will be in the oven but no more can be baked, not to be cooked in time. The cheeses hanging to be gently smoked by the heat of the ovens will not be ready; were not meant to be eaten now, so soon after harvest. We've only just finished storing the apples up in the lofts and we are still a week or more away from bloodmonth when the animals will be slaughtered. But this is something which often happens when the men come home from a hunt or a fight and we are not given fair warning. We will do what we always do in those circumstances, gathering what we can. The *briw* made of barley and flavoured with onion, garlic, cabbage and beets is bubbling away, and Steapa and I agree that we will simply have to supplement it and the daily bread with fruits and such nuts that are ready. The chickens are clucking at the other end of the yard, and it will be little work to ensure that there will be poultry on the table too.

Steapa's hand rests briefly on mine, and squeezes. This is not reassurance, but thanks. He, like the others, looks to his lady for guidance. The action sends my mind to thoughts which are not apt, amidst this sadness, and the realisation that my father will never now come to me to tell me of a wooing, that he has had a marriage agreement written up, mine to say yay or nay to. Not for me, now, young thegns at our table, offering me land, cows, trinkets; and all for me to keep, whether or not the marriage thrived. My free hand covers Steapa's. I have this vill, and these are my folk, under my protection. I will keep busy, and I will lead them.

Outside, just beyond the open doorway, Mark-mouth is looking at the children who, contrary to expectation, are still playing, as if nothing has happened, throwing acorns from the pig feed sacks and catching them. The man looks at them and smiles, a real lifting of his lips and not just the illusion caused by his scar. He sees me watching him, and points at young Ælfric. Then he taps his chest. I shake my head. He repeats the action, and makes a cradling, rocking motion with his arms. All I can do is shrug. I turn away and begin to make my way to the bakehouse and then it comes to me. Was he saying that he has a child of the same age?

A shriek, then the sound of a child wailing. A hurried conversation with Steapa about serving flat hearth cakes instead of bread, and I run outside. Ælfric is lying on the dusty ground, clutching his knee. Blood is seeping through his fingers.

"*L'enfant est blessé.*" Mark-mouth points to the child.

Blessed? How can he be blessed to have scuffed his knee? Do these Northmen have no kindness at all? Yet he scoops the boy up in his arms, his strength allowing him even so to raise his shoulders as if in query. I think he is asking me where to take young Ælfric, and I gesture for him to follow me.

"*J'ai un fils. Il s'appelle Guy. Il a cinq ans.*"

Sank on? Sank on what? He did not sink; he fell.

"Here." I open the door to the tanner's dwelling, where the child's mother is resting, heavy with the babe who will be born before year's end. The soldier places the boy, gently I notice, on the bed beside his mother. Gytha wakes and her eyes open wide briefly before falling into narrow slits of hatred. She is too loving a mother to spit the curses I know are forming in her mouth; her duty is to her son, and all her attention must rest on him, not the man who, for all we know, killed her husband only days ago.

He points at Gytha, then looks at me. "*Mère?*"

I shake my head. There are no horses inside.

He points again, waggling his finger between Gytha and the boy. "*Maman?*"

Mother? I nod. "Mother."

I clasp Gytha's hand, giving a squeeze. "I will fetch some water and a cloth. I think it is not deep. The sight of the blood upset him, that is all."

Gytha pats my hand with her free one, then swings her legs from the bed and stands up. She brushes her little finger across the child's cheek and kisses his forehead. To me she says, "I will do it." She looks into my eyes and need say no more. I hear the thought. She must keep busy or go mad with loss.

My father was her lord; now I am her lady. Her

bairns will stay with her and her man's money will be paid in equal parts to her and any of his kin. She will have her acres, and not lack; her bodily needs and those of her children will be met and none shall say that she must wed again unless she wishes. I can ensure that all this comes to pass, I can watch over her. But I cannot mend her heart.

Returning to Steapa, thinking only to make sure that there is not more to discuss, I am wrong-footed when he asks will all these men be staying?

Making my way back to the hall, Mark-mouth following me, I am tempted to dance sideways to see if he will too, just like I used to try to outwit my shadow when I was a girl. Cursing, I walk into the outstretched bramble again. Mark-mouth stops, peers at my leg with what, is that a look of worry? He spies a berry, still plump unlike the many that are shrivelled now, and he reaches out to pick it. I have to choke back a laugh as his fingers are treated to the same attack recently launched on my ankles. The difference, though, is that now the tiny spears have drawn blood. It seems that the bramble spikes wish to protect the fruit, even when it is not necessary.

Stepping into the hall, I say, "The brambles need to be cut back. Shall I do it?"

Oma stares at the hearth, but she answers me. "Yes. But only to get to the berries."

"Why do I need the berries?

Oma laughs and the soldiers seem startled, putting down their drinks to stare. "Offer them to these beasts," she says.

"But they shouldn't be eaten now. It is too late in the year and they will have the devil's spit on them."

"Indeed. But they won't know it."

I shake my head. Why must she be so difficult? She will bring the wrath of the soldiers down on us all. And yet... Mark-mouth is watching me and then he looks heavenward. If I could think of him as anything but an enemy, I would swear he was showing pity, as if he, too, knows what it is to have a stubborn old member of kin.

"I will go now to do it. And I'll gather the berries though I think they should not be eaten."

Oma nods but says, "Even so."

It is clear that they will not let me wend around the steading without an escort and this time Hairy-fingers moves to accompany me. Oma lurches forwards to grab a glass bowl, clutching it to her chest and sobbing. I've seldom seen her move so swiftly. This bowl is old, and of no value, sentimental or otherwise. Why is she fretting over it so? A snarl from Hairy-fingers and he crosses the hall in two strides, snatching the bowl from her weak hands and smashing it against the wall.

Guilt overwhelms like a wet, heavy cloak as I try to calm her, as if I am siding with them against my own kin. "You mustn't upset them."

Hairy-fingers seems to have been reminded of the sport in breaking Oma's possessions, so it is the kindlier man who comes with me.

As we step outside, he nods his head towards the hall. "*Grand-mère*?"

It sounds a little like the word he used for Gytha, which I think was 'mother'.

"She is my oma. Eldermother. Greatmother."

He gives me a little smile. I think we understand each other. But who knows? Perhaps what he really said was a rude word. Who could blame him? I wish Oma would calm herself. There is enough to worry about without her odd behaviour adding to my load.

I must do what I can to get the meal ready. I beckon Mark-mouth to follow me – as if he would not, anyway – and I point to the loft where the apples are stored. He seems to understand and fetches the ladder. There is a moment when he weighs up the wisdom of unbuckling his sword to make the climb easier, and then it is clear he sees me as no threat. With a big basket now cradled in my arms, I can demonstrate that I'll be in no position to grab the weapon. So we work together, he and I, as he clanks up and down the ladder bringing me apples which he places with more care than I'd expected into my waiting basket. It is a task that Edwin and I often performed together when we were younger.

Does this man have children who slither up and down ladders and play in the haylofts? How many kin has he left behind, to wonder about his fate? Is there a child like Ælfric waiting for his father to come home? A wife like Gytha, weeping for her man? This man might have loved ones waiting for him over the sea, but one day he will be able to go back to them. Are Father and Edwin coming back to me? He hands me an apple and I wave it and nod, to indicate that this must be the last. I might want to spit in his eye, but I cannot. For I need to live. We all do. We do what we have to do. Why can Oma not see that? He steps off the bottom rung and I don't step back in time. I can smell him, his warmth, the odour of sweat, leather, metal, strength. All men smell this way, but this is the first time that the stink of maleness has frightened me.

The yard is still full of bustling life as we make our way to the cook-house. Mark-mouth relieves me of my burden when Ceadda the hayward approaches.

"Shall I cut the hedges, Lady?"

"Let us wait and see if we can gather more berries and nuts. We might need them."

Wilburh the miller's wife calls across.

"Yes," I tell her, "we will need more wheat ground. I will send Eanflæd to help with the quern stone."

"Are they staying, then, Lady?"

I glance at Mark-mouth as he emerges from the cook-house.

"Yes, I rather think they are."

The hayward asks, "Will the slaughterman still come and help us with bloodmonth?"

"If he can. If he still lives." I suppose we must all carry on as normal. *I must carry on as normal. I* squeeze his hand. *The same as any other day.*

I tap Mark-mouth on the arm, point to the brambles and then to his sword. He understands and begins hacking at the thorny stragglers, allowing me to get to the berries, although even while I pick I have to wipe them. They really are not fit to eat. More noise wafts from the hall and it's clear Oma has not finished goading her guards. Mark-mouth and I exchange glances and I fancy that he might feel sorry for me, were we to meet in other times.

I don't care what you think. Are you going to pick me up and throw me out of my chair? Ah, so you think I shouldn't sit at the table, is that it? You're waiting for someone important to come, aren't you? Don't need a bothersome old trout causing problems. Well here's the thing. I shall keep bothering you if it keeps you here, and away from my granddaughter. Soon as I saw you I marked you out as the one who'd be harshest. So you can bide with me young man. Hmm, fingers itching to smite, eh? I don't mind losing a tooth or more. Better you take bits of me than anything of her.

I put the over-ripe blackberries on the table. "Oma, behave. They will hurt you."

The men sit for the meal, such as it is. The cereal *briw* is as good as ever, and the cooked chicken is tasty. We have the apples and some hard cheese, but my leek beds are not yet ready to harvest. It is too late in the year for fresh peas and the dried ones aren't ready yet. I serve our 'guests' as is my honour and right as the lady of the household. I gather, though, from their smirks, that they think it demeaning. It must be that things are done differently where they come from. I pour their drinks and they seem to think that I have accepted their overlordship. Is it not their custom that the lady of the house offers such hospitality? Do they not see the keys at my belt, signifying my rank? They raise their cups and there is yet more honking, but I catch among it the one name I know. *'Robaire'* they shout. Why? And why are they pointing at me and making obscene gestures? Oh yes, it would seem that some actions need no translation.

Oma begins to sing. "How many Northmen to fill my pit? Slaughter some more and make them fit."

Hairy-fingers picks up Oma's glass. He keeps his gaze on her while he drinks her wine. That glass is special. Opa gave it to her. Yet when Hairy-fingers makes as if to smash it on the floor, she shrugs. There seems to be no sport for him and he places it back upon the table. How can she be so calm and pretend it doesn't matter? How can she resist the urge now to reach out, grab it, hold it safe in her hand?

The bowl of blackberries sits at the centre of the table, along with sloes, apples, and the hazelnuts I gathered earlier. Oma laughs as the soldiers take some of the blackberries. "Ha! Eat the devil's spit."

They look up. *"Qu'est-ce que c'est?"*

Do you think that leaning forward like that will make me cringe and cower?

"Dis-le encore, Vieille."

I have a name, Northman. Does that surprise you? Huh? No, well, even my own kin scarce remember it. I'm an old woman, even if I don't feel like that inside. Do you think I fear you? One cruel leader is very much like another.

I'm not "Vee-yay", whoever she is. I'm not even English. My father was Danish. When I was a child, the English king ordered all the Danish men to be killed on St Brice's Day. Why? Because they were Danish and different and he was scared. They weren't víkingar, they were settled, farmers. But he had 'em killed anyway. Folk said it could never happen again. Not in my lifetime. And yet here we are.

Oh, settle back. I'll quieten down for a while now.

"Dis-le encore!"

They seem to want Oma to do or say something but we have no understanding. What could they possibly want from an old woman? I push the plates of bread towards them and stand up to make my rounds with the ale jug once more, hoping to take their gaze away from her.

My earliest memory is of fire. I was rooted to the spot but I wasn't looking so much as listening. I had never heard such loud flames. They were eating the timbers of the house, cracking the wood and spitting splintered sparks of illuminated heat. The roof thatch disappeared with a rustling sound that was quieter but no less cruel. This was no friendly hearth fire, where the flames danced and offered warmth and comfort. This was vicious, hungry, and heartless.

A hand grasped mine and pulled me back from the heat. For a moment I could not breathe properly, my nose pressed into my mother's breast. She scooped me up and carried me to another house. I do not recall whose house it was. I will never forget the loudness of the keening, though, as my mother howled with pain. I felt sorry for her, thinking that she had burned herself in the flames and was hurting. I sat quietly where I had been placed and watched the grown-ups moving around, as if they knew what to do, although even at such a tender age, I think I sensed that they did not. Only much later did I learn that my father had perished inside that burning building. That the fire had been set on purpose. That he died because he was different.

Oma has gone somewhere with her thoughts. She has that look about her; she stares out across the room but does not see. But now it is as if someone has wafted a lit candle across her face, for she is wearing a smile and she's beckoning me to her.

"Come, child. Let me tell you a tale. Let me tell you about your opa."

But she doesn't. She stares at the hearth and I know she sees memories in the flames.

Ælfred wasn't good-looking the way some men are. I cannot say that I ever looked into his eyes and felt my heart melt, but he was a good man and he had a merry smile which always lifted my mood. He was darker than most men, the shade of his hair the same as his Welsh mother's. Maybe that marked him out, or maybe it was bad fate that we lived in the wrong part of the town. The wrong part for that day.

We were a neighbourhood of incomers, really, and we were like a big pot of foods not normally cooked together but that gives a good flavour. My parents were settlers from Denmark, and we lived in Eastern Mercia, that some call the Danelaw. Others, like my man, grew up there after their English fathers were given land by the English kings. Ælfred's father brought his Welsh wife with him from Shrewsbury.

Ælfred wasn't rich, but he was a skilled woodworker. He was more than a tree-wright, for he would work small objects on his pole-lathe. I loved to watch him and would often get behind with my own chores. He'd say, "This one is for your mother, that will keep her sweet." And my mother grew to love him too. She had more cups and bowls than her neighbours, which might have had something to do with it. She chided me about my missed chores, but only sometimes. She was more wroth if she ever heard me speaking Danish. "We are Mercians. Even here we are not safe." And she would remind me what had happened to my father. Oh yes, even in the Danelaw it was safer to be English.

Until the day Swein Forkbeard's army came.

I was with Ælfred. He had just asked me to marry him. That is the moment in your life when you don't listen to anything else. The world and all the folk in it melt away. So only slowly did I hear the sound. Like a disturbed ants' nest, our town was all of a sudden pulsing with a life force that was not normal. There was human noise – not market traders – and the animals were squawking, bleating, bellowing. Mother came running and soldiers were behind her. In English, she shouted to us to run. "To the gates. Go!" The men looked at my man. In Danish they shouted at him. His Danish was never as good as mine and in the cloud of babble and fear he struggled to understand.

But I knew. They wanted him dead. Maybe me, too, because I was with him. And they knew that I was really 'with' him, for we had been holding hands, we were in love. My mother screamed one more time for us to leave and then she turned and faced them. I was rooted, held fast to the ground, like that night all those years ago when I was six years old. This time the sound was not of burning, but of my mother cursing. She spat and swore at them, in English. They knocked her lengthways. Her cap flew off and one of the men stood on her hair. Another forced her legs apart. She did not submit. She flailed, she shouted. And I've no doubt that she died that day.

A hand tugged mine. He took me to safety. Out of the eastern gate we ran. We stopped at his steading only to throw his tools into a cart and we fled. We took only what we needed, what we could gather in a hurry. He said we must travel lightly. I never understood how we moved so quickly, when the burden in my heart was like a millstone. My mother had sacrificed herself in order to save my life. Because being Danish was no good. Because being English was no longer safe.

We never stopped moving until we reached the sea. And I never spoke Danish or Mercian again. Until today.

We made our home in Beddingham, though I have no idea why. I think we simply decided that we had run far enough. Ælfred made all manner of useful things and we learned swiftly how to speak the tongue of the West Saxons. An old mother told me about the monastery and how it had been burned by marauding Danes back in Old King Offa's day. It wasn't so much the thought of Danes but the remembered sounds of hostile fire that kept me from the place. Our daughter kept away from it too, maybe sensing my fears, *but my grandchildren showed no timidity. There was nothing in their lives to make them fearful. Born in a time of peace, what did they know of war, of want, of hunger or degradation?*

We lived through it, but the world was a better place for them. They were safe. Oh, kings came and went, but now to be Danish was no bad thing, nor to be English. We were all English, brought together under Cnut, and then the old king, Edward. Our last king, Harold, I heard tell, had a Danish mother and an English father. All was settled. No more hatred.

Ælfred died, and I mourned. I grew into my twilight years and without a man to tell me how lovely I was, I admit that I stopped bothering to be lovely. But that was not my purpose any more. I helped my daughter, and dandled the babies, and I faded, slowly, like a footprint on a dry path smudged out bit by bit by raindrops. I'd reach out sometimes from my chair, and stroke the smooth sides of my wooden bowl. The sagging skin on the back of my hand is creased, threaded through with blue bumpy lines, but that soft turned wood underneath my fingers brings undimmed memories of Ælfred. I will carry on fading until I melt into the very walls, but inside, oh, inside, I am eighteen, I am loved, and I love. In my dreams I move with knees and ankles that are not swollen from painful old age. In my dreams I run, not fettered by creaking bones.

Now, in my hall where I have faded year on year, I must make them see me. So that they don't see her.

"La vieille est silencieuse! C'est bon!"

There is laughter. One of the men slaps his hand on the table, and this must be a way of showing approval. At least we have some things in common.

But Hairy-fingers is not laughing.

That's right. I'll keep annoying you and you'll leave her alone. I saw what the last lot did to my mother, even though she was half-Dane. Where? Where do we belong, huh? My father killed by the English because he was Dane. My mother raped by Danes who thought she was English. Now you come and you see no difference between Dane and English; you hate us all.

"*Dis-le encore, Vieille!*"

His ire seems to be rising. I think back, to before the silence. She mentioned the berries and then said no more. Now she offers the fruit to those who've not already taken some.

To me she says, "Gobbed all over by Satan. Good!"

They stop talking, and they repeat the word 'Satan' although there seems to be some debate over how to pronounce it. They say it our way, then their way, as if trying to decide if it means the same thing.

Oma chuckles. "Keep eating, Pigs, there's more. Lots more!"

"*La mort?*"

Hairy-fingers frowns in anger, brows together. Mark-mouth's brows are raised, concerned. Whatever she thought she was doing, Oma's game has gone too far. They seem to know that the berries will give them bellyache.

"Go on, take more! All nicely covered with Satan spit! More, more!"

Hairy-fingers is on his feet.

Ah no, this was not what I meant to do. To tease, to annoy, but not this. Now I cannot help her.

I barely see it. It's not how I expect the moment of death to be. Her gentle weathered smile fades to a look of regret that lingers even after his sword has gone through her. How can there be so much blood from a tiny old woman?

Some of them are thumping the table, as if what has happened is a good thing. There's that word again, '*Vee-yay.*' Why did they call her that? She had a name. Of course she bled; is bleeding still. She was a woman just like the rest of us. Not shrunken, not overlooked. She had a name.

She is lying on the floor, a tiny sprawled heap, and I want to tend her, twist some love into her hair as she once did mine.

But I haven't moved. Can't move. The honking and the braying continue. '*Robaire*' they say, and it sounds like a worrying thing.

The door opens, banging back against the wall where once our men would hang their shields and swords, for our men did not bring their weapons to the table. Aldgyth hurries in through the open space, small in the doorway, small against the men who block her path. She is back from her quest to find her man, or his body, on the battlefield. She stops when she sees the Northmen, but she does not seem surprised to find them here.

I think, dully, that they have let her through the gate because she is a woman and thus no threat. Yet here I am, standing by Oma's dead body. There is no sense to this. This is a day like no other.

Aldgyth does not even tell me whether she found her man or, indeed, if she even got as far as the battle place, as she set out to do. Instead, drawing jagged breaths, she tells me what she has witnessed at Firle, less than an hour's walk from here.

"There is a priest there who was schooled at Fleury and speaks the Norman tongue."

My wits return long enough to recall that Firle, belonging to far-off Wilton Abbey, is often host to monks and priests who are well-travelled and highly learned. What, though, is the importance of this?

"It is a rich estate. And they have sent a rich lord who will have it for his own."

I am aware of the body of my last remaining kin growing colder on the floor and care not for the riches of Firle or its new owner.

"He is taking it all. And he will come here next. And..." Her hands on my shoulders. Shaking me? No, preparing me. "He, like all the other new lords, will take an English bride."

This cannot be. We have laws. No woman can be married against her will. And my father's lands belong to me if Edwin has died too. These lands are mine by law. I think that either Aldgyth or I are mad with grief. She sees the disbelief in my eyes.

"It is true. His name, they say, is Robaire."

The word chills, setting the hairs on my arms dancing as if a wind has blown the curtain hanging on the wall behind me. This is what they have been chanting, his name said with reverence. But Firle is the richer estate. This Lord Robaire will stay there, surely?

It is as if she can hear my thoughts. "They say that they are slicing up the lands, reward for butchery of Englishmen. Robaire will be the lord, but he will not allow us to keep our lands. So each hall will have a new lord."

Now she is hugging me close, her lips next to my ear, her voice a husky precautionary whisper even though they cannot understand. "He will make you wed one of these beasts." And beyond the wisps of her windswept hair that tickle my face, I see him. Hairy-fingers. He's been the one barking the orders since daybreak.

I ease from her embrace, so that I do not hurt her with the hammering of my heart. Blood pounds against the insides of my ears, whooshing in time with the thudding, making me feel sick. When he rapes me, he will not even understand my pleas of no, my begging him to stop. So I will be mute. I can only thank God that Oma has not lived to see what will become of me. She had no idea that it would be like this, or she would not have goaded them so.

Hairy-fingers is shouting, pointing at Oma and making sweeping movements. *"Emportez le corps de la vieille."*

I look at Mark-mouth. His face is set. Kindness only goes so far. He is first and foremost a soldier. I will have no friends among these men. And no man will protect me. There will be no rescue. My only weapon is submission.

The people who lived under my father's protection now look to me. We must make tomorrow the same as yesterday. It must be like any other day. We must go on as before, as if the world has not burned. It is the only way we will keep our lives. I will be meek. I will let him have me and I will not shout, or cry, or plead. Tomorrow.

But this evening, I will roar the once. "She is not Vee-yay. She had a name. It was the same as mine. Her name was Kàta. My name is Kàta. Take our lives, take our land. Take our tongue..." I am on my knees beside her. I am stroking her hair, and tears and snot fall freely, the only things which will be released from this place. "But not our name. You will not have that."

Two men come forward; they take her from me and

one of them brushes past the scratch where the bramble bit me. It takes only one, in the end, to heft her tiny body outside. The open door brings only a glimmer of light as the day dims to night. The other man, no longer needed as pallbearer, hacks away at what is left of the blackberry bush.

© Annie Whitehead

Author's note

Vieille is French for 'old woman'. (The French used in this story is modern, not Old French.) Beddingham and Firle were Anglo-Saxon place names and Firle was part of the Wilton Abbey estate. It appears that there was a monastery at Beddingham in the ninth century, and that the land was under the control of Earl Godwine, father of King Harold, in the eleventh century. There is no reason why a leading thegn such as Kàta's father would not have held land there, and owed service to the Godwines. After the battle of Hastings, the whole area was given over to Robert, Count of Mortain. Laws were in place to protect women in Anglo-Saxon times from rape and forced marriage, laws confirmed by Cnut, even though 'Oma' didn't like him. The rights and privileges of women in Anglo-Saxon England, who were able to hold land in their own right and bequeath it as they wished, were much reduced by the Conquest.

The St Brice's Day Massacre in 1002, mentioned by 'Oma', saw an order by Æthelred the Unready to kill Danish men in England, and the townsfolk chased them into a church and set it on fire. A woman who was a child at that time could feasibly have lost a parent in that fire, witnessed the Danish invasions of Swein Forkbeard in 1013 and his son, Cnut, and lived to see the English monarchy restored with the accession of Edward the Confessor and the Norman Conquest of 1066. 'Oma' would still, therefore, have been only in her late sixties.

About Annie

Annie Whitehead is a prize-winning writer, historian, and Fellow of the Royal Historical Society, and has written four award-winning novels set in 'Anglo-Saxon' Mercia. She has contributed to fiction and nonfiction anthologies and written for various magazines. She has twice been a prize winner in the Mail on Sunday Novel Writing Competition, and won First Prize in the 2012 New Writer Magazine's Prose and Poetry Competition. She has been a finalist in the Tom Howard Prize for nonfiction and was shortlisted for the Exeter Story Prize and Trisha Ashley Award 2021. She was the winner of the inaugural Historical Writers' Association (HWA)/Dorothy Dunnett Prize 2017 and was subsequently a judge for that same competition. She has also been a judge for the HNS (Historical Novel Society) Short Story Competition, and was a 2024 judge for the HWA Crown Nonfiction Award.

Her nonfiction books are *Mercia: The Rise and Fall of a Kingdom* (published by Amberley books) and *Women of Power in Anglo-Saxon England* (Pen & Sword Books). In 2023 she contributed to a new history of English monarchs, published by Hodder & Stoughton, and in February 2025 *Murder in Anglo-Saxon England* was published by Amberley Books.

Website: https://anniewhiteheadauthor.co.uk/
Twitter: https://twitter.com/AnnieWHistory
Facebook: https://www.facebook.com/
anniewhiteheadauthor/
Amazon Author Page: http://viewauthor.at/Annie-
Whitehead

2

______

SIX POMEGRANATE SEEDS

BY JEAN GILL

A daughter's dream can be a mother's nightmare.

Sicilia 1240 – Nina

If a noble Sicilian girl had brothers, she could acquire an education in the same manner as a dog found scraps under the table. Happily for Nina's education, she did have brothers, and she gobbled up the scraps that came her way, making herself invisible in a corner of the room where her brothers were being tutored.

Latin was necessary but usually tedious, with its histories, battles and clever mudslinging. The scraps also included Greek, of course, for their island's landscape was the battlefield of ancient heroes, the place where Odysseus blinded the one-eyed giant and where followers of Dionysus drank themselves into a sacred alcoholic stupor.

Nina suspected her parents would be none too pleased at their sons receiving the latter example, given the natural inclinations of boys with wealth and opportunity. For her own part, having seen her brothers in a fug of Dionysian hilarity, she saw little attraction in being simultaneously deprived of your wits and convinced of your wittiness.

The best lessons were when the tutor, Signor Marco, forgot his charges and his duty to provide a classical education, and indulged in his passion for troubadour poetry. What he called the *real* troubadour poetry, which had travelled to northern Italy from Provence, then to Sicilia, courtesy of Signor Marco. Nobody else understood a word he declaimed but the sound of the Provençal language had a music that transported Nina's soul, even before Signor Marco translated the meaning.

Knights and their ladyloves, forbidden love and courtly manners, parting at dawn and heartache, even the vulgar puns (carefully pointed out by the tutor) were elevated to the sublime by this music. If Signor Marco had been young and dashing, instead of bald, portly and pedantic, Nina would have fallen in love with him. Instead, she fell in love with poetry itself.

Although adamant that Provençal was the true language of the troubadours, Signor Marco conceded that there were now passable imitations in Italian, such as the work of Giacomo da Lentini and his circle at King Frederick's court here in Palermo, or of the Florentine, Dante da Maiano.

"You could be among such luminaries if you work hard," Signor Marco encouraged his students.

I doubt it, thought Nina, but she absorbed every detail of the new fashion in poetry, a set pattern in fourteen lines. She joined in silently when Signor Marco made his young students compose such verse – in Latin.

Never was such an ill-assorted match made, thought Nina, *as between Latin and troubadour poetry.* She vowed to write such 'sonnets' using her own language, as the troubadours had. The boys' results, which they read aloud, were as stilted and ugly as hers, but no doubt satisfied parental expectations for their sons' education.

Unfortunately, Nina's parents also had (very different) expectations for *her* education and she found her mother more exacting as the years passed and childhood became time-she-was-married. Preparation for a suitable marriage required lessons from her mother in dress, social nuances and household management, so she could ably support her husband-to-be (nameless as yet).

When Nina was seventeen, her parents' discussion of various suitors reached an intensity she could no longer ignore but she *could* procrastinate, "Until the autumn. I will decide then." *Or have my mind made up for me.*

Nina's dowry being considerable, so was the choice of men, but she'd narrowed it down to the three who did not repel her physically. With her mother as chaperone, they had permission to speak with her. After such occasions, she used her skills in social nuances to conduct her own enquiry into these eligible men, usually when eavesdropping. She added her own findings to the judgements she overheard her parents making.

Signor Aureliu was twenty-two, heir to a grand estate in the west, where he spent his summers. The rest of the year, he graced Palermo with his wit and elegance. He would keep a young girl's interest and mature into a respectable husband. *Because he's not one bit respectable at the moment, with a string of mistresses and eyes that sparkle for any pretty pair of ankles. As ready with compliments as innuendos, all distributed as randomly as a fisherman casts his net. But we could go our own ways and amuse each other.*

Luckily, her chaperone had stayed tactfully out of

earshot, so Nina had the full benefit of Signor Aureliu's colourful language and suggestions. He clearly thought he had much to teach her, but she blushed because he was embarrassing, not because she felt an attack of modesty.

Signor Custanzu was thirty, a prosperous merchant based in Palermo and, according to Nina's parents, would prove a steadying influence on a young girl with unrealistic expectations of life. *A boring father-substitute who meted out his words as if they were gold coins. Impossible to fathom a man who barely spoke. Either he had hidden depths or was too shallow to converse with. And not one compliment from him.*

He'd said so little that, against all her mother's advice, she'd been forced to do all the talking and blushed afterwards for what she'd said. The worst of her sins had probably been explaining the scansion of the new form of poetry that was all the rage in Palermo. *What man likes a woman explaining anything to him?* And she might have mentioned her admiration for Dante da Maiano, the Florentine poet. *What man enjoys hearing a woman wax lyrical about another man?* However, Signor Custanzu remained as stolid as ever and had merely posed brief questions that, unfortunately, encouraged her to continue in the same vein. If her mother had not been out of earshot, she might have restrained herself, but this time her blushes were over her own comportment.

Signor Guiliu was twenty-seven, a clerk at the Palace, of modest means but with entry to the finest society. Her husband would be forever grateful to his wife for the enhancement to his standing that she brought him. Court life would give a high-spirited young girl every opportunity to refine her manners and conversation. *While married to someone who sees himself as* inferior and who would be subservient to all those around him, even to me and my family. If only he didn't stutter, wasn't so earnest. I could do as I wished with such a deferential husband – and be pitied by everyone. But maybe I could change him.

Her thoughts veered like a weather vane between the three men. How could you make such a crucial decision for your future, when you weren't sure who you wanted to be?

Each suitor had sent a letter to her parents, formally requesting her hand, with a personal note enclosed for Nina. In a liberal moment, her mother had passed on these notes, but Nina felt no more interest in their statements of intent to her, than in those to her parents. She could predict every word of them and they would not help her choose. The notes remained unopened in her jewellery box.

Summer allowed the whole family respite from difficult decisions by the simple process of quitting the hot, dusty city of Palermo for their summer home by the shore of Laga di Pergusa. No lessons, no council meetings, no household to manage. Instead, there were her father's groves of oranges and pistachio nut trees, which all thrived, transforming him into a peasant who smiled and grabbed his wife around the waist.

In the relaxed atmosphere of their summer home, nobody noticed Nina slip away each day to sit and dream by the lakeside in the shade of a holm oak, while the long-tailed birds whistled and swooped in dizzy loops, and skimmed the water, catching flies. Seasonal visitors, like her.

She could see a plume of smoke from the mountain the locals called Mamma Etna, which Greek myths claimed was once the smithy of the old lame god, Hephaestus. She could hear the rumblings of his bellows at work. Or was it a roar from the enraged Titan who was buried underneath a rock flung by Zeus to pin him down? Defeated but not dead, the Titan roared and spewed ash, even spouted flame whenever he could bore a hole to the surface.

Nina's imagination dived beneath the conical mountain-top on the surface to the forge of the gods below. Below the forge, the captive Titan, and below *that* – a cloud covered the sun briefly and Nina shivered. Below that, lay Tartarus, the hellish underworld of the ancients. From this very lake, so the story said, Persephone...

But no. Nina stopped herself. Here all alone in this wild place, she should not be thinking of such a tale. The cloud had passed, and the dappled sunshine soothed her, made her languorous, languid, lulled... *so sleepy...*

Persephone

How I love them, these friends of mine. The wood nymphs are wearing all the flowers they've picked, as garlands in their loosened hair and as low-slung girdles which shed yellow croci and violets as they dance. My mother would approve their footfall, the seedlings springing up as they step so lightly on the fertile ground. The ground my mother, the earth goddess, *makes* fertile.

My half-sisters Artemis and Athene are with us today and, of course, I am delighted to be outshone by Zeus' more accomplished daughters on what was supposed to be a simple maidens' outing to pick flowers and, if I'm honest, a chance to get away from my mother. She's so protective she suffocates me.

I'm not saying she's hypocritical but a woman who

conceived you while transformed into a serpent and intertwined with the King of the Gods (likewise transformed), is not the best advocate for staying with your friends and not talking to strangers. Although as *she* sees it, her experience makes her exactly the right person to give me warnings about the danger lurking in every shadow, in every flower.

Artemis and Athene suffer no such admonitions, least of all from their mere-mortal mothers. And strangers beware! If you so much as look awry at either of these two delectable and dangerous goddesses, you're likely to be changed into a stag and hunted by your own hounds.

Unfortunately, their maidenhood is as legendary as their self-esteem and they have every right to join our band of flower-plucking virgins, seemingly as unaware of the symbolism as of our hopes. We would love our flowers to be plucked but there is no hope that Artemis or Athene feel likewise. The last priestess of Athene who succumbed to earthly passion is now wearing snakes for hair, and turns to stone any who look on what used to be her lovely face.

The sisters, *my* sisters, are jealous goddesses, and when they are with us maidens, we must indeed pick flowers joyfully. I wouldn't be surprised if my mother bribes them to come. To make it worse, they always get the best flowers and pile their baskets the highest.

Well, they're not having *that* flower. Shimmering in the water is the reflection of wild narcissi, a hundred heads or more, and nodding among them is the most bewitching flower I have ever seen. Petals of white samite, gleaming and silken. A heart of pure gold, with puffs of yellow seeds so soft they could pillow honeybees. I need to touch it, to make it mine. I glance around, checking that the sisters are not watching before I hitch up my chiton and wade towards the narcissus. I don't stop to think how strange it is that this flower is growing in the water, dazzling among its companions, glowing and huge.

All I think is, *It's mine.* My robe drops into the water, forgotten, as I reach out and stroke a silken petal, insert a finger into the golden heart, bring it out flecked with gold.

Then the impulse is too strong and I grab the stem, pull with all my might. The earth cracks open in a roar that hurts my ears, sends the nymphs shrieking to find trees in which they can hide. Artemis and Athene are nowhere to be seen. *Where are sisters when you need them?*

I am holding the narcissus, evidence of my guilt, when *he* emerges from the growing fissure in the earth. He is darkness itself, driving a golden chariot and whipping four black stallions to a frenzy. I can see the whites of their eyes and the froth around their mouths as he reaches down, hoists me up beside him.

I scream.

He turns the chariot in a manoeuvre that would win me a fortune if I bet on him in the races and then we gallop down through the chasm. And down. And down. Into Tartarus itself, where souls are judged.

"Persephone, my wife," murmurs the dark god of the underworld, the lord who has many guests: Hades.

Oh, fuck. Perhaps my mother was right.

Demeter

You couldn't understand, is what she always says to me. "You've never loved someone so much you'd die if you lost them. So much you'd do anything to keep them. I mean anything. That's true love."

I started to tell her. "Once," I said quietly, "there was a man..."

She cut in. "Well, you're still here," she said, "and doing just fine, so you got over it, whatever it was. I don't want to know. I would never get over losing the love of my life." Dramatic pause. "But then I'm not the goddess of fertility." Sarcastic gesture of benison. "Blessings and bounty be upon you. Kneel a bit lower when you worship at my shrine."

A flounce and she was gone. Picking flowers, she said, but she's not back yet. I'm glad her sisters were with her. Artemis and Athene understand how precious virginity is, and how fragile. They could fend off anyone or anything that came for my matchless daughter. Except perhaps... no, he wouldn't dare. She's just a bit late back from picking flowers by the lake.

We'll make up from our latest disagreement when she gets back home. It is the way of the Fates, who love irony, that she cannot see the girl I was, the passion and pain that lives in me still, that I suppress so I can be a good mother. It is *she* who does not understand – but how could she? I have lived through youth such as hers, but she has not lived my years or known the fear and guilt and wild joy of motherhood.

Why isn't she home? Is she sulking?

I should wait, let her come to me but I can't bear the waiting, the worrying.

She's very late.

After a lifetime of hours, I hear her scream, muffled as if the air has thickened to slow down its passage so I will be too late to save her. There is no time to harness my winged serpents, the fire-breathing drakones, and take my chariot. What matters is to find her.

Quick as thought, I change into a bird and soar through the deceitful air, which holds its breath as I pass so as not to give anything away. As if I could not sense any tension in my domain, like a spider feeling one thread in her web vibrate, knowing the intruder is there. Or has been there and evaded the trap.

I start my search by the lake, calling her name until my voice is hoarse. I'm sure the trees are listening, but they rustle their leaves and tell me nothing. I'm sure the water creatures are listening, but they vanish to the deeps. I hear the gentle plops and splashes as they dive beyond my reach.

I'm sure the rocks are listening, but their stony silence hides the cause of fractures that I'm sure were not there yesterday. As if an earthquake has smashed some boulders, just here, then rearranged them much as they were before. But I felt no earthquake.

There is no other sign of disturbance, unless you count a small pile of ashes that gives off a faint scent of spring flowers, croci and narcissi. There is no trace of the maidens who should be here picking those flowers. Instead, they are long gone, at home probably, or with Persephone, wherever the hell she might be.

"Persephone!" I scream, my voice sending rabbits into their burrows and scattering birds from treetops.

"Demeter?" comes the answer. I know the voice and where to find the queen of arcana. Hecate, Queen of Witches, has something to tell me.

On the surface, all seems well. On the surface.

I spread my wings and fly to Hecate's cave, settle on a stone ledge and out-stare the black dog in the light of two torches.

"Demeter," says Hecate, sweeping aside her night-black hair and waving a hand to calm her familiar. She stands at the centre of a glowing cross, whose points multiply as I watch. "Even the gods must meet Hecate at the crossroads of their lives. I can only tell you he was powerful, the one who took Persephone. I felt them pass, heard her call out for you but know nothing more."

I take my divine form and plead with her. "Is there anything that would tell me where I should look?"

Hecate spins, her hair flying in a circle around the multi-pathed star, which dims to a simple crossroads once more.

"The all-seeing eye will know who took your daughter," she says and waits for me to work out the puzzle, which is easy enough.

The sun-god. "Helios," I tell her. She nods.

"I will go with you," she says, "in sisterhood. And we will get an answer. But whether that answer will please you, is not certain."

We both change into black birds and fly to Helios's dazzling palace. I am in no mood to admire his sunbeams and challenge him straight away to tell me who has taken my Persephone.

Hecate's words were prophetic – the answer does not please me. Way beyond the reach of my vengeance, Hades has chosen my daughter as wife, with the consent of her father, may he be cursed. They evaded my refusal with the connivance of our own mother-earth Gaia, who fashioned the trap with the very skills she passed on to me, shaping nature's beauty. There is destiny here, if Gaia thinks good for the earth will come of this union, but all I feel is humiliation on top of the crushing loss.

Helios presses the point. "What mother could object to such a husband for her daughter, the highest of us all, in his own domain?"

In his own domain. My daughter is trapped in the underworld.

"*This* mother!" I rave like a Maenad, pulling at my long gold hair till I make bald patches and what's left turns white. I drag at my face till wrinkles form, as deep as the crevasses of Hades' kingdom.

I leave the glistening palace as a crone, to wreak havoc in the world of men. I can do nothing against Hades but, without seedtime and harvest, mankind dies. And without men, the gods are not deities. Zeus has never appreciated my work and now he will see the consequences when I stop. When I unloose plague and fire, ice and tidal wave, instead of nurturing seeds and protecting the harvest. When the seeds die below ground, imprisoned with my daughter. If I withdraw my care for the earth, the excesses of the gods will destroy mankind. And I do not care.

I summon the two drakones, my fire-breathing winged serpents, and harness them to my chariot. When she was a little girl, Persephone would ride with me, her hair flying, cheeks rosy, eyes bright. The drakones loved her, made their strange hissing sounds and flickered their forked tongues when she stroked their scaled heads. When she picked fleas out of their feathered wings, they chittered like fledglings. But she grew too high and mighty for them as she became a maiden. She told me they were *my* drakones and she wanted chariot beasts of her own, that she would not take second place. I can hear her voice and I would give anything to have her back, however sullen and sarcastic.

I harness my pain, even more deadly than my drakones.

"Grieve Persephone!" I tell them, for they love her still, as I do, however much her rejection of us hurt. Growing girls test those who love them and it was my duty – it *is* my duty – to protect her, even from herself. I have failed to keep her safe.

We hope she will come back to us one day, our little girl, and we scorch the earth with fire-breath and pain.

Until the day Hades frees Persephone, the world is dead to me and my grief covers it in a lethal shroud. The mortals I once cherished should beware.

Persephone

After that word 'wife', Hades (for so I must call him now) drove the chariot like a storm-wind down below Hephaestus' furnace, which smells of sulphur and smoke, down below the captive Titan who makes the earth rumble, down to the very core of the underworld.

He swept me from the chariot onto the black rock that forms paving, walls and ceiling in this world of tunnels and caverns. Not dull black but glittering in the firelight from seams of mica, gold and diamonds – name a gemstone and Hades will thread it through black rock as decor. In a black humour, I requested jet, which made us both laugh. But he did it. And soon I could do it too.

I learned to sprinkle gold-dust and amber in the underworld rivers until the spirit of the Styx rose up in complaint, shaking glitter from the wild waterfalls of her hair. The River Lethe was more tolerant, murmuring, "Leave it go, nothing matters, forget..."

But my first steps in this kingdom were weak as a toddler's from the wild ride and he had to catch me, to stop me sinking to my knees. I shook off his help, ignored the three-headed dog-monster and found my voice, which wobbled more than my legs.

"My mother will be very angry," I said, my usual quick wits having for some reason deserted me.

"I'm counting on it," he said, with a smile, giving me his full attention for the first time. Humans have died from his attention but I was the daughter of gods and I stared him out.

Then his clothes swirled off into some shadowy

corner and he stood naked in the firelight, watching me watching him. A golden sheen limned every line and muscle, from his cheekbones and throat to his calves and toes. I was immune to the glamour of godhead but not to what he offered me, proud and confident. A man's body should always be dressed in nothing but firelight and I couldn't resist touching him.

Before the sweat had dried on the magnificent black horses (whose names I now know) I could no longer claim maidenly sorority with Artemis and Athene. So we did it again. And I swear the flames leaped higher each time.

"Wife," he said.

"Goddess," he said.

"My Queen of the Darkness," he said.

You will hear many things about me that might or might not be true (for I have never been completely trustworthy) but I can tell you that neither Hades nor I know who consumed whom in the flames of passion. From our conjunction rose a phoenix, a double-headed bird of fire, a sign that the King of the Underworld has found his queen.

The horses, those magnificent black horses, are *mine*. If I speak their names, they come to me. If they are in harness, they bring the chariot too and Hades with it. Alastor, Orphnaeus, Aethon and Nyctaeus. I shouldn't have favourites but I do. Alastor demands my attention, stamps his hooves and tosses his head in warning if the others approach me without permission. If I give this permission, so does he, though his ears flicker in disapproval.

I can walk my dark kingdom and command whomsoever I choose to visit it. They don't always realise that they can never leave and some take time to adjust. I, however, am free to leave but why would I want to? My dark lord is as much mine as I am his and my power over death runs like wine through my blood. *Nobody* treats Persephone with disrespect.

So why is my skin shrivelling, my joy paling? Why do I long for sunlight, which I have not seen for so many months? Why do I dream of my mother tearing out her hair, wasting away, dying from love? My mother, always so self-controlled, shaken by the emotions I told her she had never felt. Did my words curse her?

I have refused again and again to go above ground in case I am trapped there and parted from Hades. Then *I* would die from love. But the pull of sunlight is so strong that I am torn in two.

Then Hermes comes to our kingdom, the mischievous messenger with winged heels, to say this cannot go on. That the earth and humans are dying because my mother neglects the seeds, lays waste the harvest, spreads plague and famine in her grief over my abduction. Zeus, my father, summons Hades to an accounting.

What a hypocrite Zeus is! All he cares about is the lack of libations and respect for himself. Without human worship, what are the gods?

I laugh. That is Zeus' problem, not ours. The King and Queen of Death will always be worshipped. The population of our kingdom is increasing fast and there are such interesting (dead) people to talk to.

Hades says, "But – your mother." And I sigh. The umbilical cord tightens, woven from sunlight and flowers, seedtime and harvest.

"She'll keep me," I tell him, and the fear is as strong as the need to see her. I love them both. Why did nobody tell me this was possible? That you can leave your mother but never leave your love for her – or the hold she has on you.

My dark god brushes the back of my neck with his

lips. "I have a plan," he says. "But I can't tell you. That way you will be telling the truth to your parents."

He leaves to attend Zeus' summons and I am alone in the underworld. I should have gone with him, pleaded my case, but he asked me to trust him and I do. Together, we are stronger than Zeus (who did not make my mother his queen and who cannot visit Hades' kingdom). I think we are stronger even than my mother's grief but, a moment later, I doubt this. I doubt, and I long for her hugs and for sunshine.

I am *not* alone in the underworld. I throw burning coals for Cerberus, the dog-monster, (one for each head), and he catches them, spits fire from his mouth until his eyes glow red. Tired of play, he lays his heads on the ground in front of me, adoring.

"Good dogs," I tell him. "We'll play again later. Guard the entrance." He is trained to let visitors enter – but not leave.

I call on resident philosophers and sages, and ask each of them what they see when they look at my kingdom. Through their answers, I perceive how they valued themselves when alive. Truly, a man gets the afterlife he imagines as his desserts. Where some bask in sunlight and view the rainbow robes of Iris through the rain, others invent ravening monsters that I might bring to life if boredom takes me. The torments of Tartarus, the beauties of the Elysian fields and the oblivion of the Asphodel Meadows are all different aspects of a man's hopes and fears.

Maybe oblivion is the safest choice, I sometimes whisper to the newcomers. After all, so many of them sought oblivion in life.

I am not bored with the endless possibilities of my realm and its fascinating subjects. Imagine being able to talk to any person among the legions of the dead. What questions you could ask! I have only begun to pose such questions and from each answer springs an infinity of new questions.

Hades took his chariot. I miss my horses and their head-nudges when they think I have treats for them. Yes, treats. The fruits and flowers of our kingdom are strange and alluring, in fire colours or black. Small black fruits with blue seeds are the horses' favourite titbits.

For my own part, I have felt neither hunger nor thirst since I came to this world and am merely curious about my kingdom. I observe the transparent worms that wriggle up the cave walls, turn phosphorescent, then blink out like snuffed candles. And the black moss that spreads carpet-like, concealing pools of blacker water, into which I have dropped, whooping with shock, only to rise on the back of a finned bottom-dweller. For I am immortal and the black rock floor is not the bottom of the underworld. There are more depths to plumb.

Today I feel restless, wondering what Hades is saying, and as I pace the rocky chambers, a strange shrub catches my eye, completely out of place in its deep terracotta pot, reminiscent of my mother's cultivation above ground. I remember how tenderly she watched over the tilled fields, the precious seedlings, the harvest – the cycle of life itself. And now the upper world is devastated, like my mother. I feel proud and ashamed at the same time, at my power to bring low the great earth goddess.

I want her to see who I am now, her equal and more, for I am *his* queen while her loves are fleeting. Or rather, her *other* loves are fleeting. There can be no doubting her love for me now, not when she is willing to destroy the kosmos to get me back.

"I am so sorry. I love you," I whisper, safe in my underworld kingdom.

The shrub in its pot bears red goblet-shaped fruit, which have hardened into tough shells around the carmine flowers they came from. The fruit nearest me is ripe and has split open, juice trickling down past the tiny red seeds, which shine like jewels in their fleshy setting. A red smile, which reminds me of Hades and me, together in firelight.

I remember the first time I reached out to touch him and I wonder what the seeds taste like. I reach out and pluck the fruit as I once plucked a magical flower.

The earth does not crack open. No dark lord appears.

With one fingertip, I scoop out some of the red jelly which contains the seeds. I count as I eat them. One, two, three, four, five, six. *Pomegranate*, the name comes to me. I stop, satiated already, and look around me. Nobody is there. I feel as if I have committed a crime but that's ridiculous. I only ate six seeds.

Demeter

They are all here, the full panoply of Olympian gods, all avoiding my eye except for my antagonist; brazen, beautiful Hades who stalks the centre of the arena like a black panther about to take down whoever dares to challenge him.

I have restored my appearance to the one my daughter knows. Golden hair and smooth skin. But I still feel white-haired and wrinkled. Destroyed by grief, I turned destroyer and what I have done since Persephone was taken from me can only be forgiven by other mothers driven mad by loss.

My brother-lover Zeus covers his guilt with overdone anger. His very gruffness gives him away. "This can't go on, Demeter," he says. "For a year, the seeds have perished under the soil, which freezes or burns according to your ill-humour. You have just cause against Hades but what can you expect when a girl is attractive?"

He does not meet my eyes and many present shift nervously. I think of snakes intertwining, of being an attractive *innocent* girl and my resolve strengthens.

"You must come to an agreement with Hades," he continues. "And Hades, you must be reasonable, so we can get on with our duties. And so humans can get on with *their* duties towards us."

The epitome of a reasonable god who's never ruined a young girl's life, Zeus says, "Give her back to her mother, Hades. You've had her to wife and surely you've had enough of actually living with her by now. She's been with you months!"

And *this* is her father. My anger turns my voice to chips of ice and I can feel whole villages dying in the world of men. I do not care! *That* is my weapon. Nothing matters but Persephone. All of these years I have nurtured the earth, its peoples, even the gods and *this* is how I am repaid?

I fire the words at immortal, all-powerful Zeus. "I am the only one here who loves Persephone! If Hades does not give my daughter back, I will let the orchards and fields become deserts. The seas will boil and freeze in turn, and your precious mankind can die for all I care! As can you."

The collective silence is waiting for a thunderbolt but I have nothing to lose. No divine punishment of rolling rocks or eviscerated entrails can be worse than this torture of failing my daughter.

Athene breaks the silence, another one of our pantheon driven by guilt. "The wrong must be righted and nature must flourish again. Hades must return Persephone to her mother."

Around the circle of seated gods, the verdict echoes without demur.

Finally, Zeus speaks. "You have heard the judgement, Hades."

Hades' response is to me. "You are wrong, Demeter. I too love Persephone."

"Don't speak her name," I spit.

He says, "She is my wife and my queen." He throws a look of contempt at Zeus. "I have not tired of her in a few months and I will not tire of her in an eternity." He sighed. "But I must accept the judgement of the gods."

A sigh of relief. They can all go home.

"But," says Hades, "If she has eaten of the fruit of the underworld then she can never leave."

"So be it," yells Zeus, thunder rumbling in his voice. He's had enough.

"So be it," I mumble. My little girl knows better than to eat or drink in Hades' kingdom. I warned her, I'm sure I did. But I warned her about so many things and she's so like me at that age, rushing towards disaster. How can we protect our children from the seeds planted in them at their conception?

Persephone

"I only ate six seeds," I tell Hades. We are laughing and crying, holding hands as if we could twine into one olive tree and never be sundered.

"It is enough," he reassures me as he explains his plan. "I can wait patiently for you each year because I love you more, not less than your mother does."

I consider this, am not convinced. Surely overwhelming grief is a greater proof of love than present joy. I must discuss this with one of the philosophers. Or with one of the playwrights.

But he is cunning, my husband. He says, "You will

be queen of two worlds. When you spend two seasons with your mother in the sunshine, there will be a new shrine and more worshippers in the cult of the two earth goddesses than all the priestesses of Artemis and Athene combined. Then, when you return to me for a season, we shall ride the chariot in both worlds, unchallenged, however much Demeter cries icy tears that chill the earth."

Sunshine, I think wistfully. He knows I need the sunshine and this way I can have it all. I am tempted but there are difficulties.

"Share with my mother?" I say. I can feel my face screwing up.

"As acknowledged equal," he says. "And also as the child she loves so much she will kill the kosmos to find you."

This time I too am summoned to the gods' council on Mount Olympus when fleet-footed Hermes brings Zeus' message to Hades. I am to be handed over to my mother, as agreed.

I dressed down for the occasion to please Hades. He said that wearing snakes was provocative and baring one breast even more so. I was disappointed but settled for a black silk chiton, the clingy kind, pinned at the shoulders with silver brooches. Elegant and understated, I think. Especially with a snakeskin belt (I got that one past Hades – men never notice the detail), studded with diamonds and slung low around my hips. I'd made sure to thread flowers through my hair, for old times' sake, but they had not reacted well to the Olympian air.

Hades relishes his moment of revelation. First, he teases the gods, reminding them of the condition for my return, that I have eaten nothing in his kingdom, then he delivers the coup de grâce. Six pomegranate seeds.

"And so, as you all agreed, she cannot leave the underworld."

"Six seeds of a pomegranate," echoes Zeus, screwing up his face (so that's where I get it from).

I confirm my innocent transgression.

My mother's face crumbles and her eyes are empty pools.

"Persephone is mine forever," says Hades and his eyes lock on my mother's, "as she is yours forever. So we will share her. I propose that she spends seedtime to harvest with you and then the underworld season with me."

"Two-thirds of the year with me." My mother repeats Hades' offer, set-faced, knowing that it is generous. She looks at me then. Her eyes linger on the glittering belt slung low around my hips, and her eyes narrow. She must have realised that she will never have her little girl back because she straightens her spine in that determined way she has (I can see where I get that from) and her speech is formal.

"Queen Persephone, Goddess of the Dark Realms, we have much work to do in the world of men, if you will join me for two seasons in the sun."

"Gladly," I say, equally formal, not looking at Hades as I leave his side to join my mother. We said our temporary farewells in a tiring but imaginative manner yesterday and I will not let him see my chin wobble. Besides, we never promised we would not *see* each other while I am staying with my mother. The lake would be a fine trysting place.

I embrace her and we hug longer than is necessary. I have hurt her so much. When did I grow taller than she is?

She whispers in my ear. "Do you love him?"

"Yes," I murmur.

"Good," she says, "but he can still wait until it's his season. And I shall cry until you come back."

Good, I think. But it's not considered polite to measure love in units of pain. Hades is trying to teach me that.

She lets me go, speaks loud enough for others to hear. "Please wear green and gold and *living* flowers in your hair when you're with me, as befits the goddess of springtime."

"Yes, mother," I say, casting my eyes down. "Goddess of springtime and *seeds*." The taste of pomegranate seeds fills my mouth, the seeds that betrayed Demeter. I have so many plans. Plucked flowers are not living but dying, and Death is also my kingdom now. I shall harness the horses when I'm in the underworld and the drakones when I'm goddess of springtime.

I do not glance at Hades but I know his eyes are dancing. I feel his flames deep inside me and I know he feels mine.

Nina

Nina blinked. The sweet taste of pomegranate seeds lingered on her tongue and she still felt other-worldly. The sun was sinking fast and her mother would be worried about her. She brushed a couple of windfall acorns from her lap.

Demeter's gift.
Long shadows crept around her, a prelude to darkness. The lake had darkened with the sky but almost within her reach was the most bewitching flower she had ever seen, a golden heart with a dazzling white halo of petals. She stepped into the water, reaching out

towards the flower, to pluck it. Her movement sent ripples that broke the spell.

Out of the corner of her eye, she saw a golden chariot pulled by four black stallions, driven by a dark god. He was coming for her! She stood calf-deep in the water, hitching up her skirts, unable to move.

But when she turned her head towards him, there were only dark shrubs and a patch of fading sunlight. She looked back at the flower and saw only the golden reflection of the setting sun, with its white halo. The glittering path it made across the water gilded her hands, touched her with its magic.

Persephone's gift. The goddess who was fulfilled through marriage, not diminished. She shook the dreams from her head. Her mother really would be worried. She splashed back out of the water, picked up her skirts and ran back from the marshy shore to the safety of home, to her mother. She almost welcomed the anger that greeted her.

"Where have you been? Look at the state of you! What have I done to deserve such a reckless child? I warned you to stay away from the lake! I hope you haven't been talking to strangers. What will people think of us?"

Enfolded in her mother's arms, Nina let the words roll over her in a protective stream, until she heard the ones she'd been dreading all summer.

"It's time for you to choose which suitor you will marry. Your father and I have waited long enough."

But she was no longer afraid. She felt ready now, and she disentangled herself from the maternal embrace.

Nina nodded. "I will tell you tonight, when I have made myself presentable for the evening meal."

She went upstairs to her room, opened the wooden

jewellery casket and took out three small pieces of parchment. Their scents had mingled but she could still distinguish the ebullient perfume of Signor Guiliu so she read that first. As expected, it was lengthy and very flattering. What woman would not like to be called beautiful and have her eyes likened to starlight? But it was so predictable and – maybe she was imagining it? – there was an ink smudge over her name in the middle of the note, as if he'd started writing another's.

The next she unfolded was Signor Aureliu's, its penmanship exact and regular, its contents an accounting of what they could offer each other. He tried to tempt her with the prospect of fine clothes, aristocratic acquaintance and court fashions. He said her parents would be so proud of her. However, by court fashions, he did not mean sonnets, and it dawned on her that if she were to find happiness with Signor Aureliu, then *she* would have to change for he would not.

Finally, she opened Signor Costanzu's terse missive. There were so few words as to be insulting but she read them, in fairness to his suit. And then she thought about them.

> *Your parents will tell me if, as I dare hope, my suit for your hand is successful. Regardless of their answer, would you like to meet Dante da Maiano? I made his acquaintance in Florence this summer and mentioned you. He will be in Palermo when you return and is well-disposed towards reading your work.*
>
> *Custanzu.*

Not one term of endearment or compliment. Barely his name at the end of the message. Yet something kept Nina staring at nothing, thinking.

Of course she would like to meet Dante da Maiano,

who would no doubt join in the Palermo poets' meeting at the Palace. And her heart was thumping at the thought of the Florentine poet reading her work.

But her heart was not just thumping at the thought of fourteen-line poems. She mined Signor Costanzu's words and found gold in every sentence.

A suitor who offered her a dream come true, even if he was rejected. Such generosity and friendship.

Had he just happened to bump into Dante da Maiano in Florence, after she'd shown admiration for the poet? She thought not.

Not once had *Custanzu* (as she must learn to call him) mentioned the word *love* but it glimmered beneath the surface. He dared to hope. He had listened to her.

I am not the Queen of Darkness and yet,
he sees me as her kind, acknowledges each part
that others see as traits I should regret,
this man who dares to hope yet hides his heart.

She completed her ablutions, donned a clean linen gown, and braided her long, loose, maiden's hair. Then she joined her family at the meal-table. Sure of herself now, and heedless of her brothers' mocking gestures when her parents weren't looking, she said, "I have made my choice."

© Jean Gill

Author's note

In my 12th C *Midwinter Dragon* series, my Vikings sailed to Sicily en route for the Holy Land and I fell in love with this magical island and its layers of history.

Greeks, Romans, Muslims and Normans all shaped its cultural heritage.

While researching medieval Sicily, I came across the circle of 13th C court poets who created the sonnet form in Palermo. Among them, Nina Siciliana was credited with being the first to write sonnets in the vernacular. Yes, a woman and an innovator – I had to write her story. I am always drawn to the medieval women who achieved so much but were written out of history, especially poets – the rock stars of the Middle Ages.

Sadly, we have only two sonnets attributed to Nina. They were included in a Florentine collection published by Giunti in 1527 and are on courtly love themes, from a woman's viewpoint.

Nina's connection with Dante da Maiano (*not* the famous Dante of the Inferno, although da Maiano did mentor the younger Italian poet), is based on a sonnet he wrote 'To his Lady Nina, of Sicily'. This was famous enough to be translated by Dante Gabriel Rosetti in the 19th C. Oral tradition suggests that da Maiano and Nina inspired each other and that he loved her from afar but whether they met, and whether da Maiano's love was merely courtly posture, are purely speculative.

Some scholars dispute Nina's very existence, as is often the case when a woman's name challenges assumptions about medieval gender roles. Thanks to so many modern historians and archaeologists, women are being written back into history, using hard evidence which proves that some women in the 12th and 13th centuries had professions: including doctors, scholars, bakers – and poets. So I see no reason to doubt that Nina Siciliana was a real person.

However, nothing is known of her life, not even whether she was born in Palermo or Messina. All the details in my story are fictional: her family, suitors and circumstances; and how Nina gained an education and the opportunity to be a poet. I also wrote the lines of verse I attribute to Nina.

As for the connection with the Persephone myth, what young poet – or even old one – would sit by Lake Pergusa on the magical island of Sicily, and *not* dream of Hades, Persephone and Demeter? My classical sources, Homer and Hesiod, only refer to 'a taste of pomegranate' and Demeter keeping Persephone for 'two-thirds of the year' while later versions mention six seeds, or seven seeds, corresponding to the allocation of months above and below ground. I chose 'six seeds' as that felt right in my version. I stand to be corrected and do let me know what you think happened.

Homer and Hesiod pit Hades and Demeter against each other but never show Persephone. The goddess who became the feared Queen of the Dead surely deserves a voice, so I tried to bring her to life, as much as Nina. Two memorable women.

As I write this, sitting in my garden in Provence, I am looking at the September fruit on my pomegranate tree. They are ripe and have split open, showing the sweet seeds. If I taste them, I shall never leave. I reach out…

About Jean

Jean Gill is an award-winning Welsh writer and photographer living in the south of France with a scruffy dog, a beehive named 'Endeavour', a Nikon D750 and a man.

First published in 1988, her twenty-six books are varied in genre, including novels, memoir, military history, dog books, poetry, and a cookery book on goat cheese. With Scottish parents, an English birthplace and French residence, she can usually support the winning team on most sporting occasions. She taught English for many years and was the first woman to be a comprehensive school headteacher in Dyfed, Wales. Life has been hectic as she is also mother or stepmother to five children.

Website: www.jeangill.com
Facebook: https://www.facebook.com/writerjeangill
Amazon Author Page: https://www.amazon.com/author/jeangill

3

ONE BLACK DOG

BY MARIAN L. THORPE

A warning of Fate, or simply too much beer and a tale well told?

January 31st 1953

Dusk was falling, but it was the strangest dusk I had ever seen. The sky had a distinct yellow tinge, and the wind, coming across the Wash straight from Russia, rocked my car as I left the pine plantations of the Royal estate and entered an area of heathland and fen. Rain had slicked the metaled surface of the road, and the next gust pushed me into the other lane. My hands tightened on the wheel, bringing the car back into its proper place, glad of no oncoming traffic. No one else, I told myself, was foolish enough to be out in the increasingly bad weather, this last day of January.

Earlier, I'd been buying pints, first at a pub not too far from the coast, being regaled with stories of the sort I'd come to find. Stories of a fiddler who guided people to a smuggler's cave before disappearing, and of the sounds of battle sometimes heard at Warham Camp on a night when the moon was full. I'd recognized both –

once I'd learned to decipher the Norfolk accent – as versions of tales I'd heard up and down the land. At the next place I'd stopped, I'd been told of a golden cradle buried somewhere nearby. Whose cradle, and buried when or by whom, no one could say. At least the story was new. Maybe I could do something with it, spin it out somehow.

I steered carefully around a curve, wishing I hadn't had a last pint myself, and up a slight hill. Cottages, lights shining through windows, began to appear on both sides of the road. I could hear the wind shrieking between the buildings, like the high-pitched howl of a dog. I peered forward, trying to see ahead through the sweep of the wipers and the rain.

Perhaps I should have taken the train. But without the car, I couldn't visit the scattered, tiny villages and hamlets where I'd been sent to gather material for at least one episode of a new BBC series. The national broadcaster served the entire nation, and not all its teleplays should be set in London, or so it had been decreed. As the drama department's newest recruit, I'd been sent to the shires to find stories. I'd ended up in Norfolk in January due to my supervisor's understanding of the rhythms of rural life. "It's the slow time there, Ben. Not much happening on the land, except some shoots. Ploughing won't begin until the first Monday in February. You'll find men who'll talk your ear off in a pub for a pint or two." With one thing or another, including finding a hotel that was both open and not fully booked for the pheasant shoots, it had taken me until this last week of January to make the journey.

Something loomed in front of the car – a deer? The headlamps barely cut through the rain to illuminate it. I braked. The car skidded. I fought the wheel, slid, the car turning ninety degrees and more until one tyre caught the gravel of a forecourt. The Morris tipped, stalled, fell back onto four wheels. I sat, knuckles white on the steering wheel, hearing my heart pound.

I was fewer than ten miles from my hotel, with, I was very much afraid, a flat tyre. I peered through the car windows, twisting to see the building behind me. Was that a pub sign? A light shone through one of the front windows. I turned up my coat collar and tried to open the car door. The wind pushed it back. I struggled with it for a minute, then, with a grimace of frustration, climbed over the gear lever, and opened the passenger door.

I didn't clamp my hat to my head fast enough. It blew off and away, lost to the dusk and the wind. Would I make it to the door of the inn? I put my head down and ploughed, like a ship battling the current and tide, to the entranceway. I could barely breathe, my lungs labouring to take in air, until a few steps from the building. Then its solid, two-storey structure broke the wind a bit. I staggered to the porch to pound on the door.

Waiting for it to be opened, I glanced back at my car. In this black night, skewed sideways at the edge of the forecourt, it could be easily hit by another vehicle. Maybe, with some help, I could push it away from the road. The sounds of the door being unbolted diverted me, but as I turned back, I saw a shape – not a deer, but a huge dog – run from over the road and disappear behind the left-hand wing of the inn.

"Thank goodness," I said, as the door swung open and a middle-aged man stepped back to allow me in. "My car's damaged – I braked for a dog, and skidded. I think I have a puncture."

"Get you inside," was the response. "Nothing to be done tonight."

"But it's right at the road. It could cause an accident."

He pushed the stout door closed and shot the bolts home, top and bottom.

"There'll be no one out tonight. Take off that wet coat and come in to the fire." He indicated a bench against one whitewashed wall. I shed my coat and scarf, laid them on the bench, and, brushing water from my face, followed my host along the flagged hall, past the open door to the public bar, and into a snug little saloon. A fire burned in the grate. "Sit there," the landlord said, indicating a table close to the fire. I was glad to obey. "What'll you have?"

"Whisky," I said. I needed it. "And one for yourself, if you will." As he busied himself with the bottle and glasses, I looked around. A modern inn, not like some of the ancient places I'd been in earlier today. Modern or not, the fire was flaring and falling, the wind outside sucking at the chimney – and howling in it, the sound eerie.

The landlord brought a clean bar towel, the whisky, two glasses with a good measure in each and a jug of water, placing them on the table. I mopped my face and hair while he took a seat.

"Your health," he said, raising his glass.

"And yours," I replied, and took a satisfying, strengthening mouthful. Decent stuff, I thought.

"Bert." The landlord held out a hand.

I gave him mine. "Ben. Ben Reynolds. I was on my way to Hunstanton. I've got a room booked at The Golden Lion. I suppose I should telephone them."

Bert shook his head. "Lines are down. I doubt the road's safe between here and Huns'ton. They'll not be bothered by a guest not arriving, not tonight. I've rooms here." He didn't speak in BBC English, quite, but I was happy to note I didn't have to work to understand him.

"I don't suppose I have much choice," I said, immediately realizing how churlish that sounded. "Thank you," I added hastily, with a placating smile. "I'm sure I'll be comfortable."

"The only thing is," Bert said, "I don't do meals, except breakfast. But if bacon and eggs suits, I can manage that."

I assured him bacon and eggs would be more than acceptable. A realization struck, bringing with it a sinking sensation: my bag was in the car. I was going to have to brave the wind and rain to fetch it.

"I'll get a torch," was all the landlord said. He stood, scraping the chair along the tiled floor, and went behind the bar. The torch he handed me, a big aluminium one with a swivel head, would certainly light my way.

I shrugged into my damp coat again, buttoned it, decided to not risk the scarf, and when Bert had unbolted the door I stepped out. Rain pummelled me, but getting to the car was easy. The wind pushed me along. Reaching the Morris, I pointed the torch's beam at its wheels. As I'd thought, one tyre was flat. Tomorrow's problem, I told myself.

I retrieved the bag, and, with it in one hand and the torch in the other, bent my head against the wind and fought my way back to the inn. Just before I reached its shelter, I thought I heard a sound – not a whine, not a growl, but something in between. Under the roof of the porch I turned to shine the torch out into the night. Its beam dimmed and died, but not before I saw a dark shape cross the forecourt.

Surely a dog would know to seek shelter? Bert was holding the door open, so I mentally shrugged and stepped inside, dripping onto the tiled floor.

"I'll show you your room," he said. As I followed him, bag in hand, the lights flickered, then went out. I stopped. The corridor was as black as pitch.

"Hang on," Bert said. His footsteps receded. I stood still. Then the wavering light of a candle banished the worst of the darkness, and the landlord led me into a wing of the inn and the bedroom that was to be mine for the night.

"Just a moment." The sound of something set down, the scrape of a match, and a globe of light. The room had an oil lamp. I supposed electricity wasn't all that reliable along this coast, where the winds were so strong.

"Thank you," I said, placing my bag on the floor near a wardrobe. Bert was lighting two candles on the mantlepiece of the small fireplace. The room was cold.

"Toilet two doors down, bathroom next to it." He bent to turn the valve of the radiator. "Room'll soon warm up. There's hot water. The boiler uses coke. So does the stove, so don't worry about supper."

I thanked him again. "I'll just tidy myself up a bit."

"Do as you need to. You know where to find me."

"Oh! Bert," I called, as he pulled the door to. "Is the dog yours?"

The door opened again. His face, in the candlelight, was shadowed. "No, I've no dog. What dog?"

"The one I heard, just now. I saw it, too. Out on the forecourt. It looked like the one I nearly hit."

"What sort of a dog?"

"I don't know. Big, like a wolfhound. I thought it was a deer at first. It might have been black, but everything looks black out there."

I thought his jaw tightened, before he muttered something I didn't quite catch. It sounded like: "Abroad, is he?"

More clearly, he said, "Lots of dogs in the village. It'll find its way home, don't you worry."

———

Twenty minutes later, with hair as dry as a towel could make it and a change of socks, my feet in the slippers I'd packed, I padded down to the public rooms of the inn.

"Ah, there you are, Mr. Reynolds." Bert was polishing glasses behind the bar to the light of several oil lamps. "Did you find everything you needed?" I answered in the affirmative. There'd been good soap on the washstand, and thicker towels than I'd expected.

"Another whisky?"

"A small one, thank you." I put the candle down on a table and pulled out a chair.

He busied himself with the bottle. "I didn't ask earlier. London man, are you?"

"I am now. Brought up in Kent, though."

"What brings you to Norfolk in January? Business? Be a funny time of year for a holiday."

I took the glass he handed me, raised it in thanks. "Business of a sort. I work for the BBC." I began to explain why I was there, when an almighty howl sounded in the chimney again. Or did it? I'd have sworn the sound came from near the front door, and when I looked at my landlord his eyes were on the entranceway.

"That's the dog I saw!" I put the glass down. "It sounds terrified. Shouldn't you let it in out of this storm, at least into the hall?"

"Terrified?" Bert said. "It'll be you that's terrified, if I opened the door to that beast."

"You know it then?"

Deliberately, he turned away, to pour himself

another drink. Without adding water, he tossed it back. "I know it," he said. "I last saw Black Shuck in another January, thirty-eight years ago. I was twelve."

"That's impossible," I said. The candlelight flickered, dropping the room into deep shadows, then brightening. "No dog lives that long."

"No mortal dog, no."

"Oh, I see." I laughed. "This is a tale for my collection. A ghost story by firelight, to pass the time."

He regarded me, his face solemn. "You can think of it that way if you like. But it's not a tale for an empty stomach, neither in the telling nor the hearing. Sit you there and drink your whisky, and I'll be back with your supper in a bit."

This story sounded useful, at least. I'd better fetch my notebook. There was a recording machine in the boot of the car, but I'd quickly found it either diverted attention away from the storytelling, made the speaker stop talking immediately, or created an atmosphere where the stories became nothing more than younger men competing to tell the most outlandish tale they could think of. Even if it had been useful, I wasn't going out into the wind and rain again. Paper and pen would suffice.

Good smells were coming from the kitchen when I returned to my table, now set with cork mats, cutlery, and a bottle of HP Sauce. A few minutes later, Bert appeared, two plates held with doubled towels. "You don't mind me eating with you, Mr. Reynolds?"

"Not at all." The plate, with three rashers of bacon, two fried eggs, and a mound of fried onions, was put before me. Bert disappeared for a minute, returning with a rack of toast and a butter dish, before he retreated again, this time to bring two pints of ale. He set them on the table and took his chair.

"Eat up," he said, before slicing into his bacon. I followed suit. The heated plates had kept the food hot, and the bacon, rich in flavour, was delicious. Locally raised and cured, I guessed, and when my mouth was empty I asked.

"Yes. From the farm behind. It used to be all one, the inn and the farm, but the land was sold off nearly seventy years back. Still called The Dun Cow farm, though." He broke the yolk of an egg and dipped a piece of toast into it. "The eggs are from my chickens."

We talked of the history of the inn. There'd been a public house here for nearly two hundred years, he told me. At the edge of the village, it had started life as a drover's inn, the pasture belonging to it providing food and space for the cattle and sheep being moved from the grazing marshes to market. "You'll not have seen it in the dark," he said, "but there's a drift just south of us."

"A drift?" I didn't know the word.

"A drove, to take the sheep on and off the marshes."

I reached for my ale, the sharp taste a perfect contrast to the rich, salty bacon. "An excellent supper, Bert. I doubt I would have had as fine a meal at The Golden Lion."

"Another day, order the cockles there. Fine cockling to be had all along the Wash. But you have to know the sands and the creeks, or it's easy to come to grief."

"Were there ever smugglers?" I asked, impulsively. A good smuggling story might go down well with my boss, and I had the sense my host was regretting his earlier promise of the ghost story. Maybe a tale of smugglers would ease him back into the mood.

Bert grinned. "So they say. Supposed to be a tunnel somewhere, up near the common."

I was about to ask him more when the whistle of the wind in the chimney suddenly became a roar. Outside, something crashed, and again, even over the tumult of the storm, a dog howled. I looked at the landlord. In the dim and flickering light, it was hard to tell, but it seemed to me his face had paled to almost white.

"A bad night," he said, his voice quiet and a little hoarse. "A bad night, if Black Shuck is abroad."

I stood, and picking up his plate and mine, placed them on the bar. He didn't object. "You were twelve, you said, when you saw this devil dog?"

"Devil dog," he murmured. "Some might call it that." His voice strengthened. "Twelve, yes. It was January of 1915." He gave me a sharp look. "You weren't born." I nodded, not wanting to interrupt him. "The war had started the previous August. My father had enlisted, and my uncles on both sides, even if they didn't have to. So I was the man of the house, with a brother five years younger."

He took a pull of his ale. "We lived in Snettisham, two villages north. You'll not have seen the church, but it sits up on a hill, with a tall spire that can be seen from the sea and the marshes. Ships use it to navigate by. That night, there was a meeting in the vestry, a speaker from the Red Cross about making bandages and such to send to our boys in France."

Rain lashed the big windows of the public room on the far side of the bar, sounding like thrown pebbles. This building was new – only three years old, Bert had told me, replacing the ancient, original inn. I wondered if it would have withstood this storm – a foolish thought, really. But I was glad of a roof that didn't leak, and tightly-fitting windows and a stout door against the fury of the night.

"Anyhow, my mum had brought me and my brother along, both so she could bank the fire at home and save on fuel, and because there was going to be refreshments, and she wasn't going to have us miss out on tea and biscuits. Lots of women did the same, so there were maybe a dozen children there.

"The girls, of course, stayed with their mothers. Even the youngest were expected to help, hemming handkerchiefs or folding them if they were too small to stitch evenly, or keeping the babies quiet. Wasn't much playtime for the girls. But us boys were shooed out into the church proper, and as I was the oldest, I was told to keep the others out of mischief." Bert nodded at my empty glass. "Another?"

I'd already drunk far more today than was my usual habit. But why not? I wasn't going anywhere.

"Please."

He went to the taps, pulling a darker liquid into two fresh glasses. Setting them on the oak bar, he took our dirty supper plates and disappeared into the kitchen. When he returned, it was with two smaller plates and a board with part of a fruit cake. "Left over from Christmas," he said. "But it's still good and moist. I keep it wrapped in cheesecloth in a tin. Goes well with the stout."

Fruit cake would help mop up the alcohol, I decided. Thanking him, I cut a thick slice, broke off a piece, and tasted it. "Delicious," I told him.

"It's not bad. Not like before rationing, but that'll end some day." He cut himself a slice. I took a sip of the stout, rich, deeply flavoured, and, as Bert had said, a fine accompaniment to the cake. "Where was I?"

"Keeping the younger boys out of mischief."

"Right. Well, there was a fire in the vestry where the meeting was, but in the nave, with the ceiling so high up, and the wind out of the north strong that night, it was bloody cold. So we played marbles for a while, but even with our coats and scarves we were freezing. Someone suggested hide and go seek."

"In the church?"

"It was daring, but we were boys, and up for a bit of risky behaviour. The altar was out of bounds. Anyhow, we got to playing, and of course we got noisy."

The fire guttered. Bert got up to adjust the damper, and add a lump or two of coal. A howl, again, outside. Just the wind, I told myself. Something leapt onto the bar. I nearly overturned both my ale and my chair.

"Ah, there you are, Tybalt." Bert picked up the cat, a big striped tom made even larger by its puffed-out tail and huge, staring eyes. "You don't mind cats?"

"No, no. He just startled me." My heart stopped its pounding. I was beginning to be sure Bert was pulling my leg; that Black Shuck would turn out to be someone's pet who gave away a hiding place, or flushed a tramp from behind the altar, or some equally tame story. Well, it was as good a way as any to pass a storm-stayed evening. "Go on."

"Imagine how a shout of 'ready or not, here I come' echoed off the stones of the church. Loud enough to wake the dead, we were told. It was Sid Fowler's mother who'd come out, I recall – he was a scrawny shrimp of a boy, but she was built like a drayhorse. No one wanted the back of her hand."

The cat in Bert's arms lashed its tail, growling a little. "There, Tybs. It's just the wind," Bert murmured to it. The tom snarled and leapt from his arms, disappearing somewhere beyond the firelight.

"I don't think he believed you," I observed.

"Cats see things we don't. And hear them." Another mouthful of ale swallowed, the landlord returned to his story. "Maybe it was a good thing it was Sid's ma, because while she scared us straight, nothing ever flustered her. So when she screamed – well, we knew whatever she'd seen was something horrible."

"Was that when the dog appeared?" I asked. Bert was drawing this story out with all the art of a publican who'd told many a story to titillate his customers and keep them buying pints. I couldn't help but admire his skill. Maybe I should have retrieved the recording machine, especially with the wind howling in the background. The BBC sound men could probably duplicate it, though.

"Yes. Yes it was. And to this day I don't know where it came from. The church doors were closed tight. It was just – there, all of a sudden. Huge, and black, but with eyes as red as blood, howling and growling, jaws snapping." His voice had dropped to nearly a whisper, and his eyes were focused on something beyond the room.

He's as good an actor as he is a storyteller, I thought.

"I was in the aisle – I was the seeker, you see," he went on, barely audible. "All the other boys were among the pillars and pews. The thing – the dog – ran right by me to leap onto the lectern, still howling. The other boys were screaming, the women were screaming – and somehow one of the biggest boys got the doors open and we all ran, boys, girls, women, into the dark." He reached for his glass again, put it down. I saw his hands were trembling. He flattened them on the table top. "And not ten minutes later a lost German airship dropped a bomb on the church."

"What?" It was the last thing I'd expected.

"One of several, along the coast. Lynn got hit the worst, people killed. The bomb missed the church, as it happened, landed in a field close by. Blew the windows out. But if we'd still been there…" He shook his head.

"Injuries, maybe deaths. But we weren't, because of Black Shuck."

"So the devil-dog was actually sent to save you?" I laughed. "It's a good story, Bert. You had me believing it for a bit. And what a twist at the end!"

His face told me I'd said the wrong thing. He stood, knocking his chair over. "Get up," he growled, grasping my forearm and nearly pulling me out of my seat. He marched me – too surprised to resist – to the front door. "Don't move," he ordered. I thought it best to humour him.

He unbolted the door, swinging it open to the night. Rain lashed down. I heard the rush of water, the beat of rain, the moan of wind – and, both above and within all the sounds of the storm, the unearthly, eerie, unceasing howl of a dog.

"Do you hear him, bor? That's Black Shuck, that is, and something dreadful's happening t'night." Bert's accent thickened in his anger. "He's howling to warn us all, them's as has ears to understand. He saved you, din't he? Stopped you from goin' further." The howls grew louder. "There!" Bert said, triumphantly. "You look, bor, and you tell me what you see."

Black, and huge, eyes as red as if they reflected fire. The hound stood looking at us, its stance menacing. Then it lifted its muzzle and gave voice again, an ululation filled with grief and warning, reaching deep into my blood and bones. The hairs on my arms rose. I put a hand on the wall to steady myself, my legs threatening to give out.

And then it turned, and without another sound vanished into the night, swift as a racehorse.

"He's gone up the drift, out to the marshes." Bert looked at me. In the dim light of the hall, lit only by the distant fire, I could see no anger on his face, or fear. Only sadness. "Something dreadful's happening," he repeated. "You'll have a story for the BBC in the morning, Mr. Reynolds. But not the one you came for. You'll say nothing of what you've seen, or what I told you. I won't have us be made a laughing stock, not amidst the sorrow that'll come of this night."

"Yes," I managed. "I, I won't say anything." How could I? No one would believe me.

The landlord shut and bolted the door. "No one ever mentions him," he said. "Those who've seen Black Shuck. I knew from what you told me he'd shown himself to you, even if t'was briefly, so I could speak his name. I wouldn't have, otherwise. One more drink?"

"No," I said. "Thank you, but no. I think I'll go to bed."

He nodded. "Maybe best. Set your alarm clock for seven, if you want breakfast. Once it's light, there'll be no time for food. There'll be work to do, hard work and sad work. You can help with that, maybe, while you write your story."

"I'll be glad to."

"Good night, Mr. Reynolds." His footsteps, heavy now, echoed in the narrow corridor. I made my way to my room. Rain hammered on the slate roof, and the wind still moaned, but the howls were gone. Too much strong Norfolk ale, I told myself, and a story well told. All you saw was a lost and frightened dog, and all you heard was the wind. Your mind did the rest.

I didn't really believe myself, not then, and not in the morning, when I stood with half the village, looking out at the sea that should have been two miles away lapping at the edge of the village, at the dead animals and smashed boats and shutters and porch roofs floating in it, as the news came of the drowned and lost, the devastation and destitution the night had brought.

I stayed five days. I wrote of the storm, the deaths, the destruction, the heroism of both the local people and the US airmen stationed at Hunstanton, and those stories won me my first promotion. I stayed with Bert at the Dun Cow the entire time, along with several families needing refuge. On the day the garage finally had time to fix my tyre, I went to Snettisham to look at the church, and then as far down the road to the Wash as I could. Water still stood in the fields, the deep ditches full, and the bodies of sheep and cattle and deer lay where they had been swept by the flood.

Sheep and cattle and deer, and one black dog.

Author's note

Most of the facts in this story are true. St. Mary's, Snettisham, Norfolk did have its windows blown out by a bomb dropped by a German airship in the January of 1915, and the story of a meeting that had just finished at the church is also based on fact. The Great Flood of January 31st 1953, caused by a combination of a gale – an 'extreme extratropical cyclone' and high spring tides, killed one hundred people in Norfolk, including twenty-five at Snettisham.

The Dun Cow stood on the Lynn Road at the southern edge of Dersingham, Norfolk, and between 1875 and 1933 was in the possession of members of my family. The original 18th century building was replaced in 1950 by the modern building featured in this story. From 1950 to 1957, the landlord was Herbert Elson Crane. The Dun Cow was pulled down in 1994, replaced by a Budgens (now a Co-Op) supermarket.

© Marian L Thorpe

About Marian

A dual Canadian/British citizen who divides her year between Ontario, Canada, and Norfolk, UK, Marian published the first of her eight-book *Empire's Legacy* series, historically-inspired speculative fiction, in 2015. The series is set in a world 'on the edge of history': reminiscent of Britain, Northern Europe, and Rome in the latter centuries of the first millennium, but a world where society evolved differently after the Eastern Empire left; a world where one young fisherwoman answers her leader's call to defend her country, beginning a journey into uncharted territory.

Website: www.marianlthorpe.com
Other social media: https://mlthorpeauthor.substack.com/
Amazon Author Page: https://relinks.me/MarianLThorpe

4

———

IN THE SHADOW OF GHOSTS

BY HELEN HOLLICK

Does the fate of those who survive linger forever?

North Devon, Early Morning February 17th 1646

The February day had started bright but frosty, the cold spitefully nipping at cheeks, nose and fingers. The clear water in the shallower streams had crackled with thin crusts of ice, although the River Torridge had only been rimed at the edges where clumps of rushes grew, and autumn-dead bracken drooped bent and broken down the steep banks, the rust red fronds white-painted by the sparkle of ice.

The men, jesting and laughing, had been pleased to be on the move again at last, their horses, catching the light-hearted mood, had snorted clouds of dragon-breath, heads tossing so their bridles jingled. Wanting to jog, despite their riders holding the animals in check with chilled hands curved tight around the reins. There had been ice underfoot; now, these many hours later, there was ice within, clawing at stomachs, guts, hearts and souls as another, not so cheerful dawn would soon be peering cautiously over a solemn, grey horizon.

77

How much had changed in those hours between one dawn and the next! How had that bright, crisp morning yesterday been so full of hope and enthusiasm, only for it all to vanish into despair as swiftly as that frost had given way to torrential rain? Despair, discomfort, pain, fear? Aye, all those, but fear had thrust uppermost and lodged itself like a stuck fishbone in the gullet. They, all six of them, felt it, though not one among them was openly showing it. Hah! They were too weary, too tired – too bloody damaged to show it! And aye, 'bloody' was the right word for each of them. Six surviving men were all that was left of the small, ragged troop that had once been Sir Hugh Pollard's proud Regiment of Horse. And not one was unscathed. Bloody of body and bloody of heart. Defeat did that; tore at limb and life as deep as it tore at mind and soul.

The small troop's captain, Richard Tremayne, trudged, almost asleep on his feet along the mud-rutted lane, his exhausted mind wandering from one troubled thought to another. Some were mild, irrelevant thoughts – how would he mend the rip in his coat? Could he patch the sole of his boot which was letting in water? Thoughts that conveniently masked the important ones: was God with them or not? Where could they go? Where would they find replacement horses? How could he keep the other five, loyal men, alive? Was all this worth it?

His wandering mind returned again to another thought. How long would Sir Hugh be permitted to live now that Devonshire was lost? There had been no honour, no respect, when Hugh Pollard had been captured by Fairfax's Parliamentary men those few months ago. He'd surrendered; no choice if his men were to see another day dawn. They'd laid down their weapons and called upon the mercy of Thomas Fairfax.

He could be trusted to hold his honour. Not Cromwell, though. Few of the King's Men, from general to pikeman, thought Oliver Cromwell had a shred of decency within his stone-set soul.

Where was Pollard now, Richard wondered? Shivering in some dark, rank cell somewhere? Already executed and gone to God? Where were the men captured with him – hanged? Enslaved and transported to the Colonies to die miserable deaths in the Americas? Forgotten by all except their grieving widows, mothers, sisters or daughters?

Captain Richard Tremayne could only speculate about Pollard, for it did not matter *where* he was – Pollard was not *here* at his Devonshire manor of King's Nympton in the pouring rain. They'd needed Pollard, or at least someone, *anyone*, to be here this foul, desperate night. But as the men had ridden, exhausted, desperate, into the cobbled courtyard, no living soul beyond a scurry of rats and the startled flap of a few roosting pigeons had greeted them. The place was deserted. Had been, by the look of it, for many weeks.

Oh, but the day, yesterday – was it truly only yesterday? – had started so well with that bright sun and that glistening frost! A day when courage and hope had leapt as high as the sky. Great Torrington, with its strategic, sweeping views over the valley, fortified to the hilt, barricades built with the men – foot and horse – keen, eager and aware that this, this fine, fine day could be the last of it all. Here in North Devon, maybe it would be the final skirmish in this cursed *un*civil war that had torn loyalties asunder from high-born king to humblest peasant.

How wrong they were.

"By the Sword Divided", they said; a rapier's sharp, merciless blade slashing through truth, trust, honour, loyalty and belief. Catholic against Protestant. King against Country. Englishman against Englishman, brother against brother, father against grandfather. Husband against wife. Life against survival.

They had expected the skirmish to put an end to it all as the troop had breakfasted on cold fatbacon and chunks of rye bread, washed down by wine that was more vinegar than anything else. The horses eager, skittish. Yesterday should have been a glorious day of victory for those who were loyal to King Charles. Instead, the day *had* been an end, but it had been one filled with blood and death. And fear.

Cromwell's sour-faced rabble had marched from Exeter to join Lord Fairfax faster than expected. The tramp of boots, chink of arms and armour, rumbling of wheels, neighing of horses and curses of men, had echoed for miles along the Taw Valley road, and as dusk had approached, tired or no, Old Wart Face had thrown his men straight into the fray to batter at the stout Torrington defences which had proven not to be so stout after all.

The barricades had fallen, and the battle had raged into the narrow, night-dark streets, those still alive – on both sides – with no goal except to *stay* alive. No respite. Kill, maim, wound or be killed, maimed or wounded. Fight, keep fighting, for if you stopped you would be a dead man. Cobbles, slick with rain, blood and dismembered body parts. Smoking tar torches hissing and flaring from wall sconces, casting distorted shadows which leapt and cavorted. The push of pike, the slash of sword. Grunts and moans; not much shouting, for breath was all but spent. The Parliamentarians pressed harder, driving the King's Men further into the town. Few had chance to consider why they were there, why they were fighting, killing each other. This God-forsaken war had gone beyond sensible thought. Way beyond.

The Puritan Roundheads – an intentional discourtesy for their close-cropped hair – believed in the rigid word of God as spoken in the Bible. Were precisionists, religious persons who talked incessantly of God, Heaven, and the scriptures. Who adhered to the will of God and the will of Parliament in almost equal measure, were disciplined and punctilious. Who dressed, outside of a soldier's uniform, plainly in black or grey, broken only by a white shirt or modest lace collar. Who eschewed liquor, gambling, laughter and jollity.

While on the other side, the intended insult of the word 'Cavalier' had gleefully been embraced because it signified gaiety, entertainment, pomp, ceremony, bright clothing and bright lives. Cavaliers did not trouble themselves about the stern decrees of God, or their fate in the next world to come. Cavaliers believed in free will and, more important, were not traitors to their King. All of which was not true of all of them, Cavalier or Roundhead. Most were fighting to stay alive because they had no choice. What a god, king, lord or commander ordered, simple, ordinary men obeyed. And bugger the idea of 'free will'!

In the night-dark rain-sodden streets of Torrington, many defeated men who fought for King Charles gave way and laid down their arms. The opposing Roundheads immediately despatched each miserable one – at least a quick, clean death. Men without a coin to their name were not worth even the promise of a grave. Men of means were thrust as prisoners into the church of St Michael and All Angels for secure keeping. They were worth money, these rich folk, their lives saved to trade for ransom.

And then the gunpowder, stored by the Royalists within the church, had exploded.

———

More thoughts as Richard Tremayne trudged on through the early morning rain. What Parliamentarian idiot had decided to hold the prisoners there? Eighty barrels, someone had said. *Eighty*! From his school history he recalled Guido Fawkes had been discovered with only six-and-thirty barrels on that November night when he had attempted to destroy Parliament and all within. Eighty! As a result, the church bell tower had completely gone, and much else with it, either from the blast or the immediate spread of fire.

All fighting had ceased. Time had stood still. Those who saw, heard, the blast had stood, stunned. Sword resting against sword, pike held statue still in mid-thrust. Fists bunched but no punch thrown. All attention, all eyes, all ears, all heads turned, mouths agape, towards the explosion and the burning church, with the pitiful screams from the dying within echoing along the narrow Torrington streets.

The pause had lasted but moments. Parliamentarians sprang, furious, to tend the many among them injured by falling masonry and melting lead. Fairfax, word spread, had been knocked from his horse, clumped around the head by tumbling debris, but it was a rumour proven false. Fairfax and Cromwell had both survived the blast.

And then a different need of survival had become paramount for the King's Men. The fight effectively ended, they fled. With no high-ranked leader left alive to command them, Captain Tremayne had gathered the remaining six of their troop – six only from more than fifty – and had ridden for safety, freedom – and survival.

––––––––––

Richard saw the men and horses, all of them bone tired and weary, settled at Pollard's abandoned estate. At least they had hay and water for the horses; straw bedding for them in the stables. In one of the barns, shelter from the rain for the men, and an earth floor on which to build a fire. The pigeons sufficed for a meal.

Two of the horses had only minor wounds, another was severely lame and one, a handsome grey gelding with black mane and tail, a decent beast with good breeding, was suffering, a bullet deep into his shoulder. It was by luck alone that he'd brought his rider this far. King's Nympton was a good few miles from Torrington at the best of times, but the troop had kept to lonely tracks through the woods, kept clear of open fields, of hamlets or sign of other riders. The going had been slow; they had frequently been forced to stop, watch and listen, although most of Cromwell's men were still occupied with the carnage back at Torrington. And the King's Men? All who could would be making their way to where they might find safety... up country, the Moors or the coast where boats could take them to Ireland, Holland or France. Captain Tremayne's first thought had been to get to Pollard's estate, hoping to find fresh mounts. The disappointment was great, but stoically he continued to hide his feelings.

"What do we do now?" Cedric Cooper, the eldest of the troop, asked quietly, his face turned to look at his Captain, his expression begging for a hopeful answer, his heart knowing he would not be getting one.

Richard winced as the pain in his side caught him. A bullet had grazed him, the thickness of his doublet beneath his red coat absorbing most of the shot, but blood was staining his rose-red cummerbund which he had wound tighter to stem the flow – how bad the wound was he did not know for he'd not had time, or care, to look. His knuckles were grazed and sore from where his hand had met with the basket hilt of an opponent's sword, an opponent who was now dead thanks to Richard's own skill as a swordsman. His head ached, every bone and muscle was complaining of fatigue, but he was the captain, and he was no worse than the other men.

They were all dishevelled, muddied, bloodied. All were weary, yet they could not risk sheltering here for too long, for all the warmth and dryness this barn offered. Come daylight, Cromwell's men would start searching for waifs and strays, and this would be an obvious place to look. The risk, and hope for remounts, had been worth taking but they could not stay. What they did next would be in God's hands, in the lap of Fate. Their free will or God's direction? Huh, God was, surely sound asleep, or attentive to other matters... but they could well do with His Grace right now!

Richard took a slow, deep breath. "We have two choices: go north to find the King, which I would not counsel for I think this war is all but over, and if he has sense he will flee, join Queen Henrietta Maria and her children who are safe abroad. Which is where we should go, for there we may be of some use. Here," he paused, took a breath against the physical and mental pain. "Here we are dead men."

Cooper shrugged, "Loathe I am to agree with you, but I find I must. What shall we do? Try for Cornwall or the south coast?"

Richard echoed the shrug. In truth he had no stomach to run away, but better to run now and hope to fight again another day. Said, "I have family at

Dartmouth. My maternal uncle has several fishing boats there, and aye, before you ask it, he is for the King. From the coast we can get across to Holland or France."

But how to get as far as the coast?

"It'll be a long ride, Captain, and all of us are wounded." Cooper pointed, unnecessarily, at the dark stain on his captain's cummerbund. "And two of the horses will not take us far."

"One horse," Kenrick Mayhewe interrupted the low conversation as, white-faced, he slipped in through the barn door. "I've come from the stables. My good grey didn't make it. He be dead, and tha' bay mare? She be as lame as ever I've seen. She won't be goin' no great distance."

"Then we'll need horses from somewhere else," Richard responded decisively. "You men rest, then we'll press on. Come first light I'll slip into the village, see if there's any better luck for aid there."

As dawn slowly brightened, exhausted as he was, Captain Richard Tremayne trudged along the rain-sodden lane to the inn at King's Nympton. The Grove.

The landlord was a staunch King's Man, sympathetic to the troop's plight, but again, there was disappointment. For all his sympathy, he was no help. He'd been abed, awoken by Richard's knocking, but had welcomed the dishevelled soldier inside, out of the rain, shouted for a maid to stir herself, get the fire lit. He provided ale, bread smothered in churned butter and sweet, sticky, honey. Richard had been grateful for that, but there were no horses. All had been taken, even the shaggy but sturdy Exmoor ponies, weeks ago.

Richard propped himself against the stone wall near

the now blazing fireplace, steam rising from his wet coat and breeches, sleep begging to take him, but he had shrugged the temptation aside, supped up the ale, and taken his farewell. Now it was a new day, albeit one with a murky, mizzle-thick light, he and his men had to move on. Outside, he stood a while, listening for sounds that ought not be sounding: the chink of harness, hooves, marching men, pistol or musket shots. All he heard was a few brave birds trying out a tentative dawn chorus, their twittering drowned by crows squabbling in the woods. And the rain which was turning to sleet.

The unease did not leave him. He felt as if he was being watched, as if cold eyes stared from the rain-dripping shadows. God's eyes? Ghost's eyes? He jumped, let out an unbidden gasp, swallowed down the sudden rise of panic and fear – laughed at himself. A bedraggled barn owl had crossed his path! Huh, his own fault for thinking of ghosts – there were enough *real* shadows to be wary of, let alone spectral ones!

He walked on, back to his men, head ducked away from the skin-stinging sleet. Aye, but there would be many a ghost walking a solitary path back at Torrington – and beyond. And if he did not get his men, his friends, away to safety, then they too could end up as nothing more than the shadow figures of lonely ghosts.

As daylight strengthened, the sleeting rain, God be praised, lessened to a steady drizzle but was as miserable to bear. With great reluctance, they butchered the dead horse and stowed some of the hunks of raw meat in sacking they'd found – taboo for an Englishman to eat horse, but either that or possibly starve, for they would need meat to eat or use as barter for safe passage to wherever it was they could get to. The rest of the carcass they tossed down the manor's well after filling their own canteens with fresh water. There'd be no such sweet refreshment for any pursuing troopers.

They tight-bandaged the injured mare's damaged tendon that was as swollen as an inflated pig's bladder and led her – her rider doubling behind one of the other men, as did the horseless Mayhewe. He'd loved that grey; had bred and foaled him himself. Had loved him possibly even more than his own wife. She was dead too. Childbirth had taken her before this wretched war had started.

Making their slow, painful way through the woods to the village of Chittlehamholt, and its hopefully welcoming Exeter Inn, he was glad now that he had no living wife or child to worry about. No son to be killed by Parliamentarians. No daughter to be molested or raped. He had only himself to care for – and he cared little for that. It had taken courage, and the gentle hand of his captain, Richard Tremayne, to urge him away from deliberately joining the bloodied remains of Tom, his beloved grey horse, at the bottom of that well. He was thankful for the rain, for it hid the tears that dripped down his wet cheeks. His fingers were clutched round a braid of dark hair. Strands, taken from Tom's tail.

They were doubling back on their route, for the hamlet of Chittlehamholt was northward of King's Nympton and they needed to head south towards Dartmoor and the coast. If they could get near enough, maybe the River Dart, the longest river that flowed entirely within Devon, would take them the rest of the way? But first, they had to get that far.

The Exeter Inn was a Tudor-built coaching inn, one of several of the same name and era that linked Barnstaple to Exeter for the convenience of rich travellers or wealthy tradespeople who could afford the luxury of their own transport. And, with God's fortune, there might be fresh horses there? Fresh horses that would carry them away from the ghosts that would be haunting Torrington.

As he rode, Richard was silently cursing himself: he should have guessed that Pollard's place would be deserted. Why had he not decided on going to this inn first? Except, for all his calm assurance to the men, he could not be certain that they would be welcomed there. He knew the landlord, Charles Dyott and his wife, Elizabeth, but that had been more than a double handful of years back. Maybe they were not there now? And even if they were, loyalties changed. They had a living to maintain, an inn to run, and those who went against Fairfax and Cromwell often paid a high price for it.

They struggled up the last hill that ran with rainwater and washed-down mud. The lane at the top would have had a view to be worthy of God's praise, had it not been hidden by the thick mist that marked the course of the River Taw below in the valley. At last, ahead, looking like a mother hen shielding her brood of chicks, the thatched, roughcast-rendered stone and cob inn with a tumble of similar cottages scattered around.

By now it was past mid-day, but with the dismal rain, and not much farmwork to be done at this time of year, few locals were about, though some frowning faces twitched at unshuttered windows, and one door was hastily closed, the rasp of its bolt sliding home loud in the quiet that was broken only by the drip of the rain and the clop of hooves, though three horses had lost shoes. They would need to be reshod or they too would fall lame. The inn had always employed a blacksmith… Richard hoped he was still there.

Landlord Charles Dyott ducked below the door's low lintel, wiping damp hands on a cloth, his eyes narrowed at the sight of six weary men dismounting from even wearier mounts.

"What can I be doin' for thee, sirs? We be not currently open t'unexpected custom."

Richard handed the reins of his chestnut mare to Mervyn Brockett, a normally quiet man who kept his thoughts and deeds to himself, but who had turned even more silent these last hours. There was dried blood on his face and hands, although Richard was uncertain whether it was the man's own or spilt from others.

Smiling at the landlord, Richard extended his hand. "Good day, Master Dyott – Charles. I'm not sure you remember me? My Pa rented some good many acres down near Umberleigh Bridge 'till he died some years back and the land was passed to a new tenant. I came up here often as a young tacker. Plagued old Stafford Anning, the smith in those days, to help him with your horses."

The landlord chuckled, nodded and grasped Richard's hand in greeting. "That would be some years gone, lad, Stafford's son, Clem, be our smith now. But aye, I remember thee. A lad full o' cheek but willin' t'work in exchange for one o' m'wife's fresh-baked pasties."

"I cannot offer work now, sir, for we need desperate and urgent assistance," Richard said, his voice low, his throat tight, dreading that they would be turned away. He had no idea where else they could go without replacement horses. "I confess an awkwardness in asking, for I know not whether you are for, or against, King Charles. But…"

Dyott ran his gaze over each bedraggled man, each exhausted horse. His sense was shouting for them to be off elsewhere, but his conscience, compassion and kindly nature were arguing different. "I be for the King, though I have little sympathy for him. He ought seen sense many a moon back, but I be named Charles for him by my Pa. I had the fortune – mayhap *mis*fortune – to come into this world in 1612 in the year he became heir, followin' the death of his elder brother, Henry Stuart. Pa never liked the name Henry because of that other king. I'd've been Mary or Catharina for those Catholic queens had I been maid-born. So, aye, I be for King Charles. But I'll deny it if them Roundheads come this way agin. An' it be in m'guts that they will, sooner than I want."

Richard felt sick. Rest and refreshment was a 'no' then.

"At the least," Peter Thorne pleaded, the youngest of the troop at barely ten-and-seven years of age, "can you serve us ale and perhaps supply two horses in exchange for my lame mare? She's well bred and will fetch a handsome price once she mends. All she needs is rest, care and good grass. Or maybe breed her? Put her to a quality stallion?"

The landlord raised his hand, stopping the plea before too many tears filled the lad's eyes. "I have no horses here. Roundheads took the three we had left sevr'l days since, but take your beasts round the back and my boy'll see 'em watered, fed an' shod while thee come in for vittles and ale. Dry thyselves afore the fire and tend thy wounds. But if troops be seen, thee must be gone sharp." He nodded to one of the local men who had, tankard of ale in hand, followed him from the inn.

"Sam, get good eyes and ears sent to each end of the village, and get the boys out in search of horses. Tell 'em t'say Charles Dyott stands word for a promisin' trade, an' there'll be a pint of ale waitin' for any that 'elps out."

The man, Sam, drained the last of his ale, gave the landlord the empty tankard, nodded and sped off at a lop-sided run.

"As an inn's landlord I have no liking for this Puritan way of thinking, it seems too fastidious for my taste. Strict piety and a direct covenant with God, and living a morally pure life while rejecting worldly pleasures for relentless hard work? All based on being chosen by God to follow a godly existence without pleasure or laughter? Nay, 'tis not for me or mine. But then, unlike my Pa, I also have no care for the Catholic faith. Their idols, incense and endless mutterings? Nor, for that matter, none for this mess King Charles has mired us into."

Richard nodded, wholehearted agreed. Riding from King's Nympton here to Chittlehamholt, the same thoughts had nudged his mind. Above those thoughts, just why in God's Name – or anyone else's come to that – were they caught in this utterly futile, stupid squabble? King against Parliament? God's gift of free will against the same God's ordained rule?

Frankly he wanted none of it anymore.

Dyott ushered the exhausted men inside, poured ale for them all; slipped Richard a tot of strong rum.

Elizabeth Dyott remembered Richard Tremayne from when he had been a youth, all legs, arms and a blushing, shy, face. She had been a girl just turning into a woman. Ah, she had loved him from afar, but he had not noticed her, Seth Bater's youngest daughter, and at the end of her sixteenth summer she'd accepted

Charles Dyott's proposal of betrothal. She had a good life with a good husband, but as she bustled about doing what she could for these poor, sorry men, she could not help glancing, maybe too often, at Richard Tremayne, who had been the first love of her life.

She apologised that she had no hot food ready to serve them, but supplied bread, cheese, cold meat and the last of the autumn-fall sweet apples harvested from the orchard behind the inn. She gave each man an additional muslin-wrapped package of extra cheese for another meal. Offered to fetch warm water and bandaging for their hurts.

Richard smiled at her. He remembered her as a girl, those years back. She was still as pretty, still as kind-hearted.

"Nay, Mistress Elizabeth, we'll do well enough, but we will not linger too long. 'Tis not safe for you to shelter us. We'll move on within the hour." They'd have to take turns to walk, that was all. With his leaking boot, he didn't fancy the thought.

Elizabeth and her husband both protested, but Richard would have none of it. He propped his left elbow on the fire's mantelshelf, pewter tankard also resting there, for fear others might notice how much his hands were trembling. His flop of shoulder-length fair hair was tangled and filthy, his beard as disgraceful. He noticed that his red coat was torn in several more places than he'd realised. His sword, dangling at his left hip, should be cleaned, but he had not the energy or will to draw it. He raised his right hand to brush back hair from his eyes, noticed the grazed knuckles and the stained, dried blood. He hadn't registered the soreness until he'd looked. He tried as best he could to keep his breathing shallow, for the wound in his side was growing ever more painful. While grateful for Mistress Elizabeth's offer, he dared not inspect the wound for fear of what he might discover.

Mayhewe leaned against the wall a few feet behind, his chin drooped onto his chest, asleep on his feet. Cedric – though for some unexplained reason they all called him Cecil – sat at a wooden table, nursing the last of his ale and smoking a clay pipe begged from the landlord. Cecil swore his health was maintained by the intake of tobacco. The sweet smell of fine Virginia Blend filled the air, along with the fire's woodsmoke and the scent of lavender scattered and crushed on the spread reeds on the earth floor.

Mervyn Brockett was eager to be gone. He paced up and down, anxious, his muddied, bloodied, green coat – not so lush a green as once it had been – catching against his thighs and the chairs that Peter Thorne and Thomas Catchpole had flopped down on.

Again, Brockett glanced towards the door. Their hour was almost gone, they would have to move on – but without the extra horses...? Again he looked towards the closed door. Would no one help them? No one?

Richard inhaled, expelled the air with a long, tired sigh. Time was up. They had to be going. It was raining again and winter dusk would not be far off, but there were many, dangerous, miles ahead – and more danger to these good folk, were they to outstay this goodly welcome.

The inn door crashed open. Richard reached for his sword, Cedric almost dropped his pipe, Thomas and Peter sprang to their feet. Mervyn had a dagger immediate into his hand.

"They've as vound two!" The thick Devonshire accent of a young lad of about ten, as he burst in, slamming the wooden door behind him, his face alight with excitement, his breath all but spent from running.

"Two 'osses vor thee! Seth Bater says as 'ow 'e'll exchange 'is old cobs vor tha' mare!"

Fat-rumped cobs were not well-bred cavalry mounts, and their riders' legs would dangle near the ground, but if the animals had four sound feet and enough energy to reach the coast, then they would do. If, maybe, God had changed his mind and decided to help their riders. And if the men were lucky.

As they mounted and rode away into the fast-fading late afternoon light, young Martin Bater, the youngest of Farmer Seth's grandsons, came running from the northern end of the village.

"There be troopers comin' 'long tha low road. Roun'eads, Granpa says. Roun'eads!"

Charles Dyott ruffled the lad's hair and smiled. "Then we had best make them most welcome, ply them with strong ale, good food, an' hold them here 'til the morrow's dawn. Is the mare well away? Cain't be havin' anyone stealin' her can we?"

By nightfall it was still raining, with the temperature rapidly falling, nudged by a bitter-cold north-east wind. There would be snow again by the morrow. The hens safely locked away from any nosing fox, Elizabeth stood in the lane, her woollen cloak tight-pulled around her shoulders, arms wound about herself, not noticing the cold or wet, hoped the weather would not close in too hard for she did not want the troop of Roundheads to linger overlong. One night of their unwanted, solemn-faced company was bad enough. She looked towards where the other men had ridden away. How would she know if they made it to safety? She should have whispered to Richard to send word if he could, but why would he? She was only a face from his past, and he had more important things to think on. But still, she wished she had whispered her concern.

"God keep you all," she murmured beneath the breath that misted from her mouth. "God protect and be with you, Richard. Come back this way one day, if ever you can. You will always, always, be welcome here."

Author's note

The Battle at Torrington was a real event, and eighty barrels of gunpowder did explode, although it is not known how it happened, or why prisoners were held in the church. The heavy defeat, and probably the shock, ended the fighting in the West Country. The decisive Parliamentarian victory at Naseby on 14th June 1646 added to that ending, which effectively destroyed King Charles' armies. He was soon captured and eventually executed on 30th January 1649. Oliver Cromwell took the role of Lord Protector and governed until his death in September 1658, when Charles' eldest son was recalled to England and crowned as Charles II.

As for the men in this story, they, and their desperate plight, are portrayed as a fictional tale. Or is it?

If you believe in ghosts then these men were once alive and real. My daughter, Kathy, has the gift of being able to see those who are long dead as ordinary living people. There are several past residents in our eighteenth-century Devon farmhouse, and there are others who linger in our village pub, The Exeter Inn, Chittlehamholt. Kathy has seen a Tudor couple there, alongside Edwardian farmers, a group of women from the 1950s – and our beleaguered Royalists as described in this story. It is conjecture that these men were survivors from that battle at Torrington and the subsequent explosion, but it does seem very likely.

They appear in my book *Ghost Encounters: The Lingering Spirit of North Devon*, which I co-produced with Kathy. It delves into more encounters in different North Devon locations, but with an emphasis on *benign* spirits with no mention of uncanny, frightening hauntings, which mostly belong to the exaggerated docu-dramas of TV and film.

Kathy also saw Captain Richard (we do not, alas, know his surname) at The Grove Inn, King's Nympton, so again it is speculation as to why these men were at both locations, but I think the above story is a credible and plausible explanation.

But even if you do not believe in ghosts, I hope you enjoyed the story.

My one regret: we have no way of knowing whether the men made it to safety. Like Elizabeth, I hope they did.

© Helen Hollick

About Helen

Known for her captivating storytelling and rich attention to historical detail, Helen's historical fiction, nautical adventure series, cosy mysteries – and her short stories – skilfully invite readers to step into worlds where the boundaries between fact and fiction blend together.

Helen started writing as a teenager, but after discovering a passion for history, was initially published in 1993 in the UK with her Arthurian *Pendragon's Banner Trilogy* and two Anglo-Saxon novels about the events that led to the 1066 Battle of Hastings, one of which, *The Forever Queen* (USA title – *A Hollow Crown* in the UK) became a USA Today best-seller. Her *Sea Witch Voyages* are nautical-based adventures inspired by the Golden Age of Piracy. She also writes the *Jan Christopher* cosy mystery series set during the 1970s, and based around her, sometimes hilarious, years of working as a North London library assistant. Her 2025 release is *Ghost Encounters*, a book about the ghosts of North Devon.

Helen and her family moved from London to Devon after a Lottery win on the opening night of the London Olympics, 2012. She spends her time glowering at the overgrown garden, fending off the geese, helping with the horses and wishing the friendly, resident ghosts would occasionally help with the housework...

Website: www.helenhollick.net
Newsletter Blog: https://thoughtsfromadevon
shirefarmhouse.blogspot.com/
Amazon Author Page: https://viewauthor.at/
HelenHollick

5

———

A FATEFUL ENCOUNTER

BY ALISON MORTON

*When time turns in the wrong direction, fate will
always step in...*

Time Stitchers Headquarters, European Continent

"You have to be joking! Do you know how fricking
exhausting it is for me going through the time portal?
You're blooming lucky to be one of the eighty per cent
who don't get affected. And anyway, it's all your fault
and *you* can explain that to the boss. I'm off for a
shower and a beer."

Stannia stomped off down the causeway that ran
through the warehouse, pushing her way through
abandoned crates, reels of cable, abandoned food pods
and past the wardrobe mistress's assistant picking up
abandoned clothes. The latter recoiled from a
particularly scruffy tunic spattered with dubious stains.
Stannia gave her a perfunctory smile, too grateful that
she'd graduated from costumier to operative three
years ago.

No way was she going back to the first century BCE
just to pick up the mess Federicus had left behind.

Again. The third time if you wanted to be exact. He was supposed to be a senior operator. Ha! He couldn't even set the controls without her to check. The gods knew what time period they would have emerged in if she hadn't. Probably when the little green men had taken over Earth five thousand years in the future.

Okay, she'd been a bit dramatic when she'd left him pleading by the portal. Tough shit! They'd only just escaped with their skin from those crazed, murderous so-called Liberators. The guard of gladiators that Brutus had organised were a vicious lot. They hadn't cared whether you were male or female. A kill was a kill for them. Probably something to do with frustration at not being allowed to terminate their opponent when they were juiced up from a fight in the arena. She shook her head, causing her black curls to escape from their bun, followed by a cascade of bone pins. From the depths of the warehouse, she heard the wardrobe assistant tutting loudly at her. Stannia bent and picked the pins up. It took ages to carve the intricate patterns on them by hand so that they looked authentic – no laser cutting option allowed. She well remembered her own lacerated fingers from her costumier training as she'd wielded her carving knife.

As she switched the shower from wet to dry mode and her body was blasted with warm air, she had to admit that Federicus had tried his best, but it seemed as if the old Roman Fates were laughing at them. Well, her immediate fate was an appointment with an ice-cold glass of amber liquid in the mess bar.

"Ah, Stannia, I heard you were back." Only one person had that gravelly voice. The boss. Stannia put her drink back on the bar counter and slid off the high stool.

"Sir?"

"I'll read your formal report tomorrow but give me the short version now."

Stannia's heart thumped. Another failure to go down on her record which up to this assignment had been near perfect. She'd never get the promotion she desperately wanted. She hoped the subdued lighting hid her face reflecting the dismay she was feeling. "I'm very sorry to report that on our third attempt, we failed to prevent the assassination."

"What happened this time?"

She didn't want to rat on Federicus – poor team etiquette, although the bastard deserved it. "We couldn't prevent Trebonius from distracting Antonius," she said in the most neutral tone she could muster.

"We?"

"Senior Operator Federicus and I, sir."

"Yes, yes, I know who your teammate was. Don't treat me as an imbecile, Stannia. Details, and no prevarication. Now."

Stannia took a deep breath before she began. "I was in the crowd outside the hall by Pompey's Theatre. The Senate had been meeting there while building works were going on in the Forum Romanum. I had my dagger, but hidden inside my tunic. Mostly, I was trying to avoid getting my bottom pinched and being felt up by men in the crowd." Unbelievable how entitled they considered themselves. "Anyway, senators were starting to arrive. Cimber, who'd always been Caesar's friend, entered with that slimy bugger, Cassius Longinus." She felt heat rising up her neck at her crude words. "I mean that untrustworthy..."

"'Slimy bugger' will do very well. Go on."

"Shortly after, Antonius came along chatting with

Caesar. Decimus Brutus, who'd gone to fetch him, had hurried inside already. No sign of him. Federicus steps in, all togged up in a senator's stripes and short haircut, and makes a beeline for Trebonius who is on his mission to pull Antonius to the side and separate him from Caesar. Then Federicus trips on his toga edge and falls flat on his face. Trebonius steps over him and nobbles Antonius." She shrugged. "The rest, as you know, is history."

"Don't be facetious with me, Stannia. The rest is *not* history. When the report came in from the monitoring group about this time breach, I almost had a heart attack. Apparently, it's happened before. Several times, in fact. The monitors said the repair work was messy to the point of being botched. On this one, we now only have twenty-four hours left in our time loop during which to mend it properly. If we can't prevent Caesar's assassination this time and forever, then our timeline will diverge and go off on an alternative path. We had enough of that sort of trouble when we had to heal the enormous breach of the time continuum after the fiasco of Wellington winning at Waterloo! That took months to sort out."

"I know, sir, but I wonder about this one. We plan every move, we rehearse until we're blue in the face, we're just on the point of success, then splat, something happens that sabotages the whole thing. It's almost as if we're fated to fail."

"Oh, come on, you don't believe in all that superstitious nonsense, do you?"

Stannia thought the boss's eyebrows were in danger of meeting his hairline.

"No, of course not, but it's all a bit strange. The first time, Spurinna, the haruspex whom Caesar respected enormously, suddenly developed such a garbled voice that he sounded drunk when he warned Caesar that morning. The second time, his wife Calpurnia had almost convinced him with logical and sensible reasons to stay at home, when she – most uncharacteristically – burst into hysterical sobs which undid all our work giving her dreams of calamitous outcomes the night before. So when Decimus Brutus came to fetch him, Caesar was glad to get out of the house. This time, Federicus swore his toga was fine all the way to the meeting. He may have his faults, but he *is* good at those sort of fussy details. Now I've calmed down, I have to admit it's unlikely he was careless in that respect."

"Humph. Coincidence, I'd think." But the boss scanned around the bar, checking to see if anybody was within earshot. He looked back at Stannia. He leant in and spoke in one level above a whisper.

"Strange things do happen very occasionally that we can't remedy. And that piece of information is to go no further. If people knew the Time Stitchers were fallible, they'd be unsettled and we don't want that, do we?" His eyes bored into hers with equal amounts of threat and pleading.

"Absolutely not, sir." What the hell else had gone wrong? Time for a trip to the Archives. Or perhaps not. Things like that would have been well stitched up in every sense, then deleted. She might be reported if she even attempted to stick her nose into such secrets.

"Well, then, one last go, please," the boss said. "If Caesar ends up assassinated, I dread to think what might happen. The Roman Empire in the West may come to a premature end instead of lasting over two thousand years. The space–time continuum will be a total wreck and I'll get short shrift from the emperor, if he and I still exist at all in that alternative future."

Fine beads of sweat glistened on his forehead. He took out the folded square of cloth he always kept in the top pocket of his suit jacket and shook it out into a larger square of Egyptian cotton. He wiped his brow carelessly. Stannia looked on in amazement that he'd used his most precious antique artefact to wipe away mere sweat.

———

Federicus threw down his electronic stylus.

"I can't see a gap. In every possible scenario, we'd run the risk of meeting ourselves from one of our previous attempts and you know what that means." He gave Stannia a baleful look. She knew only too well. On her last training trip before graduation, she'd watched appalled as her training officer had gasped in horror, "Gods, I'm here already!" collapsed and vanished before Stannia's shocked gaze. No trace, not even a drop of DNA had remained anywhere in her personal timeline, present or past. Her trainer had been obliterated from time.

"Suppose you nobble Decimus Brutus in the street on his way to fetch Caesar?" Stannia said.

"With his guard around him? You're joking! There were six of them plus his secretary."

"Well, I can't be in Caesar's house again as I was fussing around Calpurnia and feeding her possets full of hallucinogens the evening before, then doing her hair that morning. Can you worm your way in as a kitchen slave and doctor his breakfast?"

"No, I'm already delivering vegetables to their house from dawn, then enjoying my own in the kitchen with a rather charming girl baking the first batch of bread."

Stannia rolled her eyes. "Road sweeper, then?"

"A possibility, or I could lurk as a member of the urban cohorts pretending to watch the crowd."

"No, you can't. You might run into yourself arriving as the senator who tripped."

"Don't remind me!" His face burnt bright red.

"Sorry."

She looked out of the window at the fields swaying with wheat. A *vigiles* patrol car with its bright SPQR logo was bombing along the main road, siren blaring. Idly, she wondered who they were chasing. Or perhaps like police anywhere, they'd forgotten their sandwiches.

"Right," she said. "We have to stop being subtle. That hasn't worked. We're going to have to do something dramatic to stop the Senate meeting at all."

"Like what? Start a riot or get the barbarians to invade? Or set the place on fire à la Nero?"

"Don't be silly. He wasn't anything to do with it. We know that really *was* an accident. Still, it's an idea."

"We could spook the augurs. Caesar was massively superstitious."

"Well, if Calpurnia's nightmares and Spurinna's warbling couldn't stop him, I'm not sure that would work. But I may have the germ of an idea…"

"Brr, it's freezing." Federicus pulled his cloak tighter against the cold wind blasting across the plain east of the River Tiber valley.

"Don't be such a wimp," Stannia hissed. "I can't help it if there's a snap frost at the end of February. At least it's not raining."

"It's all right for you – you've got a full-length wool *stola* on top of your tunic as well as a thick cloak."

"At least your boots are fur lined."

"Yes, thank the gods."

Stannia gave him a curious look. Federicus didn't

often invoke the gods either in general or any particular one like Mars or Apollo. She didn't know if he went to any temple at all. Perhaps he was getting into character. Their science briefing noted a dulling of the atmosphere and cooler temperatures throughout the period 44–42 BCE, probably due to an eruption of Mount Etna in Sicily early in 44 BCE, but please not to mention this reason to the natives of the time.

They were sheltering under an oak tree on the edge of the grove dedicated to Anna Perenna, the goddess of the wheel of time and life. Stannia thought that was rather a lovely idea. But that gossip Ovid said that Anna was an old woman of Bovillae who, after she'd become a goddess, impersonated Minerva to gain admission to Mars' bedchamber, which was why coarse jokes and ribald songs were used at Anna Perpenna's festivities. Typical man, Stannia snorted, always thinking with his dick.

"Look out, here come the priestess and her acolytes," Federicus said. A mature woman wearing long robes and a *palla* drawn up over her head so that only a few wisps of grey hair were visible, was approaching the sacred grove in a stately manner. A group of young women, girls really, followed her mostly demurely, although a few were giggling. A middle-aged woman, head also veiled, brought up the rear and was frowning at the girls.

"They're only rehearsing today, aren't they?" whispered Federicus.

"Yes, but this is the perfect moment for us to make the offer."

Stannia stepped forward to stand at the edge of the sacred spring in the middle of the grove. She raised her hand in greeting.

"*Salve*, honoured priestess of Anna Perenna. May the circle of the year be completed happily on the ides."

"Thank you. We are looking forward to it." She regarded Stannia gravely, probably wondering who in Hades was confronting her.

"I am Maia Bassiana," Stannia said. "This is my brother and guardian, Publius Bassianus. May I ask how you are celebrating this year?"

"We will celebrate at dawn with offerings, then process down the Via Flaminia and then return to eat and drink together by the river. Unfortunately, we do not have the means to go as far as the Capitolium this year as we cannot afford litters for the older members of our order." She looked down, then up at Stannia who knew what was required from a respectable Roman matron dressed up and wearing expensive jewellery.

"It will be my pleasure to provide funds for the entire procession, priestess," she replied. "Thus, *all* participants may ride comfortably in litters. I have a great affinity with the correct turn of time." She held out a heavy purse and opened the top to show the glint of gold and silver. "I have only one request of you – a small addition to your route."

"Brilliant! Well, brilliant as long as they set off in good time," Federicus said as they emerged from the time portal into the warehouse. "My turn to buy the drinks."

"Accepted. We'll be there on the fifteenth to chivvy them along. On foot, it takes about an hour from the spring in the grove to reach the hall by Pompey's Theatre. In litters, you can cut that down to about forty minutes."

Twelve days later in 44 BCE, Stannia and Federicus stepped down from their own litter at dawn in the grove containing the sacred spring of Anna Perenna. Federicus was being particularly vigilant in checking the drape of his toga. Stannia adjusted her blue silk *palla* embroidered with little gold flowers and spoked wheels. She'd worn the fine wool *stola* again as the sky was overcast, shutting out what should have been the beginning of a sunny day at this time of year in Rome.

Once sacrifices had been completed, auguries pronounced and the priestesses, attendants and hangers-on had settled in their litters, they set off for the Via Flaminia. Traffic coming from the Milvian Bridge wasn't too heavy, mostly handcarts, small herds of cattle, donkeys either packed or with riders, and occasional covered carts. Most commercial traffic would have travelled at night and had unloaded their goods in the city hours ago. As they swayed along, Stannia pulled the side curtains apart and looked across the countryside. Not bothered by the smell of dung or the clatter of hooves and boots on cobbles, she mused about how this area would become completely built over and saturated with heaving humanity in the following centuries.

"Daydreaming again?" Federicus interrupted her.

"Yes and no." She stretched her neck out to look down the road. "We're making good time – nearly at the Campus Martius."

A few blocks of *insulae* flats started to appear and they passed the Altar of Mars and the Villa Publica, the headquarters of the tax authorities, but the land stretched flat across to the Tiber where the Ianiculum Hill rose gently to the south-west. At the Porta Fontinalis, the gate into the *pomerium*, the sacred and legal boundary of the city, they turned and took the road round the base of the Capitoline Hill. Much to the annoyance of the rest of the traffic, they stopped halfway and the priestess said prayers, raising her hands and calling on Jupiter, Minerva and Juno for their blessings. At last they moved on, skirting the southern shoulder of the Capitoline and following Stannia's requested detour towards the north-west.

"Right, we're nearly on," she said.

"Just watch out for yourself in that crowd," Federicus said. I don't want to explain to the boss that you vanished in a puff of disembodied cells."

"And you make sure you're clear before your old self trips up by the Senate door."

He smiled and she gave a smile back.

She leant forward through the front frame of the litter to the left bearer. He was strong and muscled but despite the cool morning his skin was shining with sweat. The four of them had carried Federicus and herself in the litter for three quarters of an hour already. She knew what she was going to say was unreasonable, but she had to give the order if her plan was to succeed.

"Pass the message to the front litter to speed up to double pace. We risk being late." She flicked the curtain across so that she wouldn't be able to see any glare of resentment.

"Poor sods," Federicus said. "Still, if we're to ram through the crowd and snatch Caesar, then we need to be quick." He shot a look at Stannia. "How did you think this one up?"

"I watched a patrol car bombing along the road at a hell of a speed outside our HQ and thought little would stop it. That gave me the idea we could do something similar." She pulled the hem of her *stola* up and checked the portal remote strapped to her thigh for the nth time. It was already locked on to herself and Federicus. As long as they both had a grip on some part of Caesar's anatomy, he would be transported with them. Stannia reckoned that tough as he was in his own time period, the poor man would be dazed, possibly even lose consciousness for a minute or two while they reset the coordinates for a week later where he would be safely on the way to Parthia on his next campaign. He'd probably think he'd been visited by the gods or had an episode of his falling sickness.

She flicked her hem down and gripped the litter frame as the bearers started running. Was this how a sack of nuts felt when being thrown around a warehouse?

"Ready?" She looked at Federicus.

"Yes. May the Fates be with us."

She chuckled. "Well, there's not a lot they can do now to stop us."

A black raven swooped down, only just missing the litter.

"Pluto, that was near!" Federicus cried out. "Bloody thing."

"Never mind that. Look, there's Caesar coming down the street. Let's go."

Stannia leapt out of the litter, nearly losing her balance as it sped on behind the others. Federicus joined her a few seconds later. He was grasping his bundled-up toga under one arm.

"Forget jumping off a train – that's for softies. Remind me never to jump off a fast-moving litter again." He let the toga fall back into its normal draped form.

They watched as the other litters ploughed through the crowd in front of the hall by Pompey's Theatre where the Senate would be meeting today. It was chaos as the priestess shouted, the girls screamed and wept, arriving senators were jostled and their bodyguards were surrounded by a raucous mob which split into three parts with one even invading the hall itself.

Perfect!

Federicus walked jauntily towards Caesar, lifting a hand to greet him, but two paces away, Caesar vanished. Federicus turned with an accusatory look at Stannia, but she was staring at the spot where Caesar had been. Her mouth fell open and she couldn't move.

What the hell happened there?

All the group who were with him had also disappeared, including Decimus Brutus.

Instead, a tall, majestic woman was looking at them with a smirk on her lips. She wore a necklace of tiny skulls over a black robe. Her whole body seemed to shimmer. Stannia took a step back and her hand flew to the base of her throat. She tried to swallow, but her mouth was too dry. They were a myth. Just something you said. Weren't they?

"I am Morta, goddess of death and sister to Nona and Decuma who spin and measure men's fates."

The figure's lips didn't move. Stannia heard the words pound through her head.

"You seek to interfere in the wheel of time and fate. We watch you." The woman made a tiny movement of her shoulders as if shrugging and the shimmering flashed. "Much of the time it does not matter and we are sometimes amused by your little efforts." Her eyes turned black. "But today, you shall not change the weft of time. Be gone." She flicked her hand.

For an instant, Stannia found herself far above the earth and looking down on the bloody and broken body of Caesar. The next, she was crashing on a hard surface. Then everything went black.

She woke, her head aching like all the devils from Tartarus were hammering on the inside of her skull – with attitude. Pain shot through every cell of her body. She opened her eyes. The concrete floor of the warehouse in her own time. She took a deep breath and turned her head very slowly to the left. Federicus was crouching on his side like a baby, his toga twisted up round his waist and his hands over his ears.

Then she heard the laugh – full-throated, piercing, strident. It echoed round the warehouse. The technicians, costumiers, clerks, sweepers – everybody stared at the walls, up at the roof, then back at Stannia and Federicus who were taking short, sharp, panicky breaths. After a couple of minutes, the laughter faded. Stannia slowly released her breath. Then the emergency klaxon went off.

The boss ran in, covering his ears.

"Somebody turn that bloody alarm off!" He turned to Stannia. "What the hell was that?" he shouted.

"What happens when you try to defy the Fates."

Stannia sat up, her head swam. All around her, the air rippled then, gathering speed, twisted and turned into a vortex. She couldn't breathe as she was pulled into the whirling mass and everything exploded into blinding light.

Rome, present day, present timeline

"Sarah! Wake up! Are you okay? You blacked out there for a moment."

She blinked.

Federicus?

Who was Federicus? A thought hovering at the back of her brain snapped out of existence. Damn. That was always happening when she was in the middle of writing up her archaeological dig reports. A creeping cold was invading her body. She looked down. She was sitting in a muddy puddle in the bottom of a deep sectional trench where the side hall of Pompey's Theatre would have been on Ancient Rome's Campus Martius. She struggled up and was helped by a strong arm belonging to a man who seemed familiar. She shook her head. Of course, it was Jason Fredericks, her deputy.

"Thanks, Jay. I have no idea what happened there. I must have slipped. No wonder with all this bloody rain." Sarah, whose full name was Sarah Stanaway, looked round the Piazza dei Satiri at the tall orange and yellow stuccoed buildings. It had been an awkward dig in a tiny square and at the beginning of a rainy March.

"What do you say to packing it all up?" he said. "I think we're done."

"Agreed. I'll just put my tools together." She picked up her diamond-shaped trowel, brushes and bag of bags and dropped them into the lower compartment of her rectangular plastic toolbox. She slotted the finds tray in as the upper layer. It was a great box for working in compact digs. She laid the most treasured piece reverently in the tray. She was still staring at it when she realised a tall, majestic woman had appeared by her side. She wore a strange silver necklace at the neck of her sleeveless black dress but no raincoat.

"Are you finished now? It's been so interesting watching you from my window." She pointed to the third floor of one of the apartment blocks.

"Thank you," Sarah replied. "Yes, we've completed our work here. The repair crew will put the street back to as it was. My colleague and I will return to the university now to catalogue everything."

"Find anything interesting?"

"This and that," Sarah replied, trying to suppress her excitement.

"Then I look forward to hearing about it," the woman said. Not a drop of rain had settled on her bare arms or her dress. Before Sarah could comment, the woman had disappeared. How strange, Sarah thought. Didn't she want to go back to her flat in this rain? She shrugged. Perhaps the woman had some shopping to do. Anyway, Jason had been waiting patiently, but now he was fidgeting to get away out of the rain.

"Come on," he said. "I think we deserve a beer or two. And I'm buying. We've made our discovery for the week. Well, for the millennium. It's not every day we dig up one of the daggers that may have killed Julius Caesar back in 44 BCE."

© Alison Morton

About Alison

Alison Morton writes award-winning thrillers featuring tough but compassionate heroines. Her eleven-book Roma Nova thriller series is set in an imaginary European country where a remnant of the ancient Roman Empire has survived into the 21st century and is ruled by women who face conspiracy, revolution and heartache but with a sharp line in dialogue

Six years' military service, a fascination with ancient Rome and a life of reading crime, historical and thriller fiction have inspired her writing. On the way, she collected a BA in modern languages and an MA in history.

She lives in Poitou in France, the home of Mélisende, the heroine of her latest two contemporary thrillers, *Double Identity* and *Double Pursuit*.

For the latest news, subscribe to her newsletter at https://www.alison-morton.com/newsletter/ and receive 'Welcome to Alison Morton's Thriller Worlds' as a thank you gift.

Website: https://www.alison-morton.com
Facebook: https://www.alison-morton.com
Amazon Author Page: https://Author.to/
AlisonMortonAmazon

6

FOLLOWING FATE

BY ELIZABETH ST.JOHN

*A Lost Portrait, a Hidden Conspiracy, and
a Second Chance at Love*

England, Present-day

Julia Garten shouldered and shoved The Second Chance Bookshop door, jiggling the latch and ducking her head as the five-hundred-year-old blackened wood frame complained and then invited her across the threshold. Each morning, she enjoyed the same ritual: a pause and inhale as the listening silence welcomed her. Moments before, she knew her precious stock of used books had conversed, words fluttering from yellowed pages, seeping through age-softened leather bindings, and flying up into the cool air, free as they were always meant to be. One day, she'd catch those fleeting whispers, as elusively above her pitch as a dog whistle.

Beowulf drew a big old doggy Newfie sigh and shuffled to his spot by the wood burner. When her life in New York had spectacularly exploded over Mark's extra-curricular donations to a thirty-something blonde from the Met's fundraising

115

department, Julia had resolved that she would trade men for dogs permanently. Beowulf was proof of the wise decision. She flipped the crackled door sign to 'open', lit a fire to take the October chill from the air, brewed her third coffee of the morning, and pulled out her laptop.

"Okay, e-Bay, what do you have for me today?" Julia relished this morning routine, checking her bids on first editions, Stuart-era portraits, and obscure 17th-century pamphlets that had little value except to the eccentric circle of writers, readers, academics, and re-enactors she'd cultivated since opening the bookshop a year ago. Oh, and the select group of English stately homes and private country estates that welcomed a volunteer historian dedicated to searching art sales worldwide for family portraits – significant to their history but to few others.

Burford was in the heart of English Civil War country, and when in her furious online search she'd found the shop premises and its garret for sale, she'd known that fate had sent her to Right Move for a reason. Within a month, she'd sold her share of the publishing business to her partner, rented her mid-town brownstone to a Park Avenue plastic surgeon, packed up her books, and moved home to England after thirty years away.

Her laptop sprang to life, electric blue against the amber firelight and dove grey morning. She hurriedly tapped the keys, eager to see if the latest bid she'd placed on an 1806 First Edition of Lucy Hutchinson's Memoirs had been accepted – then froze and leaned toward her computer screen, where the results of her traditional daily search glowed.

A man's face stared back at her. Dark eyes gleamed with intelligence, his full beard framing a sensual mouth. A deep red jacket edged in fur emphasized his broad shoulders, one elegant hand clasping a lace-cuffed glove.

She struggled to catch her breath as she read the sparse description beneath the image:

Sir Allen Apsley (1567–1630): Of the School of Marcus Gheeraerts, 1617
Guide Price: Please Enquire

Sir Allen Apsley. Lieutenant of the Tower of London, friend of King James, cousin to the Duke of Buckingham. Father to Lucy Hutchinson. Julia's degree at Oxford had focused on the lives of Early Modern women. Her interest had never faded, and alongside a career in publishing, she had pursued her passion for Lucy Hutchinson relentlessly in her spare time. Secretly, she'd started writing her own historical fiction novel. She'd certainly had enough experience publishing everyone else's.

Now, she was face to face with her obsession's father. There were no known paintings of him. No record of his features or character, except elusive hints in the likenesses of his children. A gorgeous portrait of his wife and son existed, also by Gheeraerts, safely ensconced in the stately home of Julia's favourite client.

"Well, Allen, where have you been all this time? And where are you now?"

She scrolled down to the gallery listing and slumped back in her chair in shock, almost tipping her coffee cup over. Beowulf lifted his head, briefly thumped his tail, huffed, and subsequently resumed snoring.

Oliver Villiers Fine Arts

"*No.* No, I don't believe it."

Thirty years later and she was right back in the land of a broken heart. Oxford. She'd fallen in love with the town, the honey-coloured buildings enclosing verdant quads, even the dreaming spires that snared the woolly morning mists. And Oliver. That passionate first love, burning from freshers' week through graduation, and the subsequent betrayal and desolation. Julia plummeted back to memories she'd thought forever buried. She'd fled to New York. Oliver had built an international career – St. Petersburg, Paris, Rome – becoming one of the world's leading fine art experts with a reputation for reading hidden messages and uncovering rare treasures. He'd made a fortune deciphering a coded portrait of George Villiers, Duke of Buckingham. Or so she read in the journals.

And now he was the custodian of Sir Allen Apsley. The man she'd been seeking for decades.

Suddenly her screen blanked, her computer shifting into sleep mode. As quickly as he had materialised, Allen vanished.

Julia hurriedly tapped her mouse. Allen's face reappeared.

She reached for her phone. The receptionist connected her immediately.

"Julia Garten," he said, as if he'd been expecting her, his voice smooth and familiar, mellowed by time.

Her breath caught. "Hello, Oliver."

"It's been a while."

"Thirty years." She winced. Why was she counting?

"Thirty years." He paused, cleared his throat. "What an unexpected pleasure to hear from you."

"The painting," she rushed in. "A portrait of Sir Allen Apsley."

"Yes?"

"I'd like to see it, Oliver." She stared through the window. Burford had woken up; the first tourists were straggling along the street, peering in her door. Claire, her assistant-cum-lodger who rented the flat, clattered down the stairs, flipped on the coffee machines, and started testing locomotive steam spurts for lattes in the small coffee bar in the bay. She waved cheerily at Julia while grinding a bag-load of beans at about the same decibels as a concrete mixer.

Oliver's voice echoed in her ear. "Julia! I said I'll arrange a viewing tomorrow morning. Come to the gallery at eleven."

"I...err..."

Oliver clicked his keyboard. "There are several interested parties already registered. If you have a mind to purchase the portrait, I won't be able to hold him. Plan to stay overnight. He goes to auction on Wednesday."

Every bone in her body was warning her not to go. She'd closed the door on Oliver and his treachery long ago.

But Allen had waited four hundred years. She couldn't ignore him now.

And besides, securing the portrait for her client would bring him home to join his wife and son.

The shop bell clanged, and the first party of Americans charged in, loudly exclaiming over the darling quaint interior and Beowulf's adorable hearth-rug imitation. He sniffed their stiff new Burberry raincoats and squeaky-fresh Cotswold Wellies and went back to sleep.

"Okay," she said.

Oliver laughed, a sexy chuckle she remembered too well. "Give me your number. I'll text you my details." A pause. Then, softly, "What a curious twist of fate."

She wasn't sure if he meant the painting... or them.

Oliver Villiers Fine Arts was, of course, in Belgravia. Julia strode along Ebury Street, humming as she did when slightly anxious, after dropping her roller bag at The Lime Tree, a Georgian-fronted boutique hotel. Too quickly, she arrived at the gallery, and instead of pausing, marched straight in, following the receptionist's directions. The preview room was expensively minimalist, its polished blonde oak floors and art lighting designed to enhance the treasures on display. Oliver stood in a pool of light, the beam picking out the silver in his dark hair, muted across the broad shoulders of his grey Savile Row suit. Intentional, Julia thought. He always was one for setting a scene.

"Julia."

"Oliver."

"You haven't changed a bit."

"Flattery, Oliver? We both know that doesn't work on me."

He shrugged and grinned, unabashed. For a moment, the past hung between them, their history palpable. Then he gestured to the wall behind him. "Here's Allen. I've ordered him to be put on display. I've only just seen the piece – I normally don't deal in the less famous sitters."

The portrait of Sir Allen Apsley was a three-quarter length, its colours richer and details sharper than Julia had anticipated. Although the portrait desperately needed cleaning, his piercing gaze seemed to speak directly to her.

"Hello Allen," she whispered. "I've come to take you home."

Oliver stepped closer. "He is rather magnificent."

Julia reached for her loupe, inspecting Allen's pleated ruff, the expression in his eyes, the fine lacework on his glove.

"May I?" Oliver took the magnifier and leaned down to look at Allen's hand.

"Good Lord."

"What?"

"Look for yourself."

Julia examined the ring that Oliver had spotted.

Set deep in the gold was a ruby. And Queen Anna's serpent wrapped sinuously around the stone.

"It's Anna of Denmark's cypher," she confirmed. "And there's something else." She leaned in closer, a faint engraving on the bottom of the picture frame now coming into focus. "It's an inscription," she murmured. "But it's almost worn away."

Oliver nodded. "Can you make it out?"

Julia squinted. "*Data* is certainly the first word." She peered more, letting her eyes go slightly unfocused. She found that this was the best way to try to get a sense of an illegible word. "*Fata. Sec...*"

"...*Secutus.*" Oliver interrupted. "Is it *secutus*?"

"Maybe... I think so... yes." Julia straightened. "*Following his allotted fate.*"

"But why inscribe it on the frame?" Oliver asked. "It feels... personal, almost a dedication intended for just the recipient."

"It is very personal." Julia took a deep breath. "This is the motto of his wife's family. Sir Allen married into aristocracy: Lucy St.John."

"The Duke of Buckingham's brother, Edward Villiers, married her sister Barbara..."

"...And Gheeraerts painted Lucy and their son's portrait the same year as Allen's. It's stunning, remarkably like this style. There's no doubt they were meant to hang together. Perhaps Allen dedicated his portrait to Lucy." Julia visualised them side by side in her client's collection. It felt right. She must reunite them.

Oliver folded his arms and tilted his head to one side. "Looks like there might be some overpainting, too." He drew his finger lightly across the top left of the portrait, a blank wall behind Allen's head. "See, the brush strokes here are different, and the surface is slightly bumpy."

Julia peered at the portrait. She really couldn't see clearly what Oliver had spotted. "How interesting. Would ultraviolet show us more?"

"Probably, but that takes a while. You can send it off to a specialist once you have him. Frankly, I'm far more interested to know why Allen is wearing Queen Anna's ring."

"Why?"

"That, my dear, is a long story." Oliver glanced at his watch. "Ah, good. I've booked us a table across the road. Let's have lunch. Catch up. It's only been...what did you say...thirty years?"

"I really can't..."

"...Scared I'll bite?"

Julia shook her head. "Not after all this time. But I do want to re-look at my research about Allen."

"You can do that after lunch. I have a feeling you'll have even more to think about once I tell you about my suspicions."

"You know Apsley got his position at the Tower thanks to the Duke of Buckingham." Oliver leaned across the café table, blue eyes sharp, a shadow of beard framing his firm chin. Age suited him, Julia thought. Of course, La Chèvre d'Or, the delightful French bistro across from his gallery, was his style too. The pungent scent of Provençal herbs transported her back to their Sorbonne days – *Spring Term in Paris,* they had laughingly named it. Had he picked this place intentionally? Probably. Charm was second nature to him.

"That's part of why he's so fascinating." Julia sipped Oliver's choice of a white Bordeaux. It was delicious. "Allen was a pure Calvinist, convinced that only God set his fate, completely incorruptible. And then along came George Villiers."

Oliver lifted an eyebrow. "Are you suggesting a Villiers is a bad influence?"

Julia kept a straight face. "Well, Barbara Villiers, his grandniece, wasn't exactly full of virtue..."

"True. But King Charles was awfully persuasive..."

"And what about Elizabeth Villiers, who became King William's mistress?"

"Those are the ladies in the family."

"And Gorgeous George? King James couldn't resist the original Villiers."

Oliver spread his hands in surrender. "Alright. Enough of the name-dropping. I admit. My ancestors were actively involved in seventeenth-century intrigue and debauchery."

Julia laughed despite herself. "Poor Allen. I rather think he was way out of his depth with trying to keep up with Buckingham."

"Perhaps not." Oliver's tone turned serious. "I think there's more to the portrait. A lot more."

Startled, Julia met his eyes, cradling her wineglass as she studied him. It was uncannily familiar, Oliver telling a story, mesmerising her as he brought the past alive. "How so?"

"Allen owed everything to Buckingham. If this jewel in the portrait belonged to Queen Anna, Allen must have been connected to her inner circle, perhaps through Villiers."

"We know he was close to King James. Allen lent him a great deal of money."

Oliver nodded. "They were all short of cash. Queen Anna's jewels were said to be stolen by Piero Hugon, on Buckingham's orders to fund his wars. Apparently, they were later smuggled out of the country, but that's never been proven. Hugon was accused of the theft and imprisoned in the Tower under Allen's watch before fleeing to France. And Allen and Buckingham remained close, didn't they?"

Julia nodded. "Extremely. Allen was a witness to Buckingham's will."

"If Buckingham had Hugon steal the jewels and give them to Allen to hide, it explains why they were never found." Oliver studied his phone, Allen's portrait filling the screen. "And this surfaces now, after centuries of obscurity."

"Fate?"

"Destiny."

They smiled across the table; their old argument of splitting the difference still lingered after all these years.

Julia shook herself free of the memories. "Maybe the inscription on the frame was a way to show Allen's dedication to Lucy. There is no doubt he considered her the love of his life from the writings he left behind. Or it was a reminder, a message to whoever held the ring that they served the Villiers family, owed their destiny – or fate – to them."

"Julia, there's something I need to tell you." Oliver's serious tone caught her attention.

"Now what?"

"Someone else is looking at the portrait. She called just after you did." He had the grace to look down, for Julia knew already who he meant. "I couldn't refuse. It's my responsibility to encourage all qualified buyers to view."

Julia emptied her glass, and with the last of her

wine evaporated the misplaced sense of nostalgia and sentimentality that had grown in a French café scented with memories and romance. "Vivienne."

He bowed his head.

"Vivienne Devereaux." She swallowed. "Of course she'd know about this portrait. She's built her career at the Sorbonne on this kind of discovery. If you're correct about the jewels, she would have spotted Queen Anna's ring immediately."

Oliver stirred his coffee. "Vivienne's a seventeenth-century expert too. She has been convinced for decades that the jewels belong to France and *Les Héritiers de Hugon*."

"Who?" This just got better and better. Not only was her rival about to walk back into her life, but she had some deep academic connection that completely sidelined Julia's amateur interest.

"A French syndicate – *Les Héritiers de Hugon*, descendants of Piero. They believe the jewels belong to them and will do anything to reclaim them. You're best off letting them take what they want."

Damn it. Did Oliver really think she'd cooperate with Vivienne Devereaux? "I'm not in this for the jewels, Oliver. Allen belongs with the portrait of his wife and son, where he will be appreciated and cared for. It's about history and legacy. But if Vivienne gets there first..."

"She'll twist the narrative, discard the portrait, and pursue the jewels however she can." Oliver's eyes locked onto hers. "You're in over your head. But I can help."

She bristled. "Don't patronise me. I'm perfectly capable of bidding on Allen's portrait on behalf of my client. I'm not going to let that snake of a woman steal him to satisfy her own greedy ambition."

His amused smile was infuriating. "Still diving headfirst into impossible quests, aren't you?"

"This isn't a 'quest,' Oliver. It's fate. That portrait has been hidden for four hundred years."

"And the jewels?" he interrupted. "A myth to most, dangerously real to a few. You're thinking about Allen's portrait. Others are seeking something much more. You always were one to jump in without looking."

"And you've always arrived just in time to criticise."

His smile faded. "I'm not criticising. I'm trying to help. You called me, remember?"

"Are you helping?" she shot back. "Because it feels like you're undermining me. Again."

His expression softened, but he didn't back down. "I'm not questioning your passion, Julia. I'm questioning the risk. This isn't just an academic discovery or a family legacy. There are people who will go to extreme lengths to get those jewels. Vivienne included."

"I know what I'm doing."

"Do you?" Oliver leaned in. "Do you remember the first and last time you went up against Vivienne? Do you remember Amsterdam?"

Julia's stomach tightened. Of course, she remembered. The sabotaged presentation of her thesis that had spiralled into chaos, the wild accusations of plagiarism, the professional fallout, her academic career cratered before it began. The whispers that Vivienne had orchestrated it all. And Oliver, standing by Julia's side – until he wasn't.

"That was different," she said quietly.

"How?"

"Because I was alone." Her voice cracked and she hated herself for it. "You left, Oliver."

The words hung between them, heavier than their years apart.

Oliver exhaled, running a hand through his hair. "I didn't leave *you*. I left... us. There's a difference."

"Not to me."

The café around them blurred. For a moment, she was that younger version of herself again – naïve, hopeful, and utterly shattered when he'd walked away.

"I shouldn't have brought this up," Oliver said. "I don't want history repeating itself."

Julia met his gaze. "Neither do I. Which is why I need you on my side this time. If Vivienne is involved, I need to understand the hidden meaning in Allen's portrait, the real significance of Queen Anna's ring."

For a long moment, he was silent. Then he reached across the table and lightly caressed her hand. "Fine. But if we do this, we do it together. You trust me. Agreed?"

She hesitated, left her hand for a moment under his, and then pulled it away. "Give me reason to. And maybe I will."

She needed to see Allen with fresh eyes. Back at the gallery, she and Oliver stood before the portrait and tried to discover what else might have meaning, other than the ring. What would Vivienne be looking for? Julia ran her finger over the engraving on the frame, a thought forming in her mind. "The inscription might not just be symbolic. It could be literal. What if the ring – and the painting – are meant to direct us to a specific location familiar to Allen and Lucy?"

"If the jewels were hidden in their home in the Lieutenant's Lodgings, they might still be there – or renovations over the centuries could have buried them," Oliver mused.

"Which is why the painting is so crucial," Julia said. "There may be specific clues that point to Queen Anna's jewels – whether it was Hugon or Allen that hid them."

Oliver tilted his head. "Go on."

"Lucy St.John was very much involved in the Tower's life. She created a medicinal garden, cared for the prisoners, even funded Raleigh and the Earl of Northumberland in their alchemy, so she could learn more about curatives. There are documents, old maps and plans in the Tower – if we can locate a specific area or room, one that Lucy was familiar with too, we could narrow our search." She whipped around again, re-examining the painting. "Oh, Oliver – Allen's standing next to a table. It's almost hidden under the grime, but look closely... it's an apothecary table. Another clue to Lucy."

He grinned, his excitement mirroring her own. "We'd need access to the Tower archives and the King's House. That won't be easy. The Governor lives there and doesn't take kindly to visitors to his private residence."

"That I can help with." Julia glanced at her watch. "In fact, I'll call him now. Colonel McTaggert is a dear friend, who has been incredibly generous with his time while I've been researching my Lucy Hutchinson book. I'm sure he'd be happy to give us access to the building."

The taxi slowed as they crested Tower Hill, the fortress's ancient walls glowing in the autumn sunshine. On days like today, the Tower was benign, welcoming almost. The driver pulled to a stop, and Julia stepped out. Across the moat, the Byward Gate guarded the entrance. She'd walked in so often on research visits, exploring Allen's home, the chamber where his daughter Lucy had been born. Before, she'd had to imagine so much. Now, with his likeness indelibly printed in her mind, she almost expected him to welcome her into his lodgings. Instead, Colonel McTaggert greeted her and Oliver personally and waved them both through his private quarters to the oldest part of the building.

East through a dark corridor that led towards the Bloody Tower and the remaining patch of Lucy's garden, her stillroom was dimly lit, the scent of dried herbs and aged parchment clinging to the air. The room had a mournful disrepair about it: mops and buckets leaning against the wall, file boxes stacked under the transom window, cobwebs draping the corners. Julia imagined how Lucy would have taken such pride in this room, lined it with cabinets filled with glass bottles and earthenware jars, curatives for family and prisoners alike. She would have hung bunches of dried sage and rosemary from the ceiling hooks and sprinkled lavender buds across the floor.

Beneath the twenty-first century muddle, an apothecary chest was pushed up against the uneven brick wall, a myriad of small drawers filling its face. She and Oliver glanced at each other. He set his satchel on the floor, kneeling before the darkened wood furniture.

"It's the table from the painting," he said.

And then she saw it.

A faint inscription, hidden along the ledge under the chest top, barely visible in the dim light.

Her pulse quickened. "Oliver. Look."

He leaned in, his eyes searching the worn letters. *"Data fata secutus.* 'Following his allotted fate'. Again."

Oliver ran his fingers over the engravings that surrounded the words. Pausing suddenly, he pressed his thumbs on two small rosettes that entwined the chest's corners. With a click, a bottom drawer glided open. Carefully, Oliver pulled it out. Inside, resting on dark green velvet as fresh as the day it was fitted, lay a parchment with a red seal attached.

"Is that...?"

"The Great Seal," Oliver confirmed. He flashed his phone light onto the imprint, highlighting its intricate engraving. "From the time of James I." He looked up at her, his eyes shining. "This decrees..." He shone his flashlight again. "...An order appointing Sir Edward Villiers as Master of the Mint. In 1617."

"There's a connection here. Buckingham had everyone in place that summer. Hugon to steal the jewels. Allen to receive them. Edward to hide them. And their wives to record the missing links in case something went wrong."

Oliver placed a hand on her shoulder, his touch steadying. "You'll need to move fast. The Mint archives could hold answers, but if Vivienne gets there first..."

"She won't," Julia said calmly, turning to face him. "Her focus is on the jewels, and how she can reclaim her family's treasure. She'll take short cuts, will miss the research and evidence of pulling the history together. Just as she did in Amsterdam, forcing her to claim my work as hers. I know her style."

"And the painting of Allen?" Oliver's voice was gentle. "I know he's your real reason for chasing this."

Julia blinked at the sudden tears that filled her eyes. Blast. Would she never learn that a historian should not be sentimental? "Allen will leave with me tomorrow when I bid for him and reunite him with the portrait of Lucy and his son. They are in excellent hands. He needs to be with them, with people who will love him and care for him, through generations to come."

Oliver brushed away a tear that had spilled over to her cheek, reading her thoughts as he had often done so. "You're not an academic. You're a storyteller."

Julia flinched and pulled away, not wanting to share how her heart lurched at his touch.

He carefully slipped the parchment into an envelope he'd brought in his satchel. "I'll take this back to the gallery, keep it in the safe until I can understand its provenance and register it."

"Is that legal?" Julia looked around. They were taking a national treasure from the Tower of London.

"If I don't do it now, someone else might find it – Vivienne, *Les Héritiers du Hugon*. It could go into the Tower archives for anyone to look at," he said. "Let's get you back to your hotel. There's nothing more to be done here."

Reluctantly, she followed him, whispering a silent goodbye to the ghosts of Lucy and Allen – whose lingering presences she could still faintly feel in the stillroom.

Refusing Oliver's offer to cook her dinner that evening at his mews house in Belgravia took every ounce of willpower that Julia possessed. It was just so damn easy; they could fall back into each other's worlds effortlessly. He would make his celebrated sauce, she would boil the pasta, they would both agree on the perfect al dente, and after sharing bowls and a chianti…she shook her head to rid the images of Oliver's athletic body. He may be older, but as far as she could tell under his expensive suit, he still looked the same.

"Are you sure?" Oliver asked again, as they paused before her hotel. They'd shared a cab back from the Tower, for she didn't realise it, but apparently, she was staying just a couple of streets away from his London home. "We do make a mean spaghetti together..." he broke off in laughter as he caught sight of the restaurant next to the hotel. "Oh, no. Really?"

"What?" Julia turned and shook her head. "Oh. Ganymede. That's quite a name for a restaurant."

"I presume for the star, not the Greek hero..."

"...Aka Catamitus, from which the English word *catamite* is derived..."

"...The accusation against the Duke of Buckingham and King James..."

"...Well, James did desire him greatly..." Julia stopped abruptly. They'd even fallen back into their classic banter. She remembered long nights spent with candles stuck in empty wine bottles, lying on floor cushions debating esoteric research to the fragrance of patchouli incense and the crooning of Nina Simone vinyls on Oliver's prized record player. Her words lingered in the autumn dusk, the flower boxes on the black iron railings overflowing with the last of the stocks, drifting in through the cab's open window with a heady, seductive scent.

"I have work to do," she said firmly. "Thanks for lunch. And for warning me about Vivienne. And our find this afternoon. As soon as you have looked at the charter, we must return it to Colonel McTaggert. Or at least slip it back into the apothecary chest..."

"...Aha, an accessory to my crime..."

"No, Oliver. Don't even start that." She opened the cab door and put one foot out. "Please could you confirm Allen's provenance and any other stories or information that would be helpful before I purchase him tomorrow?"

Oliver smiled, leaned forward to kiss her, and she turned her cheek at the last moment, so his lips just grazed her face. Still, she caught the essence of him. "Of course. Goodnight, then. See you bright and early for the auction."

After a restless night of muddled dreams, where Oliver transformed into the Duke of Buckingham and Vivienne Devereaux threw the draft of Julia's Lucy Hutchinson novel off the top of the Eiffel Tower, Julia finally dozed and awoke to a blackbird singing right outside her window. That was the joy of London... hidden gardens and leafy squares where country reigned over city. She wondered briefly about Oliver's home – a mews house in Belgravia would not come cheaply – and if he had inherited the family pile in the Cotswolds. Did a Mrs Villiers preside over the Aga in a perfect Country House Magazine kitchen? Just as well she hadn't gone back to his place last night. It had been a while since she had been with anyone, and the last thing she needed was another complication in her life.

As she luxuriated with a cup of coffee in a deep claw-footed tub, Julia mentally recapped all that she had learned from her online search for Vivienne Devereaux's recent history. Oliver's remarks at lunch yesterday had reopened the old wounds of Julia's humiliation at the Amsterdam forum, where a jealous rival had deliberately sabotaged the work of Oxford's promising new star. Julia's dream of a career in academics had crumbled, while Vivienne Devereaux had ascended to a professorship in history at the Sorbonne. During her tenure the Frenchwoman had published several papers on Anna of Denmark and James I's courtship and marriage, and written widely about Buckingham's questionable influence on the king and queen.

And *Les Héritiers de Hugon*? It seemed they were deeply secret, for less than a page of results appeared about them, and most of it was old: whispers of a haul of jewels that were smuggled to Chile and later proven to be fake, funding from a Russian oligarch for them to purchase Buckingham's ancestral home

Julia took a deep breath and resisted the temptation to top up the hot water. Her mobile trilled a text, and she leaned over to look at it on the windowsill by the bath.

> I have news on provenance: Meet me for coffee at 9:30 at our French café.
>
> *O.*

Julia shook her head. 'Our' cafe? Typical Oliver. But she was happy to hear he had news on Allen's history. She stood up, stepped from the tub, sucked her stomach in and smiled at herself as she glanced in the mirror – not bad, she actually hadn't changed that much these past years herself – and hurriedly dressed.

"Sir Edward Villiers is confirmed as the connection." Oliver greeted her with a kiss on her cheek. This one landed firmly, and she didn't turn away. "The painting came from a distant cousin of mine I didn't even know about, a descendant of Buckingham's brother..."

"...Who was married to Barbara, Lucy St.John's sister..."

"...And was made the Master of the Mint in 1617..."

"...In the Tower of London."

A breathless smile, a shake of their heads. Still, they finished each other's thoughts aloud.

"And Buckingham awarded both Edward and Allen their lucrative positions. No doubt for a price," Oliver continued. He poured Julia another coffee from the pot, and broke a deliciously flaky croissant in half, handing it to her and pushing the butter and apricot jam her way. He hadn't forgotten that, either. "So it was his plan from the beginning to place incredibly loyal relatives into the Tower and the Mint, so he could rely on their complete obedience if he did anything dodgy."

Julia chewed thoughtfully. "Edward's widow, Barbara Villiers, lived well beyond their means for the rest of her life. She certainly was not short of money, and she married all her children successfully into nobility."

"While Lucy was cast out of the Tower on Allen's death and had to fight for her survival."

Oliver brushed the croissant flakes from his jacket and stood up, the wooden chair scraping on the flagstone floor. "So perhaps Allen and Lucy didn't know where the jewels were..."

"...And Barbara did." Julia stood too, and glanced across the street at Oliver's gallery. "Time to go."

Julia sat stiffly in her chair, her fingers clenched around the auction paddle. The air was thick with the scent of polished wood and wealth. Allen's portrait stood on an easel at the front, its crackled varnish catching the light. He gazed out over the half-empty room, as if searching for his wife and son. Or Julia.

I'm here. I've come to take you home. Her heart pounded as the bidding climbed.

Julia's clients had authorised her to bid on their behalf, and she'd come prepared, but now, as the auctioneer called out another increment, her confidence wavered.

"Ten thousand," he declared, his voice crisp.

This is for Allen. Julia resolutely lifted her paddle.

"Fifteen," a voice called from across the room.

She turned sharply. A man in an expensive suit, impassive behind dark-rimmed glasses. Not a collector. Not a dealer. Something about him prickled at her nerves.

"Seventeen," she countered, surpassing her budget but holding her ground. She rapidly tapped out a text to clients, seeking permission to go higher. No response.

The auctioneer barely paused. "Seventeen thousand. Do I have twenty?"

Silence. Julia's pulse pounded. This was it. Allen was on his way to be reunited with his wife and child.

"Forty thousand," the auctioneer called suddenly, eyes flicking to his screen. "We have an internet bid. Paris."

Paris. Vivienne. A cold, familiar fury coiled in her gut.

"Forty-five." She forced her paddle up. Her phone remained dark. Oliver was staring at her hard, shaking his head. God only knew how she was going to afford this. She would pay the difference, somehow.

The bid held, and for a moment, hope fluttered in her chest.

"Seventy." The screen flickered. Paris again.

Julia gritted her teeth. Vivienne wasn't here, wasn't in this room. She was hidden behind a console, playing her games from afar, pushing the price higher and higher, forcing Julia to bleed for her passion, her love. Again.

Across the room, Oliver caught her eye. "Stop." He mouthed. "Stop now." She ignored him.

Her phone stayed blank.

"Seventy," the auctioneer called, his gaze darting between the screen and the room.

Julia hesitated. She could take out a mortgage on the bookshop. Apply for a grant. She could do this.

"Seventy in Paris."

The room stilled.

The man in the dark-rimmed glasses turned slightly, just enough for Julia to see the glint of amusement in his expression.

Oliver was signalling to her again, more insistently now, pointing to the man. Stop.

She tightened her grip on the paddle while frantically looking at her silent phone. She could push further. She had to.

The auctioneer called out, "Seventy going once. Going twice..."

Julia's hand twitched.

"Sold! To the online bidder in Paris."

The gavel struck like a gunshot.

A murmur swept through the room, but Julia only heard the rush of blood in her ears.

She turned to Oliver as he reached her side. "It's her," she said. "It's Vivienne."

He hesitated. "I shouldn't tell you that, but yes."

"Get it back," she managed through sharp, ragged breaths.

"I can't," Oliver said, voice low. "It was a legal sale."

A soft chuckle sounded beside her. Julia turned.

The man in dark-rimmed glasses leaned in, his Parisien-accented whisper cutting through the hum of the dispersing crowd. "The jewels will be returned to us."

Julia stiffened.

Les Héritiers de Hugon.

He slipped away into the crowd.

She turned back just in time to see the attendants lifting Allen's portrait from its easel. The varnish caught the light for a moment before it was carried into the back room.

Gone.

Her hands curled into fists. Allen was slipping away again, stolen right in front of her eyes.

And she had no way to keep him from disappearing.

"Julia." Oliver's voice became more insistent. "Julia."

She turned on him. "You deserted me. Again. You could have stopped the bidding, withdrawn it from sale, contacted the owners, done... something!"

"There was nothing I could do. Vivienne had registered as a bidder, the owners wanted to sell, the auction was conducted correctly." He gazed down at her, sadness and regret written across his face. "I am so, so, sorry, Julia."

She slung her bag across her shoulder. "I'm leaving. I should never have thought I could trust you."

"What about the jewels? The clues? We have enough to carry on with."

"Don't you get it?" Julia stifled hot tears. "There's more to life than jewels and money and winning. There's decency and humanity and a simple quest to reunite two people who have been parted for so long." She pushed past Oliver, so close she could smell his cologne, so distant she felt nothing. "Goodbye."

Burford was quiet in the late autumn twilight, the golden stone buildings glowing softly under the fading sun. Julia sat at her desk in the bookshop, surrounded by stacks of research notes, her laptop open. Beowulf sprawled across the rug at her feet, his massive black form rising and falling with steady breaths.

Every day, she scoured the internet, searching for Allen. Every day, she found nothing.

She had called the Sorbonne, but the answer was always the same. Professor Vivienne Devereaux was apparently on sabbatical. No forwarding information. No way to reach her. Vivienne had covered her tracks well.

After a few weeks, Julia had stopped calling.

Instead, she buried herself in writing. If she couldn't retrieve Allen's portrait, she would preserve him in words. She filled her days with research, her nights with drafts and revisions. The ache of loss never faded, but she channelled it into something tangible.

Oliver had disappeared, too. No calls, no messages.

She told herself it didn't matter. She'd made it clear that she wanted nothing more to do with him.

The shop bell jingled.

Julia barely glanced up. A customer, most likely. Claire could take care of them. She stayed focused on her screen, scrolling through the same searches, the same names.

Silence stretched.

Then, a presence. Someone watching her.

She looked up.

Oliver stood just inside the door, a mix of hesitation and determination in his expression. But it wasn't just him.

At his side was a woman – tall, with sharp features and an air of quiet authority. Her dark auburn hair was swept back, and she wore an expensive navy wool coat with a gold Hermes scarf.

"Julia," Oliver said, his voice measured. "Meet Barbara Villiers."

Julia narrowed her eyes. Why was Oliver here, in her shop? And what game was he playing now?

Barbara extended a gloved hand. "I believe I owe you an apology."

Julia hesitated, then shook it. "Why?"

Barbara exhaled. "Allen's portrait – if I had known the history behind it, I never would have sold it."

Julia stiffened. "You're the original owner?"

Barbara nodded. "My husband, Edward Villiers, yes. Oliver tracked us down; we've been abroad for a month. When he told us what had happened, what the painting represented, I knew I had to make this right."

Julia's pulse quickened. "Barbara. And Edward. Villiers."

Oliver stood in silence, absentmindedly scratching Beowulf's head as he watched for her reaction. "Coincidence," he mouthed. Beowulf, blissfully content, closed his eyes and sank into his highest state of customer satisfaction.

Barbara continued, "You see, Allen is one of a pair."

"A pair?" Julia repeated.

"Yes. My father-in-law kept him in storage. We really had no idea of his connection, had no room in the house for him, so sent him to sale. You know how it goes. We needed to repair the roof. And besides, why hang two portraits that mirrored each other?"

"Mirrored?" she was sounding like a parrot. She caught a glimpse of a slight smile playing around Oliver's mouth.

Barbara nodded. "Yes. I think it's the same pose, same background, just flipped. Even to the point that as soon as Oliver sent me photos, I looked at Edward's frame."

She paused. Julia held her breath. "And it seems there's an engraving etched in the wood. The same Latin phrase..."

"*Data fata secutus.*" Julia croaked.

"So here we are..." Barbara paused, grinning.

Oliver gently stepped past Beowulf to put his arm around Julia. "I couldn't leave things as they were."

Julia shook her head in disbelief, but let him remain close. "Now what?"

"If my instincts are correct, there are clues in both portraits that must be read together," he continued. "Vivienne may have Allen, and will certainly realise Queen Anna's connection..."

"...But without Edward, the full message can't be read," Julia finished.

"Come to my home," urged Barbara. "Come and see Edward, confirm my thoughts, take him for ultra-violet testing. He may have over-painting too."

"And then we're going to confront Vivienne together." Oliver said firmly. She felt his resolve in his tightening arm. "Show the world her real intent and links to the criminals in *Les Héritiers de Hugon*. And when we do, we take Allen back."

Julia's fingers curled around her desk. After all these years, a chance to determine Vivienne's fate. With Oliver by her side.

She let out a slow breath and glanced around the bookshop. Claire was preparing cheese toasties. Beowulf had wandered over to supervise. It was almost closing time. They wouldn't miss her.

"Follow me?" said Barbara. "I'm just parked around the corner."

"Destiny?" murmured Oliver as he held the door open for Julia.

"Fate," she replied firmly. "Following fate."

Author's note

In July 2024 I discovered online an unknown portrait of Sir Allen Apsley, thought to be of the school of Marcus Gheeraerts, on sale in a London gallery. The husband of Lucy St.John, the heroine of my first novel, *The Lady of the Tower*, Allen's portrait was fortunately purchased without any drama (but a lot of excitement) and is now happily residing next to the portrait of Lucy and their son. So, this is a work of historical fiction, inspired by a fact. Well, actually, the St.John family motto really is *data fata secutus*. Queen Anna's jewels were stolen. Allen and Edward did marry Lucy and Barbara and hold their positions at the Mint and the Tower in 1617. And if you look closely, you'll see that Allen is wearing a rather nice ring on his little finger...

© Elizabeth St.John

Inspired by this short story, Elizabeth plans on writing a potential new series...

About Elizabeth

Elizabeth St.John's acclaimed historical fiction brings to life her ancestors – remarkable women linked to England's royalty – offering unique insights into

Medieval, Tudor, and Stuart times. Inspired by family archives and historic sites like Lydiard Park and the Tower of London, her novels include *The Lydiard Chronicles*, *The Godmother's Secret*, and *The King's Intelligencer*, exploring the English Civil War and the mystery of the Princes in the Tower.

Website: www.elizabethjstjohn.com
Bluesky: https://bsky.app/profile/elizabethstjohn.
bsky.social
Facebook: https://www.facebook.com/
ElizabethJStJohn/
Amazon Author Page: https://geni.us/
AmazonElizabethStJohn

7

THE BLACK ONYX BOX

BY R. MARSDEN

The Bluffer's Guide to Becoming a Famous Alchemist

17th July AD 1238 - 17th February AD 1242

Changing his name had been easy. His religion slightly less so. But, all in all, he was settling into his new identity rather well. Other things had been much harder to alter. For example, he'd had no money when he started out, and he had no money now. Not only that, but he'd had no idea how he was going to make himself famous, and had been ridiculed by his brothers and sister when this intention had first been declared. His parents hadn't been sympathetic either, for they'd paid for an excellent education for all their children. They expected obedience and diligence.

Now, three and a half years after he left India, he was still not famous, and it bothered him – much more than the lack of money, the rags he wore, the absence of prospects or the fact he had nowhere to sleep tonight. Fame would solve all those problems. Fame would lead to fortune. Fortune would amplify fame. He just needed to get himself a *reputation*.

He'd arrived in Mallrovia on 17th July, just three days ago. The weather was good, so sleeping in fields, under hedges or in empty barns was not a problem. Mallrovia, a country east of England, jutted out into the North Sea. It had a warm, dry climate, and Jahangir was grateful for that. The weather would change, of course. True, there was no monsoon season in this part of the world, but it would get cold. He'd been told about that. Cold was something he knew little about, having grown up in Nag Mandal in Gujarat. He was from a proud family. Too proud to know him now.

Five weeks later, Jahangir wandered into a small town in the south of the country. Small, and also smelly. He wrinkled his nose in distaste. His Parsi parents would have exclaimed in disgust, but Jahangir was used to European habits by now. The market square was easy to find, and it was easier still to riffle some berries and a large fish from the stalls. He was used to stealing food; his method was honed and infallible. Create a diversion, look innocent, secrete the goods under your straw hat, then stroll away. No one had ever caught him, nor would they. Normally, he would then take himself far from the market, squat down in some isolated patch of meadow or woodland and build a small fire. Then he would bake his fish or his meat, bite into his succulent fruits and wash it all down with water from a nearby stream before stretching out under the stars. One meal a day was all he needed. So long as it was a good one!

Today was different, and today was the actual beginning of his new life. He didn't realise this, having assumed his new life had begun when he walked out of that fine whitewashed Parsi house in Nag Mandal, determined to seek fame and fortune. Much later, he revised his opinion, and decided that his true new life began when he was found and befriended by some wonderful people in al-Andalus. They made him a son of the family, and they believed his every word – his new name and birthplace, and his ever-increasing catalogue of fictitious discoveries, inventions and amazing ideas. Perhaps the man of the house was a little sceptical – but Jahangir knew he'd captivated Elmira and her children. He'd stayed with them a whole year, and would, perhaps, still be there, had it not been for Husain, who'd told him it was time to move on. And move on he did, but he took the family's religion and beliefs with him, knowing it would be better than owning to a faith no one had heard of. He also took with him a small packet of rosebush seeds, for this was very precious to him.

But today, though he didn't know it, Jahangir was about to embark on his *true* new life. And that happened entirely because one man saw him pilfer the food in Hambrig Town. Never before had there been a witness, but this time, one man observed him deftly sliding the fish and the blackberries under his hat. And while everyone else was picking up the crab apples that had rolled all over the market square – which only happened because Jahangir had pretended to stumble and had kicked the barrel hard – this one man had not glanced at a single bouncing apple. He had not been diverted by the loud noise the barrel made as it rolled over the cobbles, nor had he succumbed to the entreaties the stallholder was loudly making, that everyone should help him recover his crop. So while Jahangir was hurrying away from the chaos and the confusion, this one man stood quite still at the edge of the square, and grabbed Jahangir's arm as he made to saunter past.

"Excuse me?" Jahangir said, his eyes widening in mock-astonishment. "Do I know you, sir?"

"Not yet. But I think you soon will."

There was no question of resisting. The man's grip was firm, his voice quiet but commanding and, after all, Jahangir was only seventeen years old. He wasn't tall, and had to look up into the other man's face. Mid-fifties, he decided, and a Christian, as all here would be. Jahangir wondered: should he change religion again? But his skin was too dark. He did not look like a Christian. For now, at least, he would remain a Muslim.

Sir Bernard of Hambrig introduced himself as he ushered his captive into the hall of his house. It was a large house with a very grand hall, and at one end of the hall there was an enormous glazed window. Jahangir stared at the window. The panes were bigger than any he'd seen, and the glass winked and glinted at him. The expense! He thought even his wealthy parents might have baulked at the cost of such a window.

Sir Bernard pushed Jahangir down onto a wooden stool and waved a hand at the massive glass structure. "This is my observatory. I watch the stars through that window. Stars, planets and other celestial bodies. And I write down everything I see."

"Why?"

"Because I love it. I love the night sky and everything it shows us."

"Are you going to report me?" A far more pressing question.

"Report you? For what?"

Was it possible Sir Bernard hadn't actually seen him steal the food? It was still under his hat! He'd have to get rid of it, which would mean he'd have nothing at all to eat today, but that was preferable to having his hands chopped off in punishment. He mumbled something, shrugging his shoulders.

"You can stay here for a while, young man," Sir Bernard continued, settling himself into a comfortable chair by the fire. Which wasn't lit – the day was too warm for that. "Unless you have somewhere else to go, of course?"

Jahangir began to shake his head. But he felt the fish moving on top of it, the scales no doubt catching in his hair. He stopped at once, keeping his head completely still.

"Splendid!" said Sir Bernard. "Well then, take off your hat and I'll show you where to wash and get ready for supper. We shall be eating soon. I have a housekeeper who will be here shortly to cook our meal. She's very good, you know."

Jahangir sat quite still. He could feel something oozing down the back of his neck. Whether it was fish scales or blackberry juice he had no way of knowing. He wondered if Sir Bernard could smell the fish.

"I think I'd better be going," he began to say. "I – er – I do have somewhere else to go, as it happens."

"You do? What a shame. A shame for me, I mean. I'd been looking forward to a fish supper, but I guess you'll be taking that fine mackerel with you."

Jahangir's mouth fell open.

"How about if you stay here just for now?" Sir Bernard suggested. "And my housekeeper – her name's Betsy, by the way – will know exactly how to prepare a beautiful mackerel supper for the two of us. She's a very good cook, as I may have already mentioned. And I daresay your blackberries will taste good in a pudding."

"You know I stole them?" Jahangir saw no reason to pretend.

"Of course. I was watching you. But we can't return them now, and there is nothing to be gained by throwing them out, so we shall enjoy them. And when you have told me your story we shall decide what to do about it all."

———

Betsy was a year or so older than Jahangir, and Jahangir fell instantly in love with her. It wasn't the first time. In fact, he'd been in love many times, and every time it happened he knew that, without question, this was the woman he wanted to spend the rest of his life with.

So he began an elaborate courtship of his host's housekeeper, dancing around her in the kitchen, attempting a kiss or two, wheedling her to notice him. None of which worked. In fact, the extent to which it didn't work was calamitous, as Betsy handed in her notice and disappeared from Sir Bernard's house for good.

By this time Jahangir had been in Hambrig Town for three weeks. No one had suggested he leave. He slept in Sir Bernard's great hall, and gradually made himself more and more at home there. He began to acquire possessions: a few specimens of animal and plant life, which he housed in bottles and jars placed carefully against the walls of the hall. Then there was his packet of rosebush seeds, stolen from a trader outside the curtain wall at *Krak des Chevaliers*. Jahangir put a high value on these seeds, and the packet occupied a place of honour on the high table. It was as if these items made a statement that Jahangir belonged here now. They marked his territory as surely as if he were a cat spraying the walls and rubbing against the doorpost.

"What are these things?" Sir Bernard asked curiously one day. And by now Jahangir had been living in his house for two months.

"I am creating a workspace," Jahangir replied, certain Sir Bernard would not miss the note of pride in his voice, nor the set of his shoulders. "I shall do amazing work here. And when I am famous, I will express my gratitude to *you*, Sir Bernard."

"Ah, yes. When you're famous." There was no sense of sarcasm in Sir Bernard's tone.

All the same, Jahangir flushed. "I *shall* be famous," he insisted. "I have set my heart on it."

"Famous for what?" Sir Bernard inquired. "Or doesn't it matter?" This time there was a definite fizz of humour.

"I shall be a famous alchemist." Jahangir looked at his packet of seeds, which had once bought him his life. He'd been threatened, but the seeds, with their magic powers, had been bartered for his life. Later, Jahangir had stolen half the seeds back again. Those seeds would ensure his success, and success would lead to fame. "I shall create mixtures, medicines and materials as yet unknown to man!" And he strutted around the hall on his toes.

Sir Bernard laughed. "Well then! If you are to be a famous alchemist, you will need equipment. Not just a few dried-up beetles and clumps of moss. And your Syrian seeds will need somewhere to grow!"

Jahangir blinked. Equipment! Would Sir Bernard want something in return? Apart, of course, from acquaintance with the very famous Jahangir. Which, as yet, he was not.

"Did you say your name was Jabir?" Sir Bernard asked.

Jahangir nodded. It was his alias. He'd never told Sir Bernard his real name.

"And that you come from Tusa in Persia?"

Jahangir nodded again, although he did not come from Tusa.

"So you may be a descendant of Jabir ibn Hayyan? Who also came from Tusa?"

Jahangir had the horrible feeling that a trap was being set for him. Was the correct answer that he was related to this other Jabir? Or that he wasn't? "I'm not sure," he hedged.

"You are a follower of Islam?" Sir Bernard asked then.

Jahangir assented. He was not, in fact, a follower of Islam. The sacred text that he only occasionally read was called the *Avesta*, and it had nothing to do with Islam. Jahangir was now certain Sir Bernard was concocting an elaborate spider's web of a trap, and when he, Jahangir, fell into it, it would be known he was an imposter and he would be ejected from the house. His nomadic and pointless life would resume, and fame would forever elude him.

"This equipment," he said quickly, hoping to forestall further questions. "When shall we purchase it? And from where will it come? Because I know exactly what we'll need!"

Sir Bernard smiled. "Of course you do! We will order what we need tomorrow, Jabir. And soon your alchemy will begin!"

And it actually did. Many things arrived, all within a few days of each other, brought to the house in handcarts or carried by deferential servants, to be arranged, admired and danced around by Jahangir, the self-styled alchemist and 'descendant' of Jabir ibn Hayyan.

But one purchase stood out. Superior to the retorts and glass flasks, the cauldron and the roaring furnace, the metal tubes and wooden shelving, were the *books*. Sir Bernard knew Jahangir would need information. He would need learning. He would need people to follow and texts to read. The books, therefore, arrived first, and they had clearly cost a great deal of money. Sir Bernard, Jahangir decided, probably felt honoured to have a soon-to-be famous alchemist living and working in his house.

Two months later, Sir Bernard increased his household, hiring someone to be his chamberlain. Francis didn't like Jahangir, and the feeling was mutual. Jahangir made it clear he wanted Francis to leave, but Sir Bernard found the man's services useful.

"I can't get up and down the stairs as well as I used to," Sir Bernard explained. "So Francis can fetch the things I need. He's useful to me. You don't have to like him, but don't drive him away like you did Betsy, please."

Jahangir scowled. He was hardly likely to try to kiss Francis. But Francis barely had anything to do with Jahangir, who lived, ate and slept in the great hall, which was now his workspace. At one end was the fiery furnace – the athanor. All down the long walls were wooden benches, and above them were shelves containing the many specimens he'd collected. Under the huge window was an astrolabe. But the hall, which had once been an astronomer's observatory, was now an alchemist's lair, and the large and complex instrument didn't get used.

"I used to look at the skies with my adopted son," Sir Bernard told Jahangir, although that was early on. He might have expected Jahangir to ask questions, perhaps even to want to know the young man's name. It didn't happen, and Sir Bernard rarely referred to the "adopted son" after that. But the astrolabe stayed under the window, mostly because Jahangir liked the look of it.

During the day, the alchemist made his potions. He mixed and he poured, he ground substances into coarse powders. He heated and condensed liquids, then set them bubbling in large glass retorts on top of the furnace. The seeds were not planted. That was never the plan for them.

In the evenings, Jahangir sat at the high table and wrote his reports, which were full of strange symbols and unlikely pseudo-Latin words. But, like the astrolabe, they looked impressive. Every so often, Sir Bernard leafed through the sheaf of reports. He squinted at the curious words and the mystic, squirly symbols. Then he peered into the glass jars, retorts and tubes. He stood next to the cauldron and tentatively stirred its contents. Peculiar smells sometimes emanated from his hall, and hissing, bubbling and gurgling noises now formed the backdrop to Sir Bernard's everyday life. He no longer even noticed them.

Francis kept well out of the way. He cooked drab, unappetising meals, cleaned the house and did odd jobs for his master. Jahangir and Francis hardly ever met and, by mutual consent, never spoke to one another. Nor did the 'adopted son' put in an appearance, so Jahangir worked, uninterrupted, at his alchemy. Naturally he had an aim in mind. Fame was what he sought, and ultimate fame would be acquired by the success of the ultimate quest: the creation of life.

Jahangir would not work on anything less. Not for him the conversion of base metals into gold, nor the magical manufacture of glass. He scorned finding cures for common ailments, and the invention of new cosmetics. Only the creation of new life would do, and, in the great hall of Sir Bernard's house, Jahangir worked to achieve this. But he experienced only failure.

This might have continued indefinitely, with no sign of the longed-for fame and fortune finding their way into the young man's life – until the day Jessica arrived as a replacement for Betsy, Sir Bernard having finally had enough of Francis's cooking. Jessica was ravishing, with honey-coloured hair and deep violet eyes. Jahangir's heart flipped over in its familiar somersault, and this time his advances were more subtle, and they were not rejected. It was soon apparent that Jessica was a gossip. Jessica talked to Francis, and to the stable hand, the delivery boys, the market traders, the priest and the woman who came to do the laundry. Jessica talked to everybody. Most of all, she talked to Jahangir.

"You're wonderful," she breathed wetly into his ear, one Sunday after church. Jahangir didn't attend church, so he used the time when everyone was out of the house to continue with his alchemical experiments. By now he was following the instructions of Jabir ibn Hayyan, his so-called ancestor. The household's return from Mass caused only a flicker of resentment in the alchemist, since it meant he could gaze anew on the lovely Jessica. As it was Sunday, and food had been prepared in advance, she had no work for the rest of the day.

"How am I wonderful?" Jahangir asked lazily. They were lying together on the grass. Jessica's arms were wrapped tightly around Jahangir, and her gown had somehow ridden up around her waist, exposing her plump, tempting thighs. Jahangir could have got even closer, and it was clear Jessica hoped he would, but he wanted to know more. Being wonderful? That was a given. Being famous, however, was proving disappointingly slow to transpire.

"Because you're so *clever*," Jessica said. "All those things you do in Sir Bernard's hall! How do you know how to use all that stuff that's in there? Creating life? I can't believe it! Will you make dogs, or cats, or birds? Or will you make a whole person?" She looked adoringly into his mysterious, Persian eyes.

"It doesn't work exactly like that," Jahangir told her, one hand cupping her right breast. "Life has many forms..." He left it vague. And then asked, "Does Sir Bernard think I can do it?" Jahangir knew Sir Bernard had taken him in out of pity. Had purchased the equipment Jahangir wanted out of generosity. Had let him stay out of kindness. But pity, generosity and kindness did not equate to *belief*.

"I don't know," Jessica said. "I don't know what Sir Bernard thinks. But it would surely make him happy, even if all you create is a worm! It would be nice to make Sir Bernard happy, wouldn't it? The poor man is so sad all the time."

"Why's he sad?" Jahangir asked. He hadn't known.

"His wife died. Didn't you know? Although it was *ages* ago, and I'd have thought he'd be over it by now. He isn't though, but I think it's gruesome that he keeps her under his bed!"

"Under his bed? What on earth do you mean?" Jahangir sat up, his blood racing. There was a dead body upstairs? How could there be? The smell would be unbearable!

"She's in a box." Jessica was disappointed; Jahangir had dropped his hand from her breast. But her eyes sparkled with delight that she could tell this gorgeous, clever man something he didn't already know. "And the box is under his bed! You should see it! I clean up there, and I've been told I mustn't touch it or move it. Sir Bernard can be pretty strict when he wants to be."

Jahangir stood up very suddenly. Surprised, Jessica had to tug her gown into place in order to look respectable. Which was very unsatisfactory. She'd been in hopes of not being respectable at all that afternoon.

Jahangir had learnt it was best to ask direct questions. So when he enquired about his host's dead wife, Sir Bernard took him upstairs. He'd been up here just once, when Sir Bernard had first brought him home and had shown him round the house. At the top of the stairs were the bedchambers, and the first one you came to was Sir Bernard's own. The largest.

Sir Bernard swung the door open and gently pushed Jahangir inside. The bed was huge, and hung with richly decorated brocade curtains. Jahangir caught his breath in wonder. The colours! The patterns! The textures! He danced towards the bed, his arms outstretched, long tapering fingers itching to feel the sumptuous material. He pressed it to his face, then pulled a swathe of it across himself, one elegant leg extended. He stood back to admire a mental image of himself wearing a cote made of the material, with, perhaps, striped and textured breeches...

"I have not brought you here to admire my bed hangings," Sir Bernard said crisply. "Jabir. Look at this, please."

Jahangir's attention snapped away from the fabrics, and his eyes fastened on his host. "At what must I look?"

Sir Bernard was kneeling down, feeling for something under his bed. A moment later he stood, holding a box. It was made of shiny black onyx, and it had a metal catch to fasten the lid.

Sir Bernard twisted the catch and opened the box. The inside was polished onyx, but this time a vivid red with swirls of gold. It was stunning. A blue satin cloth was folded in the bottom of the box, and on the cloth was some grey ash mixed with a white powder.

Jahangir raised his eyes. "Your box contains ash?"

"Ashes," corrected Sir Bernard. "These, Jabir from

Tusa, are my wife's ashes. Nineteen years ago, she contracted a terrible disease which killed her. She died on her birthday, the 8th November. Nobody would come near, you see. Even the priest would not bury her body; he was frightened of becoming ill himself."

"Did you also become ill, Sir Bernard?"

"I did not become ill, and, as far as I know, nobody else did either. I would have buried my wife myself, but it would not have been in sacred ground. Couldn't be, not with the scared little priest refusing to speak to me."

"So you burnt her?"

"I committed a great sin in doing so. But I could not leave her body to rot, and I would not bury her except in the churchyard. So yes, I built a pyre and I constructed a casket. I laid her body in the casket and set it on top of the pyre. Then I set light to the structure. Afterwards, I collected the ashes. Since my wife's death, I have dedicated my life to helping others."

Jahangir had no difficulty with the 'great sin'. It may have been wrongdoing in Sir Bernard's eyes, but Jahangir's own faith was not averse to cremating the dead. He made no reference to that.

"The box is beautiful."

"My wife chose it. She bought it in the market one day. Many things are brought to the market, as you know."

Jahangir nodded; he visited the market most weeks. And it was true – many wonderful things, some of which originated in strange, exotic lands, found their way to the market in Hambrig Town. It would be unsurprising for such a pretty container to catch the eye of a young woman. "What was your wife's name?" he asked.

"Carmen. From Iberia, where I met her and married her."

"You must miss her terribly." Jahangir's dark eyes were full of compassion. Perhaps even glistening with a sheen of tears. He hoped so, anyway.

"I miss her every day," said Sir Bernard. "You cannot understand, Jabir, you're too young and you have not married. But Carmen was so special and so perfect. We did not have children, but as you know..."

"Yes. Your 'adopted son'."

Sir Bernard's own eyes had misted over, as he remembered Carmen. *Carmen.* Jahangir thought it a beautiful name.

His mission to create new life now became all-consuming. Imagine if he could restore Carmen to Sir Bernard! In fact, Jahangir had no trouble at all imagining it. In his mind's eye, he saw, with total clarity, Sir Bernard's expression of awe and incredulity as his wife, once more alive, walked towards him. And as Sir Bernard's lips uttered the word, "Carmen!", the woman would fall, swooning, into his arms and declare her love for him. Then both would turn, and Jahangir would be drawn to their bosoms as they expressed their undying gratitude.

And soon, word would spread, and others would desire Jahangir's beautiful mixture. He would begrudge it to no one. All could avail themselves, and he would make more of it, so it would never run out, but the money would pour in, and so would fame. Fame and fortune. One would follow the other, as surely as summer followed springtime. And so Jahangir sought fame as an alchemist in the making of a potion which he would call "the elixir of life".

"It'll need a starter, won't it?" Jessica asked him, her fingers tracing the beautiful shapes of his nose and mouth. Eastern promise? If it existed at all, surely this was it!

"What do you mean, 'a starter'?"

"Like when I make bread for Sir Bernard. I have to use a starter, otherwise the bread won't rise. My nan says the starter gives life to the bread."

The starter gives life to the bread. In his workspace, Jahangir began to use portions of his pickled specimens, hoping they would 'give life' to his mixture. When that didn't work, he tried live plants of all sorts, and then living creatures.

For months, Jahangir tweaked, changed and rewrote his recipes. He sat at the high table, his packet of rosebush seeds by his elbow, quill pen in hand, and he inscribed his fanciest alchemical symbols onto the parchment Sir Bernard had thoughtfully provided. Elaborate curls and squirls of ink flowed across the scroll, Jahangir's nib dipping frantically in and out of his pot of ink.

Rejected recipes were thrown onto a shelf, where the pile grew alarmingly. In between sessions at the high table, Jahangir stirred the cauldron, added wood to the furnace and cut up plants and animals. He foraged in the Hambrig Woods and lurked in the market square, seeking inspiration and ingredients.

***

Towards the end of the year 1240, Sir Bernard received bad news. The nineteen-year-old adopted son had disappeared. Nobody knew his whereabouts. The master jeweller, to whom the adopted son had been apprenticed, was said to be raging. Sir Bernard was distraught, while Francis crept about as if he himself had been bereaved, tears streaming down his face and a piece of cloth permanently scrunched in his hand, so that his disgusting running nose could be dealt with. Not that he'd ever actually met the errant youth. Jahangir, whose twentieth birthday it was, eyed him with contempt. This was not the way for Francis to help his master!

Jahangir would not know how to find the missing youth, and, in any case, he had no desire to do so, but it was now more imperative than ever that Carmen be brought back to life. The faith in which Jahangir had been brought up taught that a person's fate is the result of the balance between good and evil in their life. One must outweigh the other. Jahangir was well aware he'd already done a fair amount of evil. Robbery was only part of it. Lying, another small element. Changing faith? He wasn't sure you could, even as he professed to have done so. Killing? It had been in a good cause, so perhaps he would be absolved. Then again, who knew what constituted a good cause? Jahangir would need a sizeable counterweight of good deeds. He was pretty sure that making love to Jessica didn't count. But bringing a dead woman back to life and restoring happiness to a good man? Those things, undoubtedly, would weigh extremely heavily in his favour when it came to the afterlife, and – in *this* life – would bring him fame.

That night, Sir Bernard took himself off to bed earlier than usual. Jahangir was glad to hear the heavy tread of his host's feet mounting the stairs to his bedchamber. Supper had not been eaten, for Sir Bernard was full of sorrow. In any case, Francis was too upset to cook, while Jessica, who lived in the town with her grandmother, had gone home.

Jahangir waited. Eventually he heard the slap-slap of Francis's feet on the steps as he, too, went up to bed, and soon all was quiet. Jahangir waited some more, just in case Francis had forgotten something and needed to come back down. Nothing happened. And so, as the moon rose, visible through the great observatory window, Jahangir made his silent way up the stairs.

The alchemist pushed open the door to Sir Bernard's room and tiptoed inside. Again, he waited. Would the bed hangings stir? If Sir Bernard were awake, Jahangir could be out of the room before the heavy curtains moved to reveal his presence. But, again, nothing happened.

Jahangir wanted two things, and was not prepared to leave until he had them. One was easy. The black onyx box was under the bed. With a deft movement of his arm and a rapid flick of his wrist, Jahangir had the box in his hands. He set it down by the door and returned for the second of his quests. The harder, by far, of the two. He must, somehow, acquire a length of that brocade. Jahangir made his way soundlessly around the bed, his hands feeling the curtains, his eyes gazing up at the high rail from which they fell. Moonlight streamed through Sir Bernard's window, and the hangings were clear to see, albeit with muted colours.

Jahangir tugged experimentally as he went along. All seemed firmly attached, and in any case, it would not do for one of the hangings to tumble down and land heavily on Sir Bernard. Jahangir had a knife in his belt, and it was his intention to cut the ties that secured one of the hangings to the rail. It was a pity he wasn't any taller, though. He'd have to stand on something.

Sir Bernard's clothes had been folded neatly on a small stool. Jahangir moved the pile of clothes and set the stool close to the bed. He climbed up. Now he could reach. Pulling his knife from his belt, Jahangir slit the ribbons, his other hand supporting the fabric so it didn't fall. Finally, he climbed down from the stool and arranged the remaining curtains to close the gap. Carefully, he returned the stool to its corner and replaced the folded clothing. Clutching both his prizes, Jahangir hurried back down to his lair.

The work was done at night. During the day, the alchemist devoured the *Book of Stones*, written by Jabir ibn Hayyan. He made passionate love to Jessica, and he slept just a little. But as soon as Sir Bernard and Francis were safely in their beds, he got on with the task he'd set himself. First came the robing. Over time, Jahangir had managed to fashion a kind of toga for himself out of the bed hanging. It fell around him, encasing him in the luxury of fine, exotic fabric. It even smelt spicy! Jahangir knew it was his destiny to be clothed in beautiful, colourful fabrics, and, once he was so attired, his mind swung into action and the alchemist knew exactly what to do.

Jabir ibn Hayyan had made the process clear enough, provided you understood the code he'd used in his book. Jahangir had had no trouble untangling this code, but he found it hard to rationalise Jabir's *takwin* with his own concepts of Endless Light and Absolute Darkness. From Endless Light had come the metallic sky, the purest water, the softest plants and all forms of animal life. Jahangir set aside the *Book of Stones*.

Instead, he worked to create Endless Light. If it could be done once, he reasoned, it could be done again. To be sure, he wasn't a god, but his vibrant, rich toga and his belief in his quest would, he knew, see him through. Jabir ibn Hayyan, for all his careful writing and codified symbols, had not succeeded, that much was clear from the *Book of Stones*. The creation of life, specifically one particular life, had still to be achieved, and he, Jahangir from Nag Mandal, was going to achieve it.

Meanwhile, Sir Bernard went out every day, searching for his missing son. Francis bleated about his master going mad with worry and growing thin through lack of food, but Jahangir was unperturbed. Once Carmen was back in Sir Bernard's life, the adopted son would be forgotten. As soon as Carmen showed her new invigorated form to her husband, he would no longer care about anyone else. And perhaps, Jahangir mused, that would be the time to move on. To find a new place in which to work and enhance his reputation. Unless, of course, his fame became so great he could no longer wander around at will.

The athanor was essential to the process, and Jahangir did not let the furnace go cold. The fire burned, day and night, creating and maintaining Endless Light. But there must also be Absolute Darkness. This was to be found inside the onyx box. With the lid closed, Carmen's remains were indeed in Absolute Darkness. Jahangir was satisfied he'd fulfilled all the conditions necessary. Carmen's spirit was present in her ashes; all her component parts, even her mind and her indomitable will, were waiting there in the dark.

So what was needed to make it happen? Jahangir read all his books in his quest to find the missing ingredient – the bridge between Endless Light and Absolute Darkness. Something would be needed to activate the process, transforming Carmen's dead ashes into a living, breathing woman.

Inspiration came from the packet of seeds, still in pride of place on the high table. Jahangir opened the packet, tumbling the seeds into his hands. These seeds came from roses. If planted, they would make new roses. In the moment of that thought, Jessica's bread making and Jahangir's elixir came together. *The starter!* Not crushed beetles or pulverised daisies, but – a seed! Life, whether rosebushes or people, grew from seeds. But just as a rose would need the seed from a rose, so a person would need the seed from a person. Jahangir's route to success was now crystal clear to him. But day was dawning. The procedure would have to wait until tomorrow night.

Sadly, tomorrow night was no good either. The day had been too dry. Jahangir needed rain. A week later, fortune smiled on him.

The transfer went well. Ashes were scooped from the onyx box and ladled carefully into the cauldron. Seed was added, plus life-giving pure water from the skies, collected in a pristine and uncontaminated container, supplied by Jessica. Some hopeful chanting had taken place, and, finally, a prayer, uttered under his breath in case he got it wrong. It was the sacred Ahunavar prayer, but it had been a very long time since Jahangir, now ostensibly a Muslim, had said those powerful words. Even now, although he hadn't forgotten the prayer, he wondered if his outward espousing of Islam would make the prayer less potent. Suppose it didn't work at all?

"You *have* to work," Jahangir told it, after the third time of uttering it. "And part of the reason you have to work is that I cannot now give Carmen's ashes back to Sir Bernard. They are lost, a mere sludge in the bottom of the cauldron. Carmen herself must emerge from Endless Light. I have provided light, warmth, water and seed. Together with prayers and the ashes themselves, nothing more should be required!"

But something more *was* required, and eventually Jahangir found out what it was. The extra ingredient was time. How much time? Jahangir didn't know. And to "time", you should add "patience". Since he had no way of knowing how much time was required for the procedure to work, a great store of patience was also necessary, and Jahangir, who had never been a patient person, found himself forced to become one, as days and nights drifted by, while the cauldron bubbled on and the fire never went out.

It was now three weeks since he'd begun adding the 'starter' of his own seed to the cauldron. Every night saw Jahangir on his knees in front of the athanor, intoning the Ahunavar prayer, then rising to stir the mixture in the cauldron and feed the flames beneath it. Every so often, when Jahangir thought it necessary, a fresh batch of seed would be added.

He'd had to explain to Jessica what he was doing. Their love-making was on an indefinite pause. Jessica said she understood. It was important that Jabir devote all his manly energies to bringing back Sir Bernard's beloved wife. So she told him she loved him, and she would pray for him to be successful, and as quickly as possible.

A further six weeks went by, with the alchemist, swathed in his host's bedcurtain, engaging in this ritual every night. Sir Bernard seemed not to have noticed the purloining of fabric from his bedchamber, nor the abduction of his dead wife's ashes. And this was largely due to Jessica, who, on Jahangir's strict instructions, ensured that neither theft was discovered. And, thank goodness, Sir Bernard seemed to have given up hope of finding his lost son and no longer went riding round the country searching and enquiring.

And so the summer of 1241 approached, with its short nights and long days making it harder for Jahangir to conduct his operation in complete secrecy. The venture was also beginning to pall. The same activities night after night for so long a time... Jahangir was discovering that perhaps he only had so much patience after all. And he knew he'd let his guard down when, on a bright and sunny early morning in June, Francis entered the alchemist's lair and saw what Jahangir was wearing. And also what he was doing.

Francis stood stock still and shrieked like a woman. "Sir Bernard! Oh, Sir Bernard! Come now, I beg you! Come immediately, Sir Bernard, and put a stop to this heathen person who has stolen your furnishings and whose activities I couldn't even bear to describe to you, depraved and wicked as they are, to the extent that you will not want to set eyes on the man, nor know of his abhorrent and deviant behaviour..."

He went on far more than that, but Jahangir had stopped listening. In silent fury he was disrobing himself, flinging the bed curtain under one of the benches and kicking it into a dark and dusty corner. He peered into the smoky cauldron. There was enough water, so that was all right, but some grey scum had floated to the surface, and, stirring it with his ladle, he could tell that most of the ashes were now just sediment at the bottom.

Jahangir could hear Francis's screechy voice travelling upstairs and describing in lurid detail what he'd seen. He heard Sir Bernard's deep tones in response, but couldn't make out the words. Then came Sir Bernard's uneven footsteps, as he descended the stairs. Jahangir stood very still in his shirtsleeves and waited for retribution. Which was every bit as terrible as he'd feared.

With nothing in his purse but a packet of rosebush seeds, Jahangir wandered through Hambrig Town. There were three gates you could enter or leave by, so he had a choice of direction. The Merchants Gate would take you north-west; the Hicrown Gate led to the east; Baudry Gate was in the south-west wall of the town. Jahangir stood still and considered his options, but had arrived at no conclusion when he was suddenly aware of his name being called. He turned, and saw Francis running towards him.

"You must come! Come back to the house, Jabir, and use your medical knowledge and your herbs and potions to make my master well again, for he has terrible pains in his chest and his arms, and I do not know what to do to help him, not having any training or skill of my own, although that, for all I know, may be preferable to an evil barbarian such as yourself being allowed to treat my master, which is exactly what I said to him, only he was adamant that you have more knowledge and skill than many a physician, having cured people in foreign countries of terrible diseases, even though he could barely utter the words, indeed he could hardly breathe..."

"What are you burbling on about?" Jahangir said, interrupting the seemingly unstoppable flow of noise. "How ill is Sir Bernard?"

Before Francis could begin to answer, Jahangir shot out a hand and clamped the servant's lips together, squeezing hard. "Just nod your head or shake it. Is Sir Bernard seriously ill?"

Francis, looking frightened to death, bobbed his head.

"And he's asking for me? By name? He wants me to come back?"

Another scared nod.

"I should sew your lips together," Jahangir muttered. "*Much* better like that." But he released poor Francis, who massaged his bruised mouth and glared at Jahangir with intense dislike, before once again exhorting him to hurry back to Sir Bernard's house as fast as he possibly could.

Jahangir harboured no doubts that Sir Bernard's illness had been brought on by acute distress. The knowledge that dear Carmen's ashes were forever destroyed had very nearly destroyed him too. Jahangir treated Sir Bernard, using every particle of knowledge and skill at his disposal, and all the while he cursed his own stupidity in being found out before he'd tasted success. It might be possible to create life, but bringing someone back from the dead was clearly a step too far. After all, the *Book of Stones* had had nothing to say about such a thing.

Jahangir decided he'd been a fool. As he nursed Sir Bernard back from the brink, tending him day and night, overseeing his food, the warmth of his bedchamber, the cleanliness of his utensils and the softness of the fabrics he wore next to his skin, the alchemist became more of a physician than he'd ever been, even in Murcia where he'd outdone himself in curing a man of terrible dysentery.

Downstairs, in the great hall, the athanor's flame ceased to burn and the cauldron's contents cooled and solidified. Dust lay upon shelves and glassware. Nobody was creating mixtures, medicines or materials as yet unknown to man. Francis tiptoed through the house, doing whatever Jahangir told him to do, a servant with a new master now.

And so Carmen was gone, and Jahangir could not forgive himself. As Sir Bernard slowly recovered his strength, summer turned to autumn and then bleak winter. The alchemist might have found some solace in this confirmation of a supreme healing skill, but he was well aware that he was the cause of Sir Bernard's having fallen ill in the first place. So he offered himself no congratulations, and he felt no sense of pride. For the first time he realised he loved Sir Bernard of Hambrig, and – also for the first time – he was doing something for someone other than himself.

On 8th December 1241, Jahangir stood at the foot of the stairs and surveyed his former 'lair'. It was the first time he'd seen it in six months. It was cold, for no fire burned in the athanor. Dust lay over everything. What would he do? Sell all the equipment? Leave Hambrig? For six months, he'd forgotten his goal of becoming famous…

"I have cleared out the mess," Francis quavered at his shoulder, and Jahangir spun round.

"What mess, pathetic worm? What have you done?"

"It was making a dreadful smell," Francis whined. "Such a bad odour could not be borne, and you could hardly expect that poor girl to serve food in the midst of such a stink..."

"What did you do?" Jahangir growled again, his hands clenched at his sides. But he knew what Francis had done. Striding over to the cauldron he looked inside. Empty. Wiped clean. Useless.

"Where is it?" the alchemist howled. "What have you done with my potion?"

"Gone!" Francis screeched back, his face contorted with hate. "Gone forever! As *you* should be, you accursed heathen, you disgusting pervert, you..."

"You needn't worry, Jabir," said a soft voice from behind Francis. "I have the elixir safe."

Jahangir shoved Francis out of the way, and there stood Jessica. In her hands she held the black onyx box. She gave it to Jahangir. He gazed into her lovely violet eyes. She really was the prettiest girl. And he was still in love with her. But that, like everything else, must wait.

"Leave me." He looked from one to the other. Francis was still full of hate, while Jessica's eyes held a challenge. Jahangir might have responded to either, but instead he closed the door on both of them and walked back to the cauldron hanging over the furnace. Bending down, he created a spark of fire with steel and flint, lit the kindling and waited for the athanor to roar into life. As it did so, he eased open the onyx box. The sludge had dried to a caked grey mess which lay, inert, on the blue satin cloth. Jahangir could have hated the failure which mocked him from inside the beautiful container. Or he could accept the challenge.

A month later, and just into the new year, Sir Bernard was up and about again. He wasn't the same as he'd been before his illness, but, as he said to Jahangir, at least he was alive and able to think, speak and walk again. He would use a walking stick from now on, but this did not perturb him. Francis fussed and flustered around, offering help where none was needed and causing agitation in an otherwise peaceful house. Jahangir had no idea why his host kept the servant on. After some thought, he put it down to pity, generosity and kindness.

The alchemist had worked tirelessly on his experiment. The sludge had been reconstituted with more water from the heavens. Nothing had happened. Jahangir knew he was still missing something. Water; ashes; seed; light; time; patience – *what else?*

It came to him late one February night, while he lay half-asleep on his blanket under the wooden bench. It stayed with him as he stood up to stretch the next morning. It was sewn into the brocade fabric of the garment he'd fashioned from Sir Bernard's curtain, a curtain that he knew must have been hand-stitched by Carmen herself. And so, that morning, he dressed in Carmen's handiwork and he invited Jessica into his lair. For the missing ingredient was female.

Patiently, Jahangir taught Jessica to say a line from the Ahunavar, the words both cryptic and magical. It took a long time before she felt confident, but eventually she gave a shy nod. The two of them stood next to the cauldron. They held hands, and together they intoned, although neither in English nor in Latin, *Khshathremchā Ahurāi ā yim dregubyō dadat vāstārem,* which means: The kingdom of heaven is for him who rendereth succour to the poor.

No one was more deserving of the kingdom of

heaven than Sir Bernard of Hambrig. And if heaven, to him, was Carmen, then…

They waited; Jessica in breathless anticipation, Jahangir in an agony of suspense. The cauldron hissed clouds of steam, and its bubbling intensified, becoming a heaving, frantic seething of energy; the pot itself beginning to swing from side to side. Soon the cauldron was twisting alarmingly, and Jahangir began to wonder if the chain would hold. He glanced up at the fastening in the ceiling. Would it be strong enough?

Some of the cauldron's contents frothed over the side. Liquid puddled on the floor, where it sputtered to itself. Tendrils of it flowed past their feet towards the door. Almost as if it knew the way out…

"Shut your eyes," Jahangir said suddenly. "We must both shut our eyes."

Glancing to his right, he saw Jessica had obeyed. With a final quick, silent prayer, Jahangir closed his own eyes. He breathed out slowly through his nostrils, willing the sacred breath of life to enter the cauldron. Many moments passed, and the tendrils of liquid on the floor became running streams, but for the two young people waiting by the athanor, time stood still. The cauldron was making less noise now. It was calming down, no longer at boiling point, no longer swinging, no longer spilling over. Silence stole over the alchemist's lair.

A sound came from behind them. A loud click. Then another sound – like a sharp intake of breath. Jahangir opened his eyes. He let go of Jessica's hand and whirled around. In the doorway stood a woman. Young. Beautiful. Mediterranean in looks.

"Carmen?" Jahangir was suddenly unable to move. Jessica turned. She watched, open-mouthed.

"I've come to see Sir Bernard of Hambrig," said the

stranger, her voice low and clear, with a slight but definite accent. "Will you take me to him, please?"

"I most certainly will," said Jahangir, recovering himself quickly and hurrying forward, still dressed in the toga. "He is upstairs, and he is going to be so delighted to see you!"

About R. Marsden

R. Marsden is an author and musician, passionate about the Middle Ages. He plays the gittern, a beautiful medieval stringed instrument, ancestor of the guitar; and a thirteenth century recorder, a replica of one which was excavated from medieval ruins in modern-day Poland. He also plays the piano, and there's nothing medieval about that!

Tales of Castle Rory are Medieval Fantasy Adventures, in which the demesne of Lord Rory of Hambrig is brought to life.

Set in the latter part of the thirteenth century, these stories have adventure, mystery and magic at their heart. You'll also find relationships, romance, friendship and the forging and breaking of ties between people and nations.

Running through the Tales are themes of family, loyalty, trust and resilience, together with the other sides of those coins: abandonment, betrayal, loss and disempowerment.

Website: https://talesofcastlerory.co.uk/
Facebook: https://www.facebook.com/profile.php?id=61554417124566
Amazon Author Page: https://mybook.to/TalesOfCastleRory

8

BEWARE THE CROWS
BY ANNA BELFRAGE

Beware the consequences of hatred.
Revenge can take many forms...

Sigrid Olofsdotter hated crows. Ugly things, with their black and grey plumage, and the noise they made! So when a murder of crows took up residence in the oak tree adjoining the thrall's living quarters, she took up the fight, hurling rocks and sticks at the damned birds.

"You should be careful," Gunnel One-Eye said from where she was sitting on her customary perch. "Crows are vindictive creatures. Hurt one of them, they may well hurt you."

"Pah!" She threw her mother-in-law an irritated glance. The old crone should be dead by now, but somehow, she was still here, thin to the point of being skeletal, her one good eye a glimmering blue. "What could a crow possibly do to me?"

From the thrall's quarter came a wail. Oden's toes, did she have to screech like that? Birthing was best done through gritted teeth, but then Dana was a weakling, not like her, Sigrid. Another wail, and in the tree above, several of the crows cawed.

"You never know," Gunnel replied. "Only the Norns know what role the crows may play in your fate." She extended a thin arm to pat a small child on the head. Sigrid glared. Torvald bedded his thralls and left a wake of children behind. Something twisted inside of her. She knew he blamed her for there only being one surviving child and suspected he knew just how much she detested being surrounded by his get – healthy, lively children, albeit they were thralls. She, on the other hand, had buried four miscarried babes after the birth of Gunnar.

Sigrid turned her back on Gunnel and took a couple of deep breaths, willing aside tears of anger and grief. Before her, the meadows sloped towards the lake, a faint shimmer of green announcing spring was but mere days away. A deep breath calmed her. She loved Havtun, knew every inch of its lands by heart. She'd been born here, raised here, and now, as its mistress, she ruled over it with a firm hand. She knew exactly how many lambs were born, how many bushels of rye and corn were harvested. She oversaw the annual slaughters of the pigs, directed the work in the large weaving chamber and decided what to sell at Birka's market – and what to buy.

Yet another wail from Dana interrupted her reflection. If Frigg was good, the Irish thrall would die in childbed, thereby ridding Sigrid of her constant presence. It irked her, that Torvald purchased thralls without asking her, and when he'd come home with Dana – a snivelling thing in a torn linen shift – she'd been annoyed. Even more so when it became apparent Torvald liked her too much, enthralled by that milky white skin and her big, big, eyes. Sigrid snorted. At least Dana no longer had her hair – no adult thrall was allowed to grow their hair long – but when Torvald returned from Birka and saw Dana's shaved head, he'd looked at her, Sigrid, and there had been something so black in his gaze she'd found it wise to keep her distance for the coming week or so.

Dana screamed. The crows cawed, and Sigrid stalked up to the oak and heaved herself upwards – she was tall and strong. She tore down a nest, reached for another, and a crow attacked her. She slapped it away. "Serve you right!" she yelled, tearing down a third nest. The crows went mad, diving towards her. Sigrid laughed and dropped down to the ground where she proceeded to crush the defenceless fledglings into a pulp.

"See?" she said to Gunnel. "I win."

The crow she'd struck was tottering about, dragging a broken wing behind it. She stepped on its tail. Its bright, black eyes stared up at her.

"Die!" Sigrid hissed, and stomped the bird to death just as the frail cry of a newborn child filled the air.

"Her name is Kråka," Sigrid pronounced some time later, regarding the newborn scrap of humanity with dislike. A good name, a name to remind her of just how much she detested the little bastard. Frigg knew she detested all of them, but this child, Dana's child, she already detested the most.

Dana tightened her hold on the child. "Kråka? No, this name me dislike. Me call her Finola."

The slap resonated through the dark room. "Know your place, thrall. The child is Kråka."

But in secret, she was Finola, held close to her mother's chest as her mother whispered to her in her own tongue, telling her stories of lands Kråka would never see, people Kråka would never meet. Sometimes, the stories made Kråka's mother weep. Every day, Kråka's mother would remind her that her secret name was Finola, and that she had been baptised into the True Faith.

"I baptised you myself," she told the child. "I had to – I cannot risk damning your soul to hell everlasting."

Some nights, there were no stories. Some nights, Kråka hid under the bed and listened to how the wooden frame creaked and groaned above her. Her mother always cried afterwards. Kråka didn't understand why. The master hadn't hit her, and he always left something for them when he left: some slices of smoked meat, a loaf of bread, a hunk of cheese. Once, there were even five glass beads for her, for Kråka.

Kråka's mother was strange. It was embarrassing how strange she was, with that old wooden cross round her neck and her constant – constant! – praying. Every morning, every night, Kråka had to kneel beside her while her mother whispered about a father in heaven. Pah! The only father was Oden, and he was in Valhalla, everyone knew that.

So when Kråka's mother drew a cross on Kråka's forehead, she squirmed. When she whispered that the master, the mistress – everyone at Havtun – was a heathen, Kråka gave her a blank look. She wanted to be like all the others, so if they were heathen, then so was she, and when next her mother dipped a finger into the water to draw that cross, Kråka shoved her away with all the strength she had.

Havtun was a big farm, situated on a hill that offered endless views over the lake. There was a barn, several sheds, a narrow building that housed the thralls and then there was the hall, much bigger than any other building and with a huge, carved dragon's head over the entrance.

Kråka had never been inside the hall, but she'd peeked inside a couple of times, amazed at how high the roof was, how huge the central hearth was. At the further end was the master's room – well, the master's and the mistress's – and one of the other thralls had told her they slept in a bed covered with rich furs, with chests filled with treasure lining the walls.

"Treasure he stole," Kråka's mother said, spitting to the side. "They came like wolves in the dark and they killed and burned and stole." She looked away. "They stole me and my sister, and my father they killed with an axe blow to his head."

"The master stole you?" another thrall, Mani, asked.

"No. He just bought me." Dana grimaced.

"And your sister?"

Dana just shook her head.

Close to a score of thralls worked for Torvald, the men out in the fields, the women in the dairy or at the looms. And with each passing year, more little thralls were born. Sometimes, thralls disappeared.

"Sold," the other thralls would whisper, and some would weep in fear of it happening to them. Little boys or girls would be out in the yard one day, gone the next, and their mothers would walk about with red-rimmed eyes for days.

Soon enough, their bellies would swell again, new, wailing babes pushed out into a world that Kråka's mother called evil. Evil? Kråka looked at the trees, the skies, at the stars that shone so brightly at night and found nothing evil there. No, Kråka knew exactly what was evil in Havtun, and that wasn't the world: it was Havtun's mistress.

The child was disconcerting. Sigrid frowned as Kråka entered the yard, shooing the goats before her. Disconcerting but a good worker, her thin and sinewy frame surprisingly strong for her age. Like Torvald, Kråka had hair so fair it looked white and big, pale blue eyes, which only made Sigrid dislike her even more. A thrall's bastard to look so like Torvald when Sigrid's own son didn't!

At times, Sigrid caught the child staring at her, and it made Sigrid's skin crawl. It was as if the child's name had added a taint of darkness to her, shadows clinging to her skin, her eyes. Where the other children played and talked, Kråka merely observed, a thin little thing in a worn linen smock and that fair hair in a narrow braid.

There were days when she heard Gunnel's voice mocking her, whispering that crows had long memories and would make her pay. Pah! She shook herself free of the memories – Gunnel was dead, at last – and anyway, what possibly could a crow do to her? And yet, now and then she caught Kråka staring at her, and the darkness in those bright blue eyes sent shivers down her spine

"You should sell her," Sigrid yelled one day, pointing at Kråka. "A useless mouth, is what she is!"

"Then we'd get nothing for her, would we?" Torvald bit back, before patting Kråka on the head. "Besides, it isn't true. She's quite the worker bee, this one." Sigrid wanted to hit something when he smiled down at the child who smiled back.

"I don't like her," Gunnar said one day.

Sigrid wrapped an arm round her son's shoulders and hugged him close. "She's unimportant," she said dismissively. "A mere thrall."

"She's strange," Gunnar said. "And you don't like her either."

No, that she did not.

Every single thrall child knew to stay well away from Gunnar. He especially liked hurting girls, and there were times when a thrall girl would return with her skirts bloodied, her eyes blank. And Gunnar would emerge whistling, those piggy eyes he shared with his mother gleaming. In everything he was his mother's son, from his big hands to the dark hair and his lumpy nose.

"Torvald didn't wed her for her looks," one of the older thralls said one day in an undertone that had the other thralls giggling. "Everyone knows he only wed her because of Havtun."

Kråka didn't understand, nor did she care. But she did not like it when Gunnar took to following her around, and one day he popped up behind her as she was feeding the pigs. She backed away, wary of the look in his eyes.

Up above, a bird cawed.

Gunnar stopped and pointed. "Look," he sneered, "one of your kind."

He leapt forward and had hold of her by the hair. "Time to cut this," he hissed. "Thralls aren't allowed long hair."

He was hurting her. She fought, he laughed, and then suddenly he squawked and shoved her away, arms up to protect himself from the birds. So many crows! Black and grey birds that went for his eyes, his face. He fell to the ground, screaming, and if anything, there were even more birds, cloaking him from sight as they attacked.

"Stop!" Kråka said, and it was the first word she'd ever spoken. The birds obeyed and Gunnar fled.

That night, Dana came rushing into their quarters. "Hide!" she hissed. "In the name of God and his saints, hide! Now!"

Was Torvald coming? But no, Kråka's mother might

not enjoy all that creaking and groaning, but she wasn't scared of the master. Kråka glanced at the bed. Usually, she hid underneath it, but a rustling from above made her look up. Bright black eyes stared down at her from one of the beams.

"Oh God, she's coming!" Dana gasped.

Kråka did not stop to think. She heaved herself upwards and slid along the beam until she was shrouded in shadows. The crow settled itself beside her and shook its wings. Kråka had the unsettling sensation of being covered by them – but that was impossible, was it not?

The rickety door slammed open with such force it came off its hinges.

"Where is she!" Sigrid screamed. "Where is that accursed girl?" She had hold of Dana and shook her. "Where is she?"

"What is going on here?" Torvald's large frame blocked the doorway.

"Your little bastard set her tame crows on our son!" Sigrid was spitting with rage.

Torvald snorted. "That boy lies as easily as he shits."

Sigrid glared.

Torvald crossed his arms over his broad chest. "Next you'll tell me she's a *hamnskiftare*, like Freya."

"Her?" Sigrid laughed. "No, I do not believe in such nonsense."

Kråka shifted on her perch and extended a cramping arm – except it wasn't an arm! She almost fell, but the crow beside her pressed her back against the rough timbers of the wall.

"But I will not have her hurt our son," Sigrid said.

"If a sprite of a girl half his size can hurt him, then he must be quite the weakling."

Sigrid straightened up. "He is your son!"

"Is he? He doesn't look like me – at all."

Sigrid uttered a sound eerily similar to the bleating of a goat. Was she laughing? Weeping? "Oh, he is yours," Sigrid said. "I swear on Frigg, on Oden, that he is yours."

Torvald gave her a brusque nod and stood aside, gesturing for Sigrid to leave the room. One last look at Dana and he followed his wife – but not before he hastily stroked Dana's cheek. On the bed, Dana started crying.

Kråka shook herself and dropped down from the beam. Legs, arms – no feathers. She must have imagined it.

Next day, Torvald came to find Kråka. "Come," was all he said, and she trotted after him. He led her through the woods to the shore of the lake. Golden reeds rose to well over her head, rustling and rippling in the wind. He turned due west and she followed, unnerved by his silence, by the grim look on his face. At long last, they reached a small house. Kråka shrank back: everyone knew who lived there. Mad Ulf, old like the hills and with the power to turn you into a toad should you displease him.

Torvald looked at her as if sensing her disquiet. "Ulf is my uncle," he said. "He will never hurt you."

But he could hurt others? She wanted to ask, but she could not form words – it still astonished her that she'd spoken yesterday.

The door creaked open, and a tall man stepped outside. As thin as the reeds that bordered the lake, his long hair wisps of white and grey round a balding skull, he seemed frail. Until you met his gaze. Kråka shivered inside at the sheer power blazing from eyes as light as her own.

"The crow child," Ulf said, looking her up and down.

Torvald frowned. "What nonsense is that? Yes, her name is Kråka, but she is just an ordinary child."

Ulf looked at Kråka. "Then why bring her here?"

"She's my child," Torvald said.

"They all are," Ulf muttered. "Your yard is littered with your get."

Torvald scowled. "I have urges. Besides, they're my thralls."

Ulf sucked on his teeth, his lower lip almost disappearing. "So why bring her here?"

"Sigrid hates her," Torvald said.

"As she hated my sister?" Ulf asked.

Torvald blinked. "My mother? No, she did not..."

"Gunnel starved to death, you fool," Ulf retorted.

"No," Torvald said. "Please tell me you are lying." His voice broke. "My mother?"

"Too weak to rise from her bed, she was utterly dependent on your wife and what did she do? Feed her?" Ulf shook his head, slowly from side to side. His features tightened, and for an instant, Kråka thought she could see an elongated snout, sharp fangs. She moved closer to Torvald, was reassured when he placed a big hand on her shoulder.

"You knew and did nothing?" Torvald sounded harsh.

"Like you. I found out too late." Ulf turned to look due east. "I was in Holmgård when her agony pierced my mind."

Kråka felt Torvald shiver, and when she peeked up at him, he had lowered his eyes, studying the ground. "Sigrid will pay," Torvald said in a hoarse voice.

"With her life?"

"And rile her uncles, her cousins?" Torvald barked out a laugh. "I'd be dead in a week." He urged Kråka forward. "I want you to promise you will protect her."

Ulf crouched before her and gripped her chin. He stared into her eyes, and she saw wolves and eagles lurking within him. And in her chest, wings flapped, as if wanting to break free. Ulf smiled and rose. "I will keep her safe."

They returned to Havtun. Torvald stopped her while they were still in the woods. "You go that way," he said, gesturing towards the distant meadows where the sheep were grazing. She nodded and turned away. "Wait." He dug into his pouch and produced a little amulet, threaded on a length of leather. "To protect you," he said, tugging it over her head. "And remember: if anything happens to Dana and I am not here, you run – you run like the wind – to Ulf."

Sigrid hated her husband. She would never forgive him for the beating he'd given her, screaming at her that she had murdered his mother and he'd not stop until she admitted her shame.

"My shame? The old crone was bed-ridden and useless!" she screamed back, and he had roared and swung that belt with such force she'd not been able to sit for well over a week. Even worse, he'd administered her punishment in the hall, not in the privacy of their bedchamber, and now, wherever she went on Havtun, she was met by snickers and whispers.

Torvald avoided her, sleeping in the hall when he wasn't rutting with one of his thralls. Only one thrall – Dana – and she detested seeing him interact with the Irish woman, his entire posture softening. The fool was besotted with his thrall, and it would have been hilarious if it didn't hurt so much.

"I am taking Gunnar with me," he announced the evening before he was leaving. "Time to make a man out of him."

"No," she said. "He's too young."

"He is fifteen," Torvald said. "And he wants to come with me."

Sigrid doubted that, but when she looked at her son, he raised his chin and nodded.

The next morning, Torvald gripped her by the arm and hauled her aside. "Anything happens to Kråka, I will take it out on Gunnar."

She hated him. She hated him, she hated him, she hated him!

"After all, no matter how much you swear on Frigg and Oden, we both know he isn't mine." Torvald released her with a shove. "I can count, you know."

"He is!" she yelled. Clearly, Torvald didn't believe her.

It took her weeks to reassert her authority. It took severe beatings, threats and at least three troublemakers hauled off to be sold before order was restored. Sigrid surveyed her domain with satisfaction, enjoying the frightened looks, the way the thralls bowed and crawled. Even the free women serving in the household treated her with more deference than before, but it was irksome when first Helga, then Inga, left, leaving her short-handed. Only a handful of the thralls were capable of working the loom as efficiently as Helga or Inga, and unfortunately, the most skilled among the thralls was Dana.

The woman even had the temerity to look happy as

she worked, her short hair gleaming in reds and bronze under the light of candles as she worked long into the night. It took Sigrid some time to realise there was another reason for Dana's smile: the thrall was with child. The thought was unbearable: Torvald would likely dote on this unborn child, and what if it was a son? No; that could not happen – she would not have her Gunnar usurped by a slave child. She caught sight of Kråka, crouched beside the loom and rage engulfed her. If only she'd killed her when she was a scrawny newborn! Now it was too late. She gritted her teeth. She could not put Gunnar at risk, but she could rid herself of Dana – Torvald had said nothing about *her*.

Kråka was too young to weave, but she snuck into the weaving shed as often as she could, entranced by the movement of the shuttles and the sound of the battens. While her mother wove, Kråka sorted yarn, listening with half an ear as the women talked. The thralls always fell silent when the mistress entered, and of late Sigrid was a recurring and uncomfortable presence in the weaving shed, usually staring daggers at Kråka's mother.

One day, one of the old weavers was entertaining them with stories about the Norns when Sigrid entered. "They don't weave," the old woman said, gnarly fingers efficiently sending the shuttle back and forth. "They spin. For each and every one of us, they spin the thread of fate, and sometimes we are not even aware of what events may have shaped our final fate." She snapped her fingers. "And just like that, the Norns can end our lives."

"Unless you stop gossiping and get back to work, I'll be snipping your thread of fate myself," Sigrid said.

The old woman just shrugged. "Our fate is not determined by you, Mistress Sigrid. Neither is yours."

As if in response, a crow cawed, and Sigrid jumped. "A crow? In here?"

Kråka ducked her head and smiled. Her mistress was inordinately fearful of crows.

"Where is it?" Sigrid demanded. "Where?"

But no matter how she looked, how she insisted lanterns be lifted to illuminate every nook and corner of the shed, there was no bird to be found.

"Back to work," Sigrid finally snarled. She glared at Dana, at Kråka, before stomping off. Dana set a hand to her belly and sighed. Kråka watched Dana caress the visible bump, and a dark mist rose before her, accompanied by the scent of blood. Kråka trembled and shook, while in her head the wail of an infant was cut abruptly short.

<hr>

That evening, she tried to convince her mother to leave, tugging her in the direction of the woods.

"What is it?" Dana asked. Kråka just kept tugging, wishing she could speak the words echoing in her head. Words like *flee*, like *danger*.

Dana dug her heels in. "I have no notion what is the matter with you, but you must stop." She set a hand to Kråka's forehead. "Are you ill?"

Kråka shook her head, and tugged again.

"No." Dana shook free. "I am not going into the woods."

Kråka groaned with frustration, and as if she'd conjured them, several crows came flying towards them. They circled and cawed, forcing Dana towards the woods.

"No! Holy Virgin, keep me safe from these

189

manifestations." She stared at Kråka. "It is you," she whispered, "Dearest God, you are calling your creatures from the void. Heavenly Father, save me!" She fled, and Kråka opened her mouth to call for her, but nothing came out.

She watched as Havtun sank into the night, until the flickering light of candles was extinguished. Not until all of Havtun was draped in darkness did Kråka slink into the room she shared with her mother. Dana was asleep, and Kråka carefully tugged the threadbare blanket up around her narrow shoulders. In her sleep, Dana clutched a small wooden cross. As if that would help. Kråka no longer wore hers, having replaced the symbol for the White Christ with the carved wooden hammer Torvald had given her.

She was about to crawl into bed with her mother when she heard a twig break. She froze. The door creaked open, and Kråka was suddenly just under the roof, a creature of wings and feathers. She peered down as Sigrid entered.

Wake up! Mother! The words clawed at her insides, but it came out as a smothered caw. Sigrid lifted her head, searching. But she did not see Kråka.

Kråka, however saw it all. All. She screamed inside as the dagger came down, over and over again, until the bed was drenched in blood and her mother lay lifeless.

Kråka fled. She did not know if she walked or flew, was aware of shifting mid-step between human and crow, and inside her an anguished roar grew and grew until it all burst from her, causing her to sink to her knees before Ulf's door.

"You will kill her," Ulf told her next morning. "One day, you will slay her."

Kråka already knew that. She wanted to do it now, grab an axe and slay the evil witch.

"You are not strong enough," Ulf told her.

Kråka wrapped thin arms round thin legs and hid her face, trying to blink away the image of her mother lying with her eyes wide open and her features contorted with fear and pain. She would not wait.

***

Sigrid was concerned when she discovered Kråka was missing. Would Torvald hold her responsible? Take it out on Gunnar? Not that she'd done anything to the little bastard, but if the child had seen what she'd done to her mother... Sigrid swallowed. She should have killed Dana cleanly. Instead, years of frustration had driven her to hurt, to kill her over and over again, stabbing her repeatedly in the stomach as well.

Everyone at Havtun knew who had killed Dana. Everyone at Havtun looked at her with fearful disgust. Sigrid straightened up. Let them look at her however they wanted. She was the mistress!

A week after Dana died, the first crow landed on the hall. The next day, there were ten crows, and no matter how she ordered her thralls to chase them away, the birds merely lifted for some moments before settling back down. On the third day, there were at least a hundred birds, and the thralls murmured and pointed at the cloud of black and grey shapes that hovered over Sigrid the moment she set a foot outside the hall.

She wanted to remain inside, safe from the birds with their gleaming black eyes. But she would show no fear – could not show any – even if walking over the yard had her heart racing. They taunted her, those evil winged creatures: every time she emerged into the open there was a moment of relief – no crows in sight. But as soon as she'd taken a few steps, there they were, a seething menace of beaks and sharp claws. Except they did not attack. They just watched.

———

Two weeks after Dana died, Torvald and Gunnar came home. Sigrid wept in relief. Her son was home, and soon the crows would fly elsewhere. But then she looked at Torvald, and what she saw in his eyes made her innards twist. He knew. Someone had already told him about Dana.

"Where is Kråka?" he asked.

"I do not know," she replied. Yet again, he looked at her son, and she wrapped her arms around Gunnar. "I did nothing to her!"

The next day, Torvald left at dawn.

The entire day, Sigrid and Gunnar spent inside the hall. An attempt at stepping outside had reduced Gunnar to stuttering fear when the crows came circling around them.

"It is me they want to hurt," Sigrid said in an attempt to calm her son. "Not you."

Gunnar fled for the safety for the hall and refused to set as much as a toe outside again.

Torvald returned in the afternoon with Kråka. She looked small and frail in his arms, but her eyes blazed with anger when she stared at Sigrid, and to her chagrin, Sigrid had to look away first.

"She will sleep here," Torvald announced, carrying her into the bedchamber.

"That is my chamber!" Sigrid exclaimed.

"Not anymore. Now it is Kråka's," Torvald said.

"How dare you!" Sigrid flew at him, but Torvald

just shoved her aside, turning to Gunnar. "Too craven to go outside?" he taunted. He crowded their son, herding him towards the door.

"Stop it," Sigrid said. "The crows…"

"Are everywhere," Torvald said, and from the bedchamber came hundreds of crows. Gunnar screamed and wrenched open the heavy door.

"No!" Sigrid rushed after her son. The moment they were both outside, the crows attacked. Wave after wave of birds that clawed, that pecked, and Sigrid screamed when her son went down. "Not my boy!"

"A son for a son," Torvald said, crossing his arms. "A mother for a mother," he added as Kråka stepped out of the hall to stand beside her father.

The last thing Sigrid saw was a flash of grey and black before a huge crow landed on her chest, bright blue eyes staring at her as it sank its beak into her heart. The last thing she heard was Gunnel One-Eye whispering *beware the crows*.

© Anna Belfrage

As I am sure you, dear reader, have already worked out, Kråka is Swedish for crow, a rather beautiful onomatopoeic word. And a hamnskiftare is a shapeshifter, the most famous one in Norse mythology being Freya, who now and then chose to shift into a falcon.

About Anna

Had Anna been allowed to choose, she'd have become a time-traveller. As this was impossible, she became a financial professional with three absorbing interests: history, romance and writing. Anna has authored the acclaimed time travelling series *The Graham Saga*, set in 17th century Scotland and Maryland, as well as the equally acclaimed medieval series *The King's Greatest Enemy* which is set in 14th century England, and *The Castilian Saga*, which is set against the medieval conquest of Wales. She has also published a time travel romance, *The Whirlpools of Time*, and its sequel *Times of Turmoil*, and is now considering just how to wiggle out of setting the next book in that series in Peter the Great's Russia, as her characters are demanding. . .

All of Anna's books have been awarded the IndieBRAG Medallion, she has several Historical Novel Society Editor's Choices, and one of her books won the HNS Indie Award in 2015. She is also the proud recipient of various Reader's Favourite medals as well as having won various Gold, Silver and Bronze Coffee Pot Book Club awards.

Website: www.annabelfrage.com
Bluesky: https://bsky.app/profile/abelfrageauthor.bsky.social
Facebook: https://www.facebook.com/annabelfrageauthor
Amazon Author Page: http://Author.to/ABG

9

DAME FORTUNE'S WHEEL

BY J.P. REEDMAN

Fate can be in the hands of others – or held within your own...

London 1492

The girl slipped from the postern gate of the great Benedictine Abbey into the teeming London streets. She pulled her hood up over her head, hiding her face as much as possible. She hated people staring at her, as they often did –for she bore a strong resemblance to their young, lovely queen. Strong enough to start curious onlookers questioning.

Grace did not want any questions asked. Not now, not ever.

Her mistress was unwell; she had ailed ever since the 'events' of five summers ago, and now her condition had worsened. So much had happened to the Dowager since her husband died in a cold spring four years before that time, most of it distressing and unfair. But, for a brief time, a light had shone through the darkness, or so it seemed. Messengers had come and gone in the night, bearing tidings to which only her mistress was privy, and a lightness had formed in her lady's step for the first time in years.

"My dear Grace," the mistress had said, putting hands on her shoulders, "I have taken out a lease on the abbot's house, near Westminster. A forty-year lease. I shall be near Westminster, near to the queen. You shall dwell there with me if it is your wish to stay in my service."

It had been Grace's wish, for Grace truly had nowhere else to go. So she had moved with the Dowager into the lavish home that resounded to the clang of the abbey bells. But the 'forty years never' happened…their residence at Cheyneygates ended after a few brief, blissful months.

First came the news, brought by a white-faced courier, that the mistress's son, Thomas, was incarcerated in the Tower. Words of an uprising, of a pretender to the throne, had flown about the city for months, and it now appeared that the king believed Thomas was involved. He had never really trusted Thomas, but the king was a man who trusted no one at the best of times.

He certainly did not trust her mistress. Within days of Thomas's arrest, he had confiscated her lands, conferring them to her eldest daughter, and 'suggested' she retire completely from public life. It was not so much a suggestion as a command. So her daughters left her side, at her own insistence, for they were still high in favour at the court, and she went with a few household servants, including Grace, to the Benedictines, who offered her accommodation in their abbey. It was a strange place for a woman to retire to, as it was a male foundation, not a nunnery, but at least one queen had spent her last days there not so many years ago…

Of course, the uprising, which failed, was in the past, and Thomas still had his head on his shoulders. One might have thought the king would show clemency to the Dowager now, after all this time. But he did not, and there were no visits to court, and few from it – one of two of the Dowager's daughters every now and then, sitting before her almost shame-faced, speaking only of pleasantries belied by sombre eyes.

In recent years, consumed with her private sorrows, the mistress had grown unwell. She did not have her old physicians, and the ones that came now were not of their high standard. Grace had chased one or two away after they had bled the mistress so much that she became weaker and more languid that ever. "You'll kill her, you will – get out!" Grace had cried, authoritative, her eyes blazing, and even though she was but a maid and a servant, they did.

And the Dowager, pale and limp as a plucked lily, had raised herself up on an elbow and managed to laugh. "You are like your father, Grace – although it pains me to say so. Ah, such memories..."

The Dowager's ailment, whatever it might be, had worsened during the last few nights, keeping her up and in pain, so Grace had decided to leave the abbey that morning, leaving her sleeping after receiving a calming draught from an apothecary. She planned to seek out the fruiterers in the marketplace to find out if they had any fresh, imported fruits that might cheer the mistress and make her feel well again for a spell. Maybe they might even have an exotic pomegranate or a Seville orange. Grace would have to have the fruit cooked before serving, since raw fruit was considered bad for one's humours, but that was a small enough thing to do – and the monks had a special kitchen especially for their guests and tenants.

Grace entered the busy market square, full of nuns

and monks in grey, white, and brown robes; merchants in velvet capes and long robes; ladies in tall hats with their servants gathered around them. Traders sold from stalls – a varied mix of fish, meat, vegetables, pastries, and trinkets such ribbons, furs and holy badges. Pie-men wandered about, hawking hot meat pies from wooden trays that they carried out of their shops. Children, often ragged and mud-smudged, raced giggling between the stalls, occasionally pinching an apple or two before vanishing into the bustling throng. Grace was sure a few merchants would be lightened of their purses by the end of the day, the strings on their belt-pouches sliced through by some quick-footed urchin's dagger.

Moving swiftly through the crowd, Grace found the stall she usually frequented, brimming with various fruits and vegetables and guarded by a lean, hawk-like woman with sharp eyes, who was on the lookout for thievery at all times. Mistress Lettice Warnock. Nothing untoward got past her, and she even had a dagger secreted in her boot.

The hard, hatchet face softened though, when Lettice saw Grace approach. "Ah, good to see you again, young Grace! How is the Dowager?"

"Not well," Grace admitted. "Not for some time. The physician has been, although he's not up to much. He said it's melancholy, mostly, that she suffers, but I have little faith in his word, although no doubt she bears the pain of her sorrows at all times. Poor lady; she's been through so much loss..." She closed her mouth abruptly, wondering if she had revealed too much. Mistress Warnock was kindly disposed towards her and the Dowager – but she was also known to spread gossip if she heard any juicy titbits during the market.

She didn't seem terribly interested in Grace's

comment about the Dowager's physical ailments, though. Lettice was quicker to apportion blame. "A disgrace," she said, shaking her head. "Still so much suffering despite the good fortune of her eldest daughter. It need not be this way. It's *him*, I tell you, and his sour-visaged old mother..."

Grace blinked, cheeks suddenly growing hot. "Mistress Warnock, please don't. My mistress makes no complaint. Please, do not say anything, this could bring more trouble to her."

"Oh, oh..." Lettice's wan visage grew even paler than usual. "Ah, forgive me, do, young Grace. I have a silly tongue sometimes, but the harsh treatment of your mistress makes me angry, you understand. Come..." She swept a bony arm over the fruit strewn across the table. "Choose something. Half price for the Dowager."

Grace picked up the pomegranate, counting out coins from her scrip. It was one of the more expensive fruits, since it was imported from much warmer climes, but it would make her mistress happy. Sadness gripped her, though, as she recalled how once the Dowager had lived a life of splendour. No counting coins in those heady days.

The pomegranate safely placed in a little bag she wore at her waist, Grace began to make her way back through the crowded streets to the abbey. As she passed under a stone archway, close and shadowy, a couple of lads, dressed foppishly in feathered hats and striped hose almost indecently tight, stepped out of the gloom and eyed her up and down.

To her horror, they began sauntering in her direction. She clutched her cloak tightly around her, making the hood obscure her visage even more. "What are you hiding for, sweetling?" called out one. "You haven't had the great pox, have you?"

"We've seen you before," said the other lout,

swaggering towards her. "We've seen your face, and it's not half bad. Don't know why you're always covering it. Here, give us a kiss, will you?"

He made a grab for her shoulder. She could smell his ale-sodden breath. He was drunk, no doubt having stumbled from some tavern with his odious fellow.

"Your name's Grace, isn't it?" asked the other, who seemed a little more sober. "We heard the old fruit-seller call it out. That's an unusual name. Hail Grace, not so full of Grace." He tittered stupidly and made a wobbly bow.

Grace wished he would fall over onto the mid and dung of the street.

"Just one kiss, my Grace," said the other, pulling her closer with a rough jerk. "I'd like to... see you, if you would. Proper-like. And get to know you..." His hand fumbled under her cloak.

"Get off me," she snarled, and she kneed the lout in the groin, sending him shrieking to the ground while his companion gaped.

"Never touch me again, do you understand?"

She tore away from the youths, stumbling over the cobblestones beneath the arch and into the open street. People were staring now, and fortunately the oafs made no attempt to follow. The one left standing raised a bunched fist and shook it menacingly in her direction. "Who the hell do think you are, bitch? A serving girl, a nobody. Who are you to scorn us – do you think you are royalty?"

Grace's face blanched, and she began to run faster. Rain started to dash from the sky, splashing on the street, gurgling through the gutters.

Who was she? She would never tell anyone who had no need to know. Such knowledge might bring her dire harm.

Her baptismal name was Grace.Her surname was Plantagenet.

And she was the bastard child of King Edward, fourth of that name.

Grace reached the abbey of Bermondsey as the rainstorm grew even heavier. She flung herself at the side door, banging the attached metal ring to rouse the porter, Brother Grimbold, a burly and rather elderly monk who slept in a little room high above the gate. Gargoyles on the roofline spouted grimy water onto her head; raindrops streaked the cheeks of saints' statues in elaborate niches.

A faint clatter sounded on the stairs within, and a moment later a little hatch banged open, revealing the porcine features of Brother Grimbold. He panted like a dog from his exertions of descending from his room. "Mistress Grace, what ever ails you? You were banging so loud, I thought it was a dire emergency. I nearly fell down the stairs!"

"Forgive me," she said, "but look at the downpour, and if that wasn't bad enough, I was set upon by two drunkards."

The monk's eyes widened. "Set upon? What is this wicked world coming to? Are you hurt, child?"

She shook her head. "No. I think my attackers fared worse than I. Well, one of them did anyway."

There was the sound of a lock engaging, and the door into the monastery grounds creaked open. Brother Grimbold beckoned Grace inside. "Come in, come in. Terrible that a decent maid cannot fare to the market without being harassed by varlets!"

Grace stepped over the threshold into the

monastery's precincts and hurried to the Clare chambers where the Dowager lived. Wet cloak dragging, she ascended the flight of stairs to the guest apartments and rapped on the door.

"Enter!" The voice behind was soft but bore a faintly regal air, woven with a trace of haughtiness.

Grace entered the chamber and performed a swift curtsey. There, by a crackling little fire, wrapped in a warm robe, sat her mistress, the Dowager Queen, Elizabeth Woodville.

The woman Grace's sire had married – but who was not Grace's mother.

The Dowager was no longer in the first bloom of youth. She had suffered much since King Edward had died in 1483, and the pain of her various losses showed in the traceries of lines around eyes and mouth. Yet, in the soft light of the cressets, the delicate curve of cheek and chin, the sweep of long lashes, still told of bygone beauty. And, unbound within the privacy of her apartments, her hair flowed down, silver-gold, touched by the moon, kissed by the sun, although the silver-blonde was now growing grey along the temples.

Elizabeth glanced listlessly towards Grace. Hectic colour dappled the older woman's cheeks. It was not a healthy rosiness but a look of feverish illness. "Ah. You are back, dear Grace," she sighed. "Is all well? You are wet through; and you appear quite bedraggled."

Grace had decided not to tell the Dowager Queen about her unfortunate encounter with the ruffians on her way back to the abbey. It would only worry her, and she had enough woes to deal with. Her little period of unexplained happiness had died away after Stoke Field, which Grace never fully understood, for surely Elizabeth was glad that her daughter's throne as queen consort was secure? That the plots of the last of

King Richard's supporters had been thwarted, with a pretender called "Simnel," like the cake, taken into King Henry's kitchens to turn the spit, young John, the Earl of Lincoln, slain in the field, and Lord Lovell last seen fleeing through a river and never heard from more?

But it appeared there were other secrets that her mistress would not impart to her. Once Elizabeth had said, while running a fever, "The boy taken on the field of battle was not the same one Henry now parades in his court. There never was a 'Lambert Simnel'." But when Grace had enquired what she meant, the Dowager had shaken her head and turned her face to the wall.

"The rain falls heavy today, madam." Grace pulled off her cloak and hung it in front of the fire. "I ran as fast as I might to keep from getting too wet, but alas, all my efforts were in vain."

"Sit and warm yourself then." Elizabeth nodded toward a stool near the fireplace. "It would not do well for you to become ill."

Grace flopped down upon the quilted stool, stretching out her cold legs to the warmth of the fire. "I managed to find a pomegranate for you today, your Grace. One of good quality, neither too green nor overripe. It was Mistress Warnock's last one."

"I am pleased to hear it. How delightful. I have not had such a fruit for many months. I bid you take it to the kitchen to be warmed. I will let you have some of it once I am done."

Grace rose, curtseyed again, and hurried off to the guest kitchens, set separately from those of the brothers, where she asked that the pomegranate be peeled and warmed for the Dowager. She then went to the chapel to say a few prayers for Elizabeth's health while she waited for the cook to finish. She always felt the monks were uneasy to have a girl her age in close proximity, so she avoided them when she could. The chapel was always a sanctuary between masses.

She entered through the heavily carved doorway into a smoky dimness that smelt vaguely of incense mingled with tallow. A few small cresset lights flickered below a large painted statue of the Blessed Virgin and illuminated a large painting on the wall.

The painting had always fascinated Grace: the Wheel of Dame Fortune. A beautiful golden-haired lady stood beside a vast, spoked wheel, which had four struts upon which four men sat. On the left was a youth wearing a coronet; next to him was written *regnabo*, I Shall Reign. On the top was a king, crowned, sceptred, and robed. The words above his head read *Regno*, I Reign. On the right-hand side was a more sombre figure, still crowned, but old, weary, battered. *Regnavi*, I have Reigned. Last was a corpse in a loin cloth, lying under the wheel with worms issuing from its pallid flesh. *Sum Sine Regno*. I am Without a Kingdom.

Grace's hand stretched out to touch the painting, musing upon how true it was that Fate was fickle and also implacable. In an eye's blink, the great could be thrown down to despair or raised to the highest dignity. So it had happened to her kingly sire, taken swiftly after an ague caught while fishing. And so it had happened to Elizabeth, a commoner made a queen, but now living as a recluse in a monastery.

Grace knelt before the altar, not praying so much as thinking about the strange course her life had taken. When she was a little maid, growing up near Clarendon, if anyone had told her that she was a king's daughter and would one day serve his widow, she would have laughed and thought them moon-mazed.

She sighed. Her mother, Catherine, had died when she was very small, too small to remember much of her: a gentle voice, a coil of honey-hued hair. Her clearest early memories were of a herald in a bright tabard speaking earnestly to her old, white-haired grandfather. "The king wants to do right by the child. She is of the royal blood, even if baseborn." She had seen her grandfather nod, wipe his eye. Then she was placed in a chariot and whisked away, like a maiden in a fairytale, to a castle she now knew to be Eltham Palace.

A giant of a man had come to welcome her, clad in robes of purple trimmed with ermine. "My little Grace!" he had boomed, his voice loud as thunder, and he had picked her up as if she were a child's doll, and she felt as if she were flying up to touch the very sun.

King Edward, her father. Called the Rose of Rouen for his masculine beauty, the victor of many battles, the Sun in Splendour.

She'd also met Queen Elizabeth for the first time that day, but their meeting had been much different than Grace's encounter with her sire. Elizabeth, dripping in white seed pearls and crystals, had seemed a woman of ice seated on her throne, a gaggle of her sisters, all married to dukes or lords, circling round her in a protective ring. Her green eyes, beneath heavy, sultry lids, were not friendly.

And as an adult, Grace understood why. What worse than to have the fruit of your husband's infidelity thrust into your face? But Edward had wanted her there, and so too Grace's half-brother Arthur, begotten on a courtesan called Elizabeth Wayte. The two baseborn children did not stay long at court, however, and were soon given into the care of noble families to be educated.

But life had a strange way of throwing unexpected

turns, and as the King's ardour towards his wife had cooled with the advent of a new mistress, the flirtatious Jane Shore, Grace had been summoned back to court, a young woman now, joining her royal half-sisters in a lowly but not menial position. Gradually, Elizabeth's coldness towards her evaporated. They became friendly, if not actual friends, and that bond had deepened after the events that followed King Edward's unexpected death in 1483.

And now here they were, both sailors of the sea of fate, weathering the winds and storms. But whereas Elizabeth failed and withered like a leaf plucked from a tree, Grace had begun to thrive and blossom in their new world, the world of a Tudor king. And her heart changed, matured. At one time she had craved the life of court, the dancing, the glittering gems, the music played by minstrels...now she could not bear the thought of its intrigues and lies, the hate and suspicion that followed any interaction. She had heard that King Henry VII had spies everywhere, ears flapping to catch any rumours of dissent, and that Margaret Beaufort, styling herself 'The King's Mother' was every bit as suspicious as her son, never leaving Grace's half-sister Elizabeth of York alone with any foreign dignitary lest she say something that might be deemed inappropriate.

Rising from the cold tiles of the chapel floor, Grace made her way back to the guest's kitchens. The cook had finished warming the pomegranate and handed it to the girl in a pewter dish. Hurrying so that the fruit would not grow chill, Grace made her way back to the Dowager Queen's apartments.

Elizabeth had moved from the fireplace to a window embrasure. She was gazing out over the monks' herb gardens towards the gate, towards all manner of life that went on in the great city beyond. To

Grace's embarrassment, she saw a tear trickle down the parchment skin of the old queen's face. Grace put the pomegranate on the table and coughed loudly. "Madam, here is the fruit from the market. I can see you are...indisposed. I will return later." She gathered her skirts and took a stride towards the chamber door.

"No, Grace, come back." Elizabeth turned on her cushion and gestured with her hand. "You must not mind me. I just am consumed by the foolishness of age – and the sorrows of my life that never leave my mind. But all those troubles are coming to an end, as surely as autumn slides into winter."

"Madam, I beg you do not say such things! You are not old, nor is your life ending."

"Ah, Grace, you are still so innocent and so full of hope, as it should be at your age. But I have had signs. What ails my body is more than mere melancholy. But come, slice open that pomegranate and let us dine."

Grace took a little knife and deftly cut the fruit into two halves. The red seeds, plump and jewel-like, spilt into the bowl. She carried it to her mistress and proffered the fruit. Elizabeth picked at it, delicately lifting the pomegranate seeds to her mouth. They stained her lips like fresh blood, and Grace could not suppress a shudder at the sight.

Elizabeth finished and passed the bowl back to Grace. Then, rising stiffly from her seat, she went to a wooden chest, opened it, and brought out a little bag. It jingled as she lifted it.

"Grace." The Dowager approached her, taking her hand and pressing the bag into it. "A little something for your good service. I give this advice: when I am gone, leave London and go far from here. Find a life for yourself. Marry. Marry someone of your choice and do not chase princes. Forget that you are of Plantagenet line."

"But I am proud of who I am." Grace began. "I know that I am baseborn, but..."

"It is right that you are proud," interrupted Elizabeth, "but I do not believe Plantagenet is a safe name to bear in these times, and I know not what is to come. I think only of your future happiness and safety . I could do little for my daughters, as they are princesses, but I can do something for you."

"Your Grace, I am so grateful." Grace dropped a low curtsey, clutching the bag of coins to her breast. "Your kindness will never be forgotten."

"Good. Now come, help me to my bedchamber. I am feeling both weak and weary."

<hr>

The bells tolled mournfully in the tower of Bermondsey Abbey. Grace knelt in the chapel, head on her arms, weeping. The Dowager Queen had rapidly declined over the previous days and weeks, and she had written out her final will. She had asked to be buried with her husband, Edward IV, King of England, in St George's Chapel at Windsor Castle, a change in plans, for once she had expressed a wish to lie in Westminster, in the chantry she had founded almost twenty years before. She also asked for no pomp, no ceremony – although it went without saying that this request, frequently found in the wills of the highborn, would be ignored. After all, she had been a queen and was the mother of a queen.

The Abbot of Bermondsey appeared at the chapel door, clearing his throat. "Child, she is calling for you. Come, do not tarry, for I fear there is not much more time."

Grace clambered up and ran down the cloister and then up the worn stone stairs to the Dowager's apartments. Elizabeth lay in her bed, still and pale, her breathing shallow. A doctor stood at the bedside holding a pan that Grace thought at first was rich red wine; then she realised that the physician had bled her mistress. It made her feel angry, for both she and Elizabeth had denied this useless treatment before. As she stared, transfixed by despair, her mistress's eyelids fluttered and her thin fingers twisted, signalling the doctor to leave the chamber.

He hesitated. Grace glared at him. "Leave," she whispered, pointing at the door. "You've done enough."

His mouth twitched into a grimace of annoyance, but he bowed his head and dutifully left in a rustle of black robes.

"Come closer, Grace," the old queen said, her voice a rasping whisper.

Grace came over and knelt at the bedside.

Elizabeth glanced over at her. The green eyes that were so famous, a dragon's eyes half-lidded and seductive, were now dull and unfocussed, as if she already gazed into the afterlife. "I have designated you as my chief mourner, Grace," she murmured.

"But Madam!" cried Grace, surprised. "I am not worthy of such an honour. It should go to one of your daughters; as the queen cannot attend, what about Cecily, Catherine, or Anne? Or even young Bridget?"

"Cecily is with child and cannot travel. Bridget will come, but I would not place her under the duress of mourning; she is but twelve years old. The others, I do not know; they have not written to me or visited for such a long time. I fear that because I fell out of favour with Henry, they would not be quick to associate with me, even in death. He is a suspicious, cold man, as you know. At least he does seem to love Elizabeth, though; that is my one consolation. Even if the other girls do attend, it is you who have stayed with me to the end. A daughter not of my blood but of spirit. Ned's child."

She closed her eyes, and a ripple of pain raced over her face. "Grace... hold my hand... please."

Grace clasped her hand; so frail, so cold.

"My boys," she whispered. "My sons, Edward and Richard. I wish I could see them one last time."

Grace's half-brothers, missing and presumed murdered in King Richard's reign. "They await you in heaven, madam, of that I am certain."

Elizabeth managed to make a little gasping laugh. "Oh, no, Grace, the day will come when we will indeed meet at the Almighty's throne, but it is not yet."

"What do you mean, mistress?" asked Grace with a frown, but Elizabeth spoke no more. Her head rolled to one side. A few moments later, a long, rasping breath escaped her lips, and then she fell still. The coverlet over her breast ceased to rise and fall.

She was gone.

Grace pressed her face into the cover and wept as the tapers in the bedchamber melted into puddles of wax and the darkness of night took hold

---

"It is time, Mistress Grace." A monk rapped on the door of the bedchamber, the sound cutting through the stillness.

The girl climbed groggily from her chair next to the guttering fire, disoriented, heavy with sadness. As swiftly as she could, she donned a cloak over her sombre mourning garb and adjusted her plain hennin with its trailing black veil.

She was ready for this last task for her mistress.

Back straight, she left the Clare apartments and walked briskly to the monastery's chapel, where the body of Elizabeth Woodville lay in state before the altar. The dead queen, features stroked by the warm glow of flickering candle flames, looked strangely young in death, the lines of care erased from her beautiful features. Her hands were folded in the Christian manner, her hair arranged on a pillow stuffed with fragrant herbs and spices.

Grace bit her lip to control her emotions. She had been wrong when she thought Elizabeth would have a regal burial despite her last request, that King Henry would relent in his seeming dislike and bury her in a style fitting for a Dowager queen – and the mother of his own wife. But he had not; he had sent nothing. And so Elizabeth had a cheap, flimsy coffin, crudely made of the poorest wood; no encasement in lead as was common for those of high estate. A small bier held her remains, not the large funeral hearse decked with banners and regalia that one might expect. A pittance for a few tapers had arrived secretly, not enough, but the monks had kindly donated a few more to light her last journey.

Grace knelt and prayed in silence for a while, then raised her head as she heard the sound of footsteps in the corridor outside the chapel. The pallbearers had arrived. She rose and stood aside, head bowed, as sturdy, black-clad men filed into the chapel and lifted the bier on which Elizabeth's body lay in the open coffin.

They carried it out through the cloisters, and Grace followed, casting her gaze back once to the wall-painting of Dame Fortuna. The candlelight struck on the lowest part of the wheel and on the words written there. *Sum Sine Rego.* I Am Without a Kingdom. And so it came to every king and queen that had ever reigned upon the earth: the slip of years, the dip of good fortune, the grievances of old age, the eternal quiet of the tomb.

And as for Grace, she knew not which way the Wheel might spin for her, for as the poet Thomas Malory had written in his tome on King Arthur, one of the Dowager queen's favourite romances, *Fortune is so variant, and the wheel so moveable, there is no constant abiding…*

The pallbearers traversed down to the Thames with Grace close behind. It was dark still, and the stars were hard, jewelled eyes in the blackness of the firmament. Reaching the riverbank, wreathed in a haze of night fog, the funeral party headed to one of the many wharfs jutting out along the riverbank. A small barge was moored there, with a black canopy drawn over it, and a single sickly lantern hanging on a hook near its prow.

The pallbearers carried Elizabeth's coffin onto the barge, then knelt around it like a troop of guards. Grace lit more tapers and sat down at her mistress's feet as the barge pulled away from the dock to begin its long journey to Windsor.

Shivering in her cloak, Grace felt she had entered a mystical world of fog, smoke, and candlelight. All down the riversides, she saw night-fires blaze, men and beasts moving before the flames, and above, the silhouettes of spires, crenelations, and turrets stood dark against the slightly lightening eastern sky. The journey felt surreal, the faint chants of monks and nuns from various monastic houses throughout London carrying over the water like the lamentations of ghosts.

But then the dawn came, heralded by singing birds, and the heavens grew crimson, and the city faded into the fog, and there were only green fields and distant spires and the faint clang of church bells for miles around. And for Grace Plantagenet, on her way to

Windsor to bury her royal father's wife, this was both an ending and a new beginning. A death – and the chance of a new life with the money Elizabeth had bequeathed her.

Dame Fortune's Wheel turned yet again.

213

© J.P. Reedman

Author's note

Grace Plantagenet was a real person, the daughter of Edward IV and an unknown mistress. She appears in records of Elizabeth's Woodville's death and was indeed the only member of the York family to accompany the dowager queen's body on its journey from London to its very low-key burial in Windsor. After this event, Grace completely disappears from the historical record.

About J.P. Reedman

J.P. Reedman lives in Wiltshire near to Stonehenge. Born in Canada, she has had a lifelong interest in ancient and medieval history, and is often found lurking around prehistoric sites, ruined castles and abbeys, and interesting churches with camera in hand. She became a full-time writer in 2018. Series include I, Richard Plantagenet, five books chronicling Richard's life from childhood to Bosworth, and Medieval Babes, a set of standalone novels about lesser-known medieval queens and noblewomen.

Facebook: https://www.facebook.com/ IRichardPlantagenet/
X/Twitter: https://x.com/stonehenge2500/
Amazon Author Page: author.to/REEDMANHISTFIC

10

SAINTS ALIVE

BY DEBBIE YOUNG

When children are not quite the saints we'd like them to be!

Sina

The thing about me is, I know stuff. Not just the sort of thing your mum tells you, or what you learn at the village school. One reason I know more stuff than most kids my age is that my big brother Tommy tells me interesting things all the time. Even though he says secondary school is boring, most days he has something clever to share with me. Last week, he told me about this thing they did in Biology called ozzymozziness, or something like that. It means you can absorb stuff just by being next to it. It's sort of like magic. That night, I slept with my Spellings book on my pillow, and the next day I got ten out of ten in my Spelling test. See what I mean?

The other reason I know so much is because my brother and I hang out a lot in our village bookshop, Hector's House. It's rammed full of books stuffed with useful things to know. Unlike my brother, I sometimes read books.

Sophie

"Miss Mabbs says we never learn from history," declared Tommy to the small group gathered in the bookshop after Saturday closing.

Together, we were assembling strings of green and white bunting. Later we'd use them to festoon the High Street, ready for the next day's celebrations of St Bride, the patronal saint of Wendlebury Barrow village church. While we worked on the bunting, the flower rota team was busy decking the church out in matching colours. Other volunteers were delivering home-made cakes and biscuits to refresh Sunday visitors. After the morning service, St Bride's was to be open to visitors and tourists for the rest of the day.

As the pile of bunting grew, we were enjoying a bit of banter.

"So, if we never learn from history," Tommy continued, "I don't know why Miss Mabbs bothers teaching it. I mean, we could use that lesson time for something more useful, like athletics practice."

Tommy may not have won any prizes for academic prowess, but he was the fastest sprinter in his year group at Slate Green Secondary School. His record for the fifty-metre dash at Wendlebury Barrow Primary remained unbroken.

"You misunderstand her, Tommy," said Hector. "She's not talking about school history lessons. She means the bigger picture. People continue to make the same mistakes, despite plenty of examples in our history to teach us otherwise."

"That's why they say history often repeats itself," added Kate, Hector's godmother. She rolled a newly-completed string of bunting into a tight coil and secured it with an elastic band.

"Miss Mabbs repeats herself all the time," Tommy grumbled.

As a trained teacher, I sympathised with Miss Mabbs.

His little sister Sina chimed in. "But you have to have history, or else there wouldn't be a future. It would only ever be now."

That silenced us for a moment.

Carol, village shopkeeper and wardrobe mistress to the Wendlebury Players, looked up from her sewing machine. She lifted its needle and broke the thread hemming her latest green triangle.

"You mean like in that film, *Wombat Afternoon*?"

"*Groundhog Day*," I clarified. I'm used to interpreting Carol's malapropisms.

"We also need to plan for the future," said Hector, folding photocopied service sheets ready for the morning. "If we only ever learned from yesterday, we'd be no more advanced than cavemen."

From beneath his dark eyelashes, he shot me a surreptitious wink.

Tommy's face lit up. "I wonder what we don't know now that we'll know in the future," he said.

"Medical things," said old Billy, licking the froth off his coffee spoon as a hint for a refill. So far, Billy had done nothing to help our preparations, but he liked to be on hand whenever free refreshments were on offer.

Kate nodded. "I can think of lots of examples of medical advances. Tommy and Sina, did you know, once upon a time, people thought foul smells rather than germs spread plague? So, they carried posies of fragrant flowers as a deterrent, with the same faith that we had in facemasks during Covid, without the same scientific merit."

"Ring-a-Ring-a-Roses, A pocket full of posies," I sang. "You know, like in the nursery rhyme?"

Sina nodded with a sagacity beyond her years.

"Remember those sailors who got scurvy because they didn't know about Vitamin C? All their teeth fell out, and then they died." Billy spoke with as much conviction as if he'd been a fellow traveller of Magellan's.

I interrupted before Billy could be tempted to emphasise his point by removing his false teeth, something he did at the slightest provocation.

"By the time you're Billy's age, you will look back and laugh at what we currently believe to be medical truths. With any luck, by then, diseases that are now fatal will be curable."

Setting down the string she'd been threading through bunting flags, Sina balanced her chair on its two back legs. "Like if you swallow chewing gum, it'll wrap around your heart."

Kate reached behind Sina and gently righted her chair.

"Like if you cut yourself between your thumb and your finger, you'll get lockjaw," added Tommy.

"My Great-Uncle Alf died of lockjaw," said Billy. "But you don't hear of no-one dying from lockjaw nowadays."

Tommy thought for a moment. "I suppose that's why Walt Disney had his head cut off."

I pushed my half-eaten jam doughnut away from me.

"Really?" Sina's shrill voice rose to a squeak.

Noticing our eyes upon him, Tommy eagerly elaborated. "To freeze it until they find a cure for cancer, of course. When they've done that, they'll thaw his head out, stick it on a new body, and bring him back to life."

Sina tutted her disapproval. "You'd think a man that rich would pay to freeze his whole body," she said. "I bet he never had to worry about his electric bill like Mum does."

"This business of freezing people is a load of stuff and nonsense, if you ask me," said Billy, although nobody had asked him. "It's just the work of charlatans to separate rich fools from their money. The only good use for a severed head is to make head cheese."

The children gawped at him.

"How do you make cheese out of someone's head?" demanded Sina. "Walt Disney wasn't made of milk."

"Head cheese is also known as brawn," said Kate. "I always think brawn sounds less grisly."

Although Kate's an excellent cook, I was glad she'd never served Hector and me with such a gruesome dish. I doubted I could force any down for the sake of politeness.

"You boil the meat off the bones, add spices, and when it cools, it sets to a jelly," she continued brightly, as if we might note down her recipe for future use.

"I hope they're not giving us that sort of stuff at the church tea tomorrow," said Tommy, who will usually eat everything put in front of him.

"Don't worry, Tommy, there won't be so much as a hint of Disney on the menu," said Hector, his lips twitching in amusement. "Just the usual array of cakes and biscuits, as per tradition."

"Tradition," scoffed Tommy. "If we're meant to learn from the past so we can move on, why are we still doing the same thing for St Bride's Day that they did when Billy was a boy?"

"Ah, but we're not," Kate corrected him. "Some years ago, we moved our celebrations from winter to midsummer. The official Saint's Day for St Bride is 1st February. When Billy was a boy, they still celebrated her on her proper patronal day. Not long before you were born, the Vicar persuaded the village to mark the event in June, to give our church's patron saint the time and attention she deserves. Before that, St Bride's Day tended to be overshadowed by Candlemas on the second of February. That's the day of Christ's presentation in the Temple."

"I suppose the Son of God would trump a mere saint," said Hector.

"But the change upset traditionalists," Kate continued. "Even those who only ever go to church at Christmas, and maybe Easter."

I confess, that would have been me until the Vicar roped me in to run the Sunday School, not long after I'd moved to the village. Our Vicar is the sort of person who can persuade anyone to do anything, then send them away thinking he's done them a favour.

"It caused quite a ruckus, I can tell you," said Kate. "It took about ten years before certain people stopped boycotting the midsummer event to express their outrage."

"I still think it's a daft idea," muttered Billy. "Either a day's a saint's day or it's not. Saints aren't like the king, having two birthdays each year. One's the official birthday for the sake of ceremony, and the other is the day he was actual born on."

"King Charles has two birthdays?" echoed Sina, hands on hips. "Lucky duck!"

"No wonder he looks so old," added Tommy.

In the distance, the church clock struck half-past six. Carol whisked the plug of her sewing machine out of the electric socket on the wall.

"Come on then, boys and girls," said Hector. "Let's get this bunting up in the High Street. Then we can go home and have our tea."

Sina

Of course, I already knew about saints, because Sophie's always going on about them at Sunday School. At first, I thought they were a bit like superheroes, what with all those miracles they go around doing. I'm not sure why superheroes don't get made into saints, too. They're always saving people from burning buildings, and stopping asteroids destroying the Earth.

I asked Sophie about this at Sunday School once, and she said the saints don't just do miracles. They also lead selfless holy lives, and they only get made saints when the Pope says so.

Apparently, the saints' miracles aren't the sort of thing you see in Marvel films. They're things like St Patrick sending all the snakes out of Ireland. That's tough on you if you love snakes, like I do, or if you happen to actually be a snake. Then there's St Christopher, who gave the Baby Jesus a piggyback across a river. We have piggyback races every sports day at school, with the top class carrying the little ones from Reception. But all the winner gets is a rosette and a lollipop, not a special celebration every year.

Earlier today, when I was helping to fill the font for Ginny Hastings' christening this afternoon, I chatted to the Vicar about saints.

"So, what did Saint Bride do that made her so special?"

I was expecting him to say something unimpressive, like she went shopping for her mum. He stood back as I emptied my seaside bucket into the font. I like watching the pale stone turn dark wherever I splash it.

"We can all try to follow in the footsteps of the saints and aim for a holy life like Jesus," said the Vicar.

"And so we should. Each of us is a saint in the making, on our own journey through life."

"So, I could be Saint Sina? I like the sound of that."

He replaced the big wooden lid on top of the font to keep the water clean. He always worries that if he doesn't do that, one of the little birds that gets into the church occasionally will use it as a birdbath. Personally, I'd have thought a baby would love sharing its bath with a bird.

"In the olden days, people were often made saints only after they'd been martyred." He looked at me for a moment. "That means someone had killed them for their beliefs."

I shuddered.

"Maybe I won't bother, then."

He smiled.

"No, I wouldn't, if I were you. But you can still be inspired by the lives of the saints. Many people admired St Bride for her wisdom and her kindness. When she founded a convent, people respected her as much as any man in the church. That was rare in those days. Consequently, all kinds of people still admire her. She's patron saint of blacksmiths, babies, poets, and scholars, amongst others."

"Clever of the babies to get together to choose their own saint," I said.

The Vicar crossed to the central aisle and pointed to the stained-glass window at the sunset end of the church. It showed a picture of St Bride in a white dress. She wasn't wearing any shoes. Her long orange hair hung down to her waist. I thought she was very glamorous. In her right hand, she held a green cross with a chunky middle.

"You know about the special St Bride's cross, don't you?" said the Vicar. "She wove one from rushes to help her teach people about the Christian faith. I think Sophie told you about it at Sunday School last week."

"Yes, we wove some out of grass."

I liked St Bride's green cross. Having her own symbol, like Superman, was very cool. I wondered whether she had it on her vest underneath her white dress.

"I wanted to take mine home, but we weren't allowed. Sophie said they were to stay in the church as part of the decorations for tomorrow. Not like the palm crosses you give us at Easter. I've still got mine at home. It's sticking out of the chimney of my dolls' house."

"It's so much easier to gather enough greenery for her crosses in midsummer than in winter," said the Vicar. He glanced at his watch. He was probably thinking about stuff he had to do somewhere else. He's always too nice to tell me to go away, but now he headed for the exit.

"I like St Bride," I said, as I skipped beside him. "I think I'd like her to be my patron saint, too. Perhaps I'll start a St Bride's Gang for my friends at After-School Club. What sort of gang should it be? Obviously, me and my friends are too big to be babies. And I don't think we'd be allowed to do blacksmithing at school because of health and safety. They're always stopping us doing fun stuff because of health and safety. So, that leaves poets and scholars. Which do you think me and my gang should be?"

The Vicar held the porch door open for me to go out in front of him.

"If they're all clever girls like you, scholars, for sure."

Kate

As churchwarden, it fell to me to organise the decoration of the church for our celebration. As ever, the flower rota ladies did St Bride proud. They chose a simple green and white colour scheme, with accents of orange to reference St Bride's beautiful auburn Irish locks. The nave was hung with swags of white roses, while urns of white lilac topped the altar. The windowsills were decked in ropes of ivy, shot through with orange gerbera and white Shasta daisies. Either side of the south porch door, the main visitors' entrance, pots of bright early marigolds drew attention to wooden trugs of woven grass crosses. Handwritten cards invited visitors to help themselves to a St Bride cross as a souvenir. This stunning floral display – and the cakes and biscuits – would tempt plenty of villagers to visit the church, whether or not they attended the morning service.

All things considered, our St Bride's Festival event was a much-needed fundraiser to supplement the collections from our dwindling congregation. Sadly, that's the lot of just about every country church these days. Fortunately, whenever we appeal for donations of cakes for such things, the community responds with generosity. By the end of Saturday, copious home-baked goodies had been delivered. A WI sub-committee had arranged them beautifully on borrowed platters and cake-stands. They had also filled the tea-urn and arranged the crockery ready for the off. All that remained to be done on the Sunday morning was to turn on the urn and bring in fresh milk.

Leaving the menfolk to put the completed bunting along the High Street, I set off to lock the church for the night before returning home. After a busy day, I was looking forward to a restorative glass of dry sherry as an apéritif to the chicken casserole simmering in the Aga.

Standing in the church porch, fishing inside my wicker basket for the keys, I was distracted by a screech coming from the High Street. Hoping it was nothing serious, I dashed back down the path and through the lychgate to discover the cause. I am always willing to offer my first-aid skills if needed.

Fortunately, the source of the screech was only Tommy's mother, standing at the foot of a telegraph pole and gazing upwards open-mouthed. Far above her head, legs wrapped around the towering wooden post, Tommy was hammering a nail into the end of the last string of bunting.

"Thomas Crowe, come down from there before you fall down!"

For now, her voice was cracked with terror rather than anger, but I suspected she'd change her tune once Tommy was back on the pavement. He climbs like a monkey and is often to be spotted up trees or even on the roof of the village hall. Now he scampered down to ground level.

"What?" He held up his hands in puzzlement. "You said I'm not allowed up ladders anymore, so I'm not."

He pointed to the telegraph pole. It was so full of holes from thumbtacks used to pin up event posters over the years that it looked like a woodworm hostel.

"Besides, lots of men climb those things all the time, so why shouldn't I?"

I stifled a laugh at the mental image of Wendlebury Barrow's menfolk habitually scaling telegraph poles, like ascetic hermits trying to literally rise above temptation. Simeon Stylites, I'm looking at you.

"That's different," returned Mrs Crowe. "You're talking about telephone engineers, and they're meant to. It's their job to fix things up poles, and they have special equipment and health and safety training and everything."

"Health and safety, my –"

Billy, sitting on a nearby wall smoking a roll-up, changed tack when Mrs Crowe gave him a hard stare.

"Well done, boy. All finished now. He's all yours till the morning, Mrs Crowe."

Billy was ever generous with things that didn't belong to him, but Mrs Crowe was not as easily soothed. "And where's Sina?"

As one, Tommy and Billy shrugged.

"I dunno," said Tommy. "I haven't seen her since she was making bunting with us at Hector's House. Do you want me to go round the village looking for her?"

"Only if she isn't home by her eight o'clock curfew."

Now that we were enjoying the longest periods of daylight of the year, few parents in Wendlebury Barrow minded their children playing outside until late. That was especially true on a Saturday evening, with no school to worry about next day.

"She'd better just hope I don't eat her tea for her before then," said Tommy, turning to follow his mother home. "I'm starving. Mum, what's for tea?"

With their knack for finding offers of cakes and sweets at Hector's House and elsewhere, if there's one thing these wily children aren't in danger of, it's starving.

Remembering my own tea in the Aga awaiting my return, I turned to head home. Billy trudged companionably beside me, but only as far as The Bluebird.

Sina

When I decided Mum and Tommy were out of earshot, I came from my hiding place behind a tombstone. I'd be better off hanging around outside for a bit longer. That would give Mum a chance to cool down after she'd been shouting at Tommy.

When Tommy had mentioned tea, my tummy rumbled. It seemed a long time since we'd been eating doughnuts at Hector's House, but I suppose doughnuts are mostly air, so no wonder I was feeling empty.

Hector and Sophie would have shut up shop by now, so there was no hope of any more snacks there. I scrambled up onto a nearby table tomb and sat cross-legged while I thought where to go instead. When the church clock chimed a quarter past seven, it was like St Bride sending me a message. She was reminding me of where else I might find a little something to keep me going until tea time.

As I jumped down from the tomb, the cushiony lichen that grows there brushed the backs of my legs, turning them green. It made them look a bit like Shrek's, only skinnier, and I liked it. After I'd glanced around the churchyard to make sure no-one was watching me, I darted over to the north porch. I hoped the big church door was still open, and it was. I'd seen Kate get her keys out to lock it, but she had dropped them back in her basket when she heard Mum screaming. She must have forgotten to lock it.

As I lifted the thumb latch, I remembered the Vicar telling me once that the village blacksmith made it hundreds of years ago. That blacksmith must have been one of St Bride's fans too. The door was too heavy to push open with my hands, and I had to lean my shoulder against it before it budged.

"Helloey!" I called as I entered the church, to check no-one was in there to see what I was about to do.

It was much cooler inside than outdoors, but still the evening sunshine shone down through St Bride's stained-glass window. It was sending a beam of light along the centre aisle onto the silver cross on the altar. It was like the green cross in her hand was a light sabre. Impressive. Spread out on a table beneath her window, shaded from the sun by the thick stone wall, lay a feast of cakes and biscuits, ready for our celebrations the next day.

I was just about to lift the cling film covering a plate of green and white macarons when I felt a cold hand on my shoulder. Someone shrieked in alarm. Then I realised it was me. Why hadn't I heard any footsteps approaching?

I turned round to see who had touched me. A lady in a long, plain white dress like Mum's summer nightie stood behind me. She wasn't wearing any shoes, which explained the lack of footsteps. Her bare feet must have been freezing on the cold stone floor, but she didn't seem to mind. Her long red hair was hanging loose, with not a single scrunchie or hair clip to keep it tidy. It looked as if she had trouble combing the tangles out of it. That's why Mum usually makes me tie mine back.

"Hello," I said. She looked familiar, but I couldn't think of her name. "You're a day early. We don't start celebrating until tomorrow. If you're here for the cakes, that is. Or the service."

At the sound of a loud rumble, I patted my tummy. Then I realised it wasn't mine that had made the noise. I hadn't felt that funny gurgling that usually goes with a rumble. It must have been the lady's tummy.

"That's a shame," she said.

She looked far hungrier than I felt. Perhaps she hadn't even had any lunch.

"Although if you're really hungry, you can have a cake or two now. I can teach you how to make sure no-one ever finds out."

This was another thing I'd learned from Tommy.

"If you rearrange the cakes on a plate to hide the gaps left by any you've taken, no-one will ever know. And here's another good trick. Press down on the top of a sponge cake, and its filling will ooze out around the middle. Then you can run your finger round to gather it up and eat it. The cake will still look exactly the same, just a bit shorter."

"Really?"

I nodded. I wouldn't have taught any old grown-up these important tricks, but I thought she was a bit different to the usual boring sort. She didn't say any more, so I went on. "Besides, after all the trouble the cake ladies have gone to, it would be a shame if they had any left at the end of St Bride's special day. You'd just be helping them avoid any embarrassment if you ate some. I've seen some of these ladies getting upset if nobody wants to eat their cakes. It's like being picked last to be in a team in school sports. It makes you feel sad and left out."

I hoped the nice lady would agree. I was ready to join her in a little something, if it would make her feel better about helping herself.

"If you're sure," said my new friend. "Perhaps we could have a little picnic together."

"I love picnics," I replied.

Before I knew it, we'd taken a plate of cakes to up by the altar. We sat down cross-legged on the carpet, just in front of the gleaming cross. "I'm Sina, by the way," I told my new friend as we each chose our first cake from the selection we'd put together. We'd taken one from each plate on the table, just to be fair.

The lady blinked at me for a moment. She looked a

bit sunburnt, and I wondered whether the bright sunshine outside today had hurt her eyes. I looked up to see which bit of the St Bride window the sun was coming through now. Would she prefer to sit somewhere in the shade?

Then I realised. She didn't have to tell me her name, because I already knew. She'd expect me and everybody else in the village to know it, same as someone really famous like Taylor Swift would. (Not that Taylor Swift has ever been to Wendlebury Barrow, but I keep hoping.)

"Happy Birthday for tomorrow, St Bride," I said, glad to be the first to say it to her this year. "What a shame the cake ladies didn't bring any birthday candles."

St Bride pointed at the wire stand beside the nave that holds tea lights like the ones Mum gets in Ikea. The Vicar once explained to me that lighting tea lights in church makes you feel better if you're sad or worried, especially when you say a prayer at the same time. I told him lighting tea lights anywhere makes me feel better, especially if I'm allowed to blow them out.

I jumped up to grab the nearest tea light and the box of matches from beneath the candelabra.

"Look, it's just the right size to fit on top of your macaron."

I let St Bride light the match. Mum doesn't like Tommy or me playing with matches.

Only when the church clock struck eight did I realise how long we'd been at our picnic. No wonder there were only a few crumbs left. I leapt to my feet.

"Sorry, St Bride," I said, brushing the crumbs off my t-shirt onto the red carpet. "Mum goes mad if I'm not in by eight, even though it'll be light for ages yet. I expect I'll see you again tomorrow."

"Not if I see you first." St Bride gave a naughty

smile. She'd turned out to be much less stuffy than most grown-ups. Maybe that came from being a saint. I'd have to ask the Vicar next time I saw him.

With a little goodbye wave, I jumped down the altar steps and skipped along the aisle and out of the porch door. As I ran the rest of the way home, I hoped I hadn't eaten too much cake to manage whatever Mum had made for our tea.

St Bride

As soon as the funny little girl had gone, I gathered up the crumbs from the carpet onto our empty plates. Then I headed for the vestry down the carpeted central aisle, enjoying the soft touch of the blood-red wool beneath my bare feet. I was glad the vestry had a proper hinged door, unlike the curtained affairs I've seen in other churches, like dress-shop changing rooms. A Vicar should have privacy as he slips in and out of his robes, and I'd appreciated it too when I arrived.

Not wanting to get the kind little girl into trouble, I washed our plates in the hand basin in the corner of the vestry. Then I dried them on the tea towel hanging from a brass hook in the wall and returned them to the stack of clean crockery on the cake table. As the child had taught me, I rearranged the cakes to fill any gaps and carefully reapplied the cling film. No-one would detect our private party – the first birthday party I'd had since I was fifteen, just before...

Abruptly, I turned on my heel to head for the font, where I lifted the carved oak lid to retrieve my soaking laundry. After wringing out as much water as my stiff hands could manage, I hooked the damp washing along the iron railings surrounding a nearby tomb. What a way for the poor soul to spend eternity, imprisoned behind iron bars, caged as if for some dreadful crime.

Even though the church would grow chillier overnight, the worst of the damp would likely be gone from my clothes by morning. The reddening sky behind the west end window told me the next day would be a shepherd's delight. Any lingering damp in my clothes would be bearable as I headed off to wherever fate decreed.

Before I left in the morning, I planned to fill my pockets and my backpack with more cake, again taking care to conceal the gaps. The instinct that had told me to stop here for the night had been a good one. I should probably navigate by churches more often, especially in this season of summer fetes and festivals. This one had been easy pickings.

Finally, I borrowed another of the Vicar's robes – a purple silk affair, heavy with gold embroidery. That would keep me cosy while I slept. This white surplice had made me decent while I was laundering my own clothes. If the little girl had recognised it as the Vicar's, she was too polite to say.

Patting my full stomach – a rare phenomenon – I returned to the altar, picked a needlepoint kneeler from the choir stalls to use as a pillow, and set it down on the red carpet. Spotting the tea light we'd blown out together a little earlier, I picked it up and dropped it back to fill its space in the candelabra. Then I lay down on the floor, the kneeler beneath my head, and draped the purple robe the length of my body. Its weight, as well as its warmth, would be a comfort that night. Knowing the dawn light would wake me and send me on my way before anyone arrived for the Sunday morning service, I relaxed into the deepest night's sleep I was to have that summer.

The Vicar

On Sunday morning, it was my turn to unlock the church for the day. When my key met no resistance, I realised it was already unlocked, and presumably had been all night. In the hubbub of organising the festivities for our special day, poor Kate must have forgotten to lock up the night before. My wife tells me I lean too much upon my dear churchwarden.

To my relief, nothing inside was amiss. The spectacular floral tributes radiated freshness and scent in the morning light, and the refreshments table groaned under the generous baked donations. The cake ladies couldn't have fitted another bite on the crowded platters and cake stands if they'd tried. The cleaning brigade had also done St Bride's proud. Long summer days made it easy to spot dusty corners and streaky windows, and everything looked immaculate.

I gave a little bow to the gaily decked altar, a delightful contrast to the honey-coloured walls and scarlet carpet. After I'd said a quick prayer of thanks for the blessings of this special day, the candelabra of offertory tea lights caught my attention. All the tea lights were gleaming white from wick to wax, except for one. At its heart, a blackened wick had dropped ash into a dimpled hollow where a small amount of wax had burned away.

Crossing the nave to look more closely, I saw the burned wick was at an angle, as if blown out by a prevailing wind. How bizarre in this still church. Odd too when Kate had insisted that for our celebrations, any partly burned tea lights should be replaced with new. Another little oversight on her part. It was about time she had a rest from her church duties. I made a mental note to ask Sophie to stand in for Kate as churchwarden for a couple of weeks. She never seems to mind me asking her to help out, dear girl that she is.

I cast a grateful smile at the great west window, where St Bride presided, as ever, in her snow-white robe. For an Irish saint who doubtless never set foot in our Cotswold parish, she looked remarkably at home.

The noisy arrival of young Sina Crowe shook me from my morning reverie. Bowling in through the door on shiny pink roller skates, she made me wince at the potential damage to the red carpet. The Friends of St Bride's had spent so much money installing it just a couple of years before.

"I hope no-one catches you roller-skating in church, or you'll be in trouble," I admonished her.

Grinning, she plonked herself down on the carpet to unlace the skates and slip them off. Standing up in her mismatched socks, she surveyed the church, clocking every feature from altar to vestry. Then she skipped up to me, apparently bursting to tell me something.

"Yesterday at Hector's House, all the grown-ups were saying we never learn anything from history."

I nodded, wondering what she was leading up to.

"Well," she said, hands on hips, "sometimes, history can learn from us."

I had no idea what she was talking about, but she seemed pleased with her conundrum, so I let it go.

Then she pivoted on the toes of one foot – she's a little star at ballet lessons in the village hall – to gaze fondly at the west end stained-glass window.

"Happy Birthday again, St Bride," she said sweetly, and galloped away to be first in the queue for the cake stall.

© Debbie Young

Author's note

Although I'm inspired by the Cotswold village community where I've lived since 1991, I always say I make my stories up and invent all my characters. I was therefore startled to receive from our churchwarden, the day after I finished writing this story, photographic evidence that a stranger had spent the night inside our parish church when one of the keyholders forgot to lock up. The uninvited visitor had made themselves comfortable, creating a cosy den beneath the altar with a hassock for a pillow, just as 'St Bride' does in my story, a long seat cushion from a pew as a mattress, and an old curtain from the vestry as a cover. I didn't dare ask whether our visitor had also done their laundry in the font or worn the Vicar's surplice as a nightie!

About Debbie Young

Debbie Young is the author of three series of cosy mystery novels set in the Cotswolds. The Sophie Sayers series starts with *Best Murder in Show*; the Gemma Lamb series begins with *Dastardly Deeds at St Bride's*; and the Cotswold Curiosity Shop series kicks off with *Death at the Old Curiosity Shop*. She sometimes sends characters from one series to visit those in another. She also writes short fiction, not all of it crime-related, set in the same world, eg *Christmas with Sophie Sayers*. Her novels are published by Boldwood Books in English, by DP Verlag in German, and by Antonio Vallardi in Italian. She has recently written her first murder mystery play for performance by her village amateur dramatic group. She is a frequent speaker at events for writers and readers, a course tutor for Jericho Writers, and the founder and director of the Hawkesbury Upton Literature Festival. She lives in a Victorian cottage with her Scottish husband, her student daughter, and three cats, and she writes in a little hut at the bottom of her garden.

Website: www.authordebbieyoung.com
Facebook: AuthorDebbieYoung
Instagram: DebbieYoungAuthor
You'll find links to buy Debbie's books here:
https://authordebbieyoung.com/books-2/

ENDWORD

BY HELEN HOLLICK

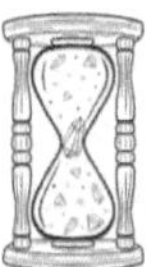

Any anthology of short stories inevitably produces one or two that are more popular than the others – but it all comes down to a matter of personal taste, particularly where several genres are involved. Perhaps you prefer historical fiction rather than a story about magic or fantasy? Maybe you enjoy exploring new themes or prefer sticking to the familiar? Historical fiction can often inform, imparting knowledge of the past, of its events and its people. Stories of mystery exercise the 'little grey cells' as Poirot would say, while fantasy and magic create new worlds and awed wonder.

Whatever result, this is where anthologies come into their own, and where short stories are often appreciated as enjoyable, entertaining, quick or easy reads shown through the eyes of a variety of extraordinary characters and situations. In this instance: an Anglo-Saxon woman facing the consequence of conquest, the pursuit of alchemy, the concern of a mother for her daughter, the shifting of time, the necessity of hidden identity, souls who will linger as ghosts, a warning from the supernatural, the necessity for (justifiable?) revenge. All mingled with the rekindling of romance through a mutual quest, and the preparations for a Cotswold village celebration. (Along with a good tip if illicitly snaffling cakes.) The binding theme? The effect of Fate or Destiny… *Kismet*.

As authors, we find writing these short stories to be as much of a challenge as any full-length novel, possibly even a greater challenge, for there is not the page space in a short story to develop the characters, background events (and plot) in lengthy detail. A short story has to start with the immediate grabbing of the reader's interest from that very first sentence, and must not let go until the very last word… I hope that, between us, we have successfully completed our mission.

If so, and you have enjoyed any (or all!) of these stories, please do leave a review for us on Amazon at: **https://mybook.to/FateAnthology** we would greatly appreciate it.

BEFORE YOU GO

You might also like some other recommended anthologies:

Exile: Stories of Exile

1066 Turned Upside Down:

1066 Turned Upside Down

Betrayal (free e-book): Betrayal

Thank you!

www.ingramcontent.com/pod-product-compliance
Lightning Source LLC
Chambersburg PA
CBHW020654120726
47906CB00001B/260